ralph higley and the illuminatus

Jimmy Griggs

Cover Illustration by
Chris Fisher

Text © Jimmy Griggs 2016
First Published by CreateSpace

Jimmy Griggs has asserted his right under the Copyright,
Designs and Patents Act 1988, to be identified as the author of
this work.

ISBN-13: 9781519669209

Dedicated
to
Ann Martin and Rebecca Meeres.

acknowledgements

To be a writer you need a pen, to be a published writer you need a team. And for my team I would like to thank Sue Medway, for support and encouragement. Les Weatheritt, my friend and first editor. Gill McLay, my agent who has spent many hours crafting me into the writer I longed to be. And lastly, Liz Burcher, my proof-reader and final editor.

contents

one: the raven

It was the week before Christmas Eve in the sleepy town of Broomfield and the festive illuminations glittered throughout. Yesterday's snowstorm had settled like a thick white blanket over rooftops and passageways and the heavy clouds were gone leaving a clear and bright morning.

Today was Saturday and, as on most Saturdays, Ralph Higley was reluctant to get up. He lived in an old house in Twizzle Street. It had large rooms upstairs and down but lacked many of the comforts taken for granted in modern houses. The windows were draughty. The heating was old and the pipes rattled noisily. The bathroom was often damp and always a refuge for spiders.

Ralph was lazing in bed waiting for one parent or the other to come up the stairs and yank him from his slumber. However on this Saturday morning things were going to be very different.

He was daydreaming under warm blankets about his 13th birthday. There were only four days to go. Ralph had asked his mother for a book on Nocturnal Animals and was desperate to have it. He was convinced that their garden was getting nightly visits from some very unusual animals. This was the first time Ralph had asked his parents for a serious book. Greatly relieved and surprised that he showed an interest in reading his parents awaited an improvement in his behaviour.

Ralph was drifting back into that pleasant state of half-sleep when a persistent loud tapping at his window brought him wide awake. He rubbed his eyes as he struggled to see the source of the noise. Disbelief flooded his face. A large bird was hammering its beak on the windowpane. Ralph stared. Staring back was the all-seeing, all-piercing, beady eyes of a beautiful jet-black bird; bigger and more magnificent than the crows and rooks he was used to.

Ralph waved his arms to shoo the bird away, annoyed that his peace and quiet had been spoilt so early. But his shooing had the opposite effect. The magnificent bird squawked more and deliberately flapped its powerful wings. Baffled, Ralph threw back the bed covers and rose to his feet, groaning furiously at having to get up.

"Go away! Just shut up and leave me alone!"

But the bird took no notice. Ralph stomped to the sash window and threw it up with the start of a bad temper.

With a single flap of its immense wings the bird swooped into the room and perched on the end of the bedpost. Cawing at Ralph it looked back towards the outside world.

"It looks like a crow or even a rook," Ralph thought, "but it's different and grander. I think it's a raven."

Ralph peered through the open window but saw nothing unusual to explain the bird's arrival in his bedroom. Suddenly he had a brilliant idea. He would keep the raven. He smirked knowing that not even his friends Evan or Tom had a pet like that. He stretched out his hands to stalk the bird and edged closer and closer. He was almost upon it. Then quick as a flash he threw himself forward, eyes tight shut, scooping both hands together. He was holding thin air. The raven had flown straight out the open window.

In the garden Ralph saw the raven perched calmly on the gate. How could he have missed it? But then it dawned on him that the bird had not flown away as he expected. It was as though the bird had waited for him, to give him a second chance. He wouldn't let it slip. He was determined to be quicker this time.

Calmed, Ralph closed the window with more care than he opened it. He threw on his clothes and checked that the raven was still perched on the gate. Then he seized a small length of string he kept in his bedside cabinet. This would be a good tether for the bird, if he caught it.

Leaving the house like a tornado, he had the bird in his sights. It flew and flapped along the pavement. It was if it were taunting him.

When the raven swooped from tree to tree Ralph still followed. Near the end of the street, it stopped in a tall fir tree that stood in the garden of Gloomstone Lodge. This was where Ralph's best friend Evan Gordon lived. As much as Ralph liked Evan he didn't want him to have the raven.

Nearing the house he planned to climb the high wall and reach into the fir tree but his raven vanished. There was no more cawing. No more flapping of wings. There was nothing except the whoosh of a bitter winter breeze.

Full of disappointment that the raven had gone, Ralph didn't give any thought to where or why it had come in the first place. He pulled the string from his pocket and chucked it down in anger. He was left with the faint feeling of what it might have been like to have a raven on his arm, ready to play tricks and show off to his friends.

At that same moment, Alice Moore, a small, gentle ten-year-old, has taken some bread crusts down to Oak Apple Lane to feed the hungry birds. Head down, she concentrated on scattering the crusts. She thought she was alone. A sudden movement and a glint of silver caught her eye. She looked up and stood before her was a strange man who wore a large floppy-brimmed hat. He had a brooding look on his face. In his hands was a small silver box. It was the shape of a perfect cube and polished so bright it was dazzling.

When the man pushed up the brim of his hat Alice saw dark circles under tormented, hollow eyes. His voice was slow and deep and gravelly but the words flowed from his mouth as soft as buttermilk.

"Look at what I have found. A little robin with a broken wing! Come. See if we can mend him."

The man waved his free hand in a circle over the silver box, tempting Alice closer.

Alice's eyes were drawn into the stranger's hands. The thought of the little robin in pain filled her with grief. But though she concentrated hard all she saw was a strange light that glistened around the silver box.

She looked up at the man and again down into his hands. But the curiosity in her eyes had turned to anxiety. Something was wrong. This was all too odd. A warning voice in her head urged her to "Run, Alice, run!"

A strong instinct made her turn on her heels and flee for her life. But the strange man was quick. He snatched at her with a grasping hand. Alice felt a swish of air rush past her cheek as his hand missed. Now she knew the danger was real. She ran towards home for all she was worth.

Alice's heart pounded faster and faster. Fear griped and spurred her on. She hardly slowed as she charged out of that lane and turned the corner into the next street. In her headlong rush she didn't see the tall woman in the bright red coat. The woman had her head down, preoccupied with a small cloth bag, and showed no sign of having seen Alice turn the corner. Alice swerved but couldn't stop herself as she bumped into the tall lady.

"Sorry!" Alice gasped.

The lady looked up as though she was about to give the girl a good telling off, but her foreboding expression changed when she noticed how troubled Alice was.

"Why," the woman said kindly, "whatever is the matter? Why are you running like that?" The woman's voice was gentle and kind but the look on her gaunt face hid the fact that she was scheming.

Alice stopped and caught her breath. In the security of finding an adult she thought she could trust she told the woman what happened in a rush of words.

"There was a horrible man with a big hat and he tried to trick me. He said he had a little robin with a broken wing but really all he had in his hand was this weird silver box! And when I ran he tried to grab me!"

"Oh, my dear. That is awful!" the woman said in a shocked tone. She looked around as though she wanted a word with that frightening man. "You are safe now, with me," she said reassuringly. "I know what we must do. We must report this man to the authorities. Come with me."

The tall woman closed her bag, carefully hiding the silver box nestled inside and took the hand of the trusting little girl. Alice gratefully held the woman's hand as they walked down the snow-covered street. This was the day Alice Moore went missing and made the headlines in newspapers the following day.

That night, a few streets away, a tall elegant man called Greystone and his powerfully built younger colleague Black-Bob were outside an old house in the quiet little road of Twizzle Street. Greystone and Black-Bob were members of the Binders. Indeed, they were two of the leading investigators and tutors of that secret guild. They were dressed in smart evening suits and looked as though they had just arrived from somewhere they had never left.

"Is this where the boy lives?" Black-Bob asked as he looked up at the old house. It was like other houses in that part of town. Old fashioned. Substantial. Built in brick but with stone framing the doors and windows. It seemed too ordinary a place for a special person.

"This lad has a rare talent, of that I am sure. I have witnessed things covertly. Remember that whistling invisible cat? He saw it!" said Greystone. Black-Bob raised his eyebrows and said nothing. In full flow, Greystone continued, " The lad is nearly thirteen and on that birthday strange events will unravel his fate." Black Bob smirked and replied, "There are others who think differently."

"Given time, Ralph will prove his worth. I don't know where this talent comes from or why it has settled on him but I believe it is possible that he could be a Twister." Greystone spoke with quiet confidence.

"A Twister, no less," Black-Bob said. A Twister carried a gift of immense significance to members of the guild. "A watcher of the invisibles," he continued, deliberately letting Greystone hear the sarcasm in his voice. "Even though it is more than three hundred years since the last Twister was among us. Your Ralph will have the gift to see things no one else can, not even a Master Binder!"

"Almost certainly," Greystone retorted.

Black-Bob's face clouded with doubt and he frowned. He would like to have discovered a Twister instead of Greystone.

"If you're right, he will be unpredictable," Black-Bob sniped. "We call them Twisters for good reason. Remember the last one, an alchemist and a magician. He was a bender of light. I wonder what surprise powers your young Twister Ralph will show us!"

Greystone shrugged, once again ignoring Black-Bob's sarcasm. He leaned closer and made a delicate point. "I want all this to be between us and us alone. No one, not even the High Council, must know of Ralph's potential until I am ready," he said forcefully.

What passed between them next would have made no sense to eavesdroppers. It had meaning only to them. Black-Bob's doubt had grown into bafflement and he was angry.

"So be it!" Black-Bob said. "But there are dark servants loose and especially in this town. Any time we waste with your splendid new discovery – this Ralph – may cost us heavily later."

Greystone smiled reassuringly. "My dear friend, remember the Oaks, remember the Great Seal. The scrolls tell us that the Great Seal has been forged and by this seal the evil creatures of Ragna Doom will forever be held at bay."

Black-Bob shook his head in dismay. He was angered by what he saw as Greystone's procrastination.

"And if Wychen should fall to the dark servants, what then will stop the Great Seal from cracking open? What then will save the Oaks? Their broken boughs will surely lead to broken hearts. Mark my words, Greystone."

Greystone changed the subject to soothe his friend.

"But you have your own promising understudy Miss Harwood. Rebecca, isn't it? How are you faring with her?"

"She is excellent," Black-Bob told Greystone.

"I hear she is a mathematical prodigy," Greystone murmured.

Black-Bob, who had always wanted to be recognised as a serious mentor, didn't notice his friend was gently teasing him. His serious face almost smiled.

"Rebecca has a talent for our subject. At most times she is a fine student of logic. Such promise. If she would only concentrate more!"

"Oh, I've heard that Professor Pumpkin thinks she is a bit of a scatterbrain," Greystone replied, more mischievous.

Black-Bob looked at Greystone sharply, suspecting he was poking fun.

"Scatterbrain? Ha! That old Pumpkin head can talk, as well you know," Black-Bob said emphatically. "I am sure that with a little discipline she will make the top grade. I wouldn't be swapping my Rebecca with your Ralph just yet, thank you very much, Greystone!"

Greystone rocked on his heels and said, "It's nice to see you're so confident."

Black-Bob nodded politely in firm affirmation.

A cloud of white steam billowed at the other end of the street and out burst a large white car. Its bright headlights the size of dinner plates pierced the darkness and threw shadows before the car. The car sped straight up to the two men and stopped abruptly. It was sleek and low with wide tyres and a sloping back, built like a speedster from decades ago. The engine growled and hummed, but its source of power was from a very advance technology. The rear door sprung open with a distinctive hissing of air under pressure. Yet incredibly there was no driver.

The meeting of the two Binders was over. Not another word was spoken. Black-Bob stepped solemnly into the car. The door closed slowly of its own accord. Air hissed loudly as the car sped away into the night like a phantom.

Calm descended on the street. Darkness embraced everything. Greystone stood alone, silent and still, like a ghostly spectre on the crisp snow. In that bitter cold he watched the house closely for any tiny movement. Not even a mouse went unnoticed that night. Eventually Greystone was ready to leave. Without a sound he stepped backwards into the blackness and melted away, vanishing like an apparition.

two: strange events

Sunday arrived and Ralph woke to the same tapping noise on the window as he heard the previous morning. The raven was back! Oliver, the family dog was also asleep on Ralph's bed. He was a terrier named after Oliver Twist on account he always begged and asked for more. In his prime he had been a good rat catcher. Now too old for fights, he barked.

"Not now," Ralph shouted at Oliver then scrambled to the window and looked down. Once again this beautiful bird was perched on the garden gate.

"This time I'm going to make you mine, if it's the last thing I do," he muttered. He threw on some clothes, grabbed his last piece of string from the bedside cabinet and again made off down the stairs.

On his way though the hall, Ralph remembered he'd get into trouble if he didn't collect the Sunday newspapers for his father. So he quickly snatched the money from a small dish on the sideboard and shoved the change in his pocket as he whizzed from the house.

He was so pre-occupied with his second chance to catch the raven that he forgot to close the door properly. It was not the first time Ralph's careless urgency had caused mistakes. He sprinted for the gate without a thought of the front door. Hard on his heels was Oliver, who bolted through the open door.

"Get back," Ralph shouted at the dog as he looked intently for the raven.

He shut the gate hard and Oliver was stranded. Again Ralph's eyes fixed on the raven and he burnt with excitement. He had read ravens were very clever and already he was imagining how to teach that raven to count and speak. Perhaps he would train it to tell the time too.

"I could be the famous 'Ralph Higley and his Stupendous Raven'. Better than The Unknown Ralph Higley and his Stupid Dog," he thought.

He looked down over the gate at Oliver and a warm smile crossed his face.

"It's alright, Oliver. I wouldn't swop you for anything," Ralph promised.

Ralph looked up to search for the bird and saw it had flown to the other side of the road. It was heading in the same direction as it did on Saturday. He was not going to let that bird out of his sight for a second. He followed it tree by tree as it flew towards the big fir tree again. Suddenly he saw his friend Evan coming along the pavement towards him.

"You look in a hurry," said Evan.

Ralph was caught flatfooted. He still saw the bird but if he pretended it wasn't there he would lose it again. And if Evan saw how magnificent that bird was he would want it. Ralph then had a stroke of genius and said, "I'm trying to catch um….. 'Blacky', my pet raven."

Evan's mouth dropped open.

"You have a raven," he said with astonishment. Ralph smiled and pointed up at the bird then said, "Yes, he's mine. Blacky must have undone his catch and escaped. Ravens are very clever, you know!"

"I know they are!" Evan replied, not wishing to appear dim as well as raven-less. Sounding put out, he continued, "You didn't tell me you had one."

"That's because I only got him yesterday," coughed Ralph as he covered up his little fib by making it larger.

The big fir tree swayed and the raven swooped across.

"Look where he's gone. He's in your garden now. Will you help me catch him?" Ralph asked.

"Sure, but not if he pecks!"

"He's tame as anything," Ralph replied with another lie as big as a house.

As they walked towards Evan's house Ralph noticed his friend's father, Mr Gordon talking to another man at the gate. What struck Ralph, however, was the strangely rigid way Mr Gordon was standing, like a mannequin.

"Nice day, Mr Gordon," Ralph called. "I say, it's a nice day, Mr Gordon," he repeated more loudly, but again there was no sign from Mr Gordon. Fed up, Ralph was not inclined to ask again.

By contrast, the other man seemed much more agreeable. He turned cheerfully and wished Ralph a good morning.

Puzzled, Ralph looked at Evan and whispered, "What's up with your dad?"

Evan shrugged his shoulders and whispered back, "He's fine. Let's go and get that bird of yours."

By then Mr Gordon had managed to turn his head slowly and was looking directly through Ralph with not a sign of recognition. Ralph saw Mr Gordon's face. It was ashen grey as though all human expression had left it.

Evan walked through the gate while Ralph hung back.

"I'll just check the tree from this side," he said excitedly.

Ralph nodded and, with the raven no longer visible, his attention turned to the two men. Suddenly, a dark shape on Mr Gordon's shoulder caught his eye. It was like a black lump of slimy tar about the size of a tennis ball, but shapeless. At first Ralph thought it could be a bat, perhaps like a vampire.

But this was no bat. Ralph looked slyly from the corner of his eye for he couldn't stare openly. To his horror, the lump moved. Its shapeless form followed Ralph's every movement. It was alive! Strange dark thoughts whirled as his mind was gripped in panic.

Evan called his friend into the garden. But Ralph had other ideas.

"My raven's gone. I have to go. My father's newspapers need collecting," he said after a last look up the tree.

He then took to his heels as fear gripped him. He dared not look back in case that black creature was pursuing him. Only after he safely reached the corner of Twizzle Street did he look round again.

Mr Gordon and the other man were no longer insight and neither was Ralph's magnificent raven. They had all vanished, except Evan who was stood at the gate. He was dumbstruck by Ralph's odd behaviour and his quick departure. But Ralph's thoughts were else-where, why had no one noticed the creature on Mr Gordon's shoulder? Did they not see it?

Ralph soon reached the newsagents and was relieved. He pushed the door open and it pinged like a doorbell. Inside he shuffled round to the shelf where he picked up the Sunday papers for his father. At the counter, Ralph held out the money but the gum-chewing girl was too busy reading a dreamy girls magazine. He rustled his papers to attract her attention.

Ralph was tall for his age, as he took after his mother, yet he had not filled out like his broad-shouldered father. The girl looked up with a flash of interest, but when she saw how young he was she rolled her eyes, as if to say she would serve him only on sufferance. When she asked for the money her manner irritated Ralph and as he handed her the coins a wicked thought popped into his head. He imagined the strange foul creature on its way to gobble up that insolent girl. The wicked thought cheered him and he smiled sweetly at the girl but already she had turned another page of her magazine as he left the shop.

In Swinepen, the blackest and grimiest part of Broomfield, a man trudged down a crooked alleyway between two old warehouses. The derelict buildings had once been thriving woollen mills. There, loom after loom ran their length and continuously turned like a pauper's millstone that ground the corn for the penny loaf.

The man moved swiftly, hunched tight against the bitter cold. He wore a large floppy-brimmed hat and a long dark coat, perhaps for concealment. He knocked loudly on a half rotten door on the gloomiest side of the warehouse and waited. A moment later, metal bolts slid back and there was the clink of a latch being undone. The door opened cautiously. A tall woman stood partially obscured from view by the door itself. On the wall behind hung her bright red coat.

"About time," she grumbled. She was gaunt, her face wrinkled and her lips taut with a sullen meanness. There was no welcome for the man. He lifted his head for a brief moment to show a young yet weathered face. He was perhaps much older than he looked. His voice was muffled under the hat.

"I got here as soon as I could, Mrs Ridley. I do hope this one will prove useful."

"Oh yes, especially if some obedience is knocked into the little madam," the woman said with a surly voice, sneering at the man. "I'm sure this one will be useful. I found things very risky owing to these difficult circumstances. Nevertheless I did my best. None of them are easy to catch as you probably know."

Impatient, Mrs Ridley jerked the door wider and beckoned him into the dungeon-like room.

She closed the door behind the man and crossed to a small table. She carefully drew back a dirty rag. Beneath it was the perfect cube of a silver box, big enough to hold a large ring. Strange carved markings glowed and shimmered with a mysterious pulsing light. Mrs Ridley grasped the box in both hands. Delighted the man looked on in admiration.

"Excellent," he said eagerly. "Do you have two little mites or just the one inside?"

Mrs Ridley took the box in her left hand and stroked the edge of the lid ever so tenderly with the index finger of her other hand. As she savoured that moment of triumph her voice softened.

"There is only one. Little Alice," she said as she hissed out the girl's name like a snake. "It took hours before I managed to get her in the box. She is a darling even though she wriggles and kicks. Don't be tempted to open it!"

The visitor's eyebrows lifted slightly as though he didn't need to be told.

"Don't worry, Mrs Ridley. This one is going straight down to Ragna Doom."

Almost smiling, the sullen crone handed him the box. The stranger slipped it under his long coat. A terrible grin lit his greedy face as he tapped the box beneath his coat.

"They need more. More is what they like, Mrs Ridley!"

Mrs Ridley shifted her gaze from the man's coat. Her eyes glowered fiercely from the flickering light of the old oil lamp.

"Don't worry, my dear," she said, with all the menace of her blackened heart, "we do have more coming. Those silver traps are about to be set again. Call round to Gloomstone Lodge tonight. Make sure you come after midnight. You will meet our good friends the Gordons. If all goes well they will have two more little darlings for you."

The man tensed and clenched his fists with anticipation.

"Mrs Ridley, your efforts will not go unnoticed or unrewarded. You have my solemn oath on that."

The crone's stone face grew livid.

"I work for them too, you know!" she said, her voice filled with distrust. "Don't you dare cross me! Remember, I will not suffer a fool, Mr Thorn."

"That's a name not to be mentioned, not here nor anywhere. Do you understand, Mrs Ridley?" The stranger snapped at her cold and sharp. His long face furrowed as though reliving the chilled agonies of some forgotten tragedy and a needlessly lonely life.

"I keep quiet as long as I am well paid!" the woman said. Her soured face spat venom at him. "I could as easily drown these little brats like a bag of kittens. It's only that I have seen such a nice warm winter coat to buy with that money."

The man acknowledged her vicious warning with a nod. There was no warmth of friendship between them. He forced a smile, tugged down his hat and slipped from the room without a word. At the door, Mrs Ridley watched him trudge away warily. She had the upper hand in their shared business. But for how long?

As the door closed on the bitter cold Mrs Ridley pictured all the things she could buy with the money she would earn. She often ran those pictures through her mind to enjoy the cruelty of her work. It mattered nothing to her that others suffered to advance her material comfort.

three: tea at the gordons

As Ralph walked home he wanted to avoid the Gordons' house. This meant going the long way round, along Old Smithy Road. On the way he read the front-page head-lines of the local paper. "Girl, ten, vanishes in Broomfield. Has anyone seen Alice Moore?" Below there was a big picture of a smiling Alice.

"I didn't know the girl but Swinepen is a bad place," Ralph thought. He looked at the headlines and again at the picture. "How many kids go missing in this country?" he wondered. " How many go missing the whole world over? I bet it's thousands and thousands."

By the time Ralph reached home he knew the day wasn't going to get any better. His mother gave him a frosty welcome as he opened the front door. He quietly followed her to the kitchen.

"Your father's not best pleased with you, Ralph" she said sternly. "You have turned this house into an icebox.

You left the front door wide open. Don't you care?" Hardly pausing to breath she continued, "This house will take ages to warm up again."

They had put up with a lot from Ralph in the past few months. Windows in nearby streets had been broken and neighbours claimed Ralph was one the vandals. The problem ended when the local parents, including the Higleys, confiscated catapults from their children. Although Ralph was not one of the culprits, he didn't like the shame of fingers pointing at him.

Feeling glum his mind returned to the raven and he was glad he never caught such a royal bird. What would be the point? His parents wouldn't have allowed it in the house. They wouldn't have appreciated its power and elegance and wisdom. He could hear his mother now: "What's this? More mess for me to clear up." And his father would complain, "Take that thing out! I can't put up with its squawking." Ralph grumbled to himself that there were times when his parents were no fun, but when he saw his mother so cold that she was wearing an extra thick sweater he felt a twinge of guilt.

"I am sorry," Ralph said, "but I did fetch Dad's papers."

"You'd better leave them on the kitchen table," his mother told him sternly. "And if I were you I would stay out of your father's way until lunchtime." She then took a knife to peel the potatoes and continued in a severe tone: "Best if you go outside and play till lunch is ready. And have you combed your hair yet?"

Ralph had to find somewhere else to play. He would have gone to Evan's house but he couldn't be sure that creature wasn't still lurking. Better if he went to see Tom Moffat, another friend. Tom lived in a terrace house four streets away in Marsh Lane. He was three months older than Ralph and liked to play the big boy, bossing Ralph around. Not that Ralph minded as long as they were having fun.

Tom's house was in the centre of the terrace and could be seen clearly from the top end of Marsh Lane. You could see him standing on the path of his house, wrapped up in a navy blue coat. He wore woollen gloves and the earmuffs on his woollen hat were tied up so he could hear. He kicked about in his welly boots to keep warm, as he talked to a tall woman in a bright red coat. Her features were bony with a haggard look. She was not someone Ralph knew. Without knowing why, Ralph felt anxious and the more and more anxious he became the more his steps dawdled. He had an impending sense of yet more trouble ahead. When he arrived and said hello to Tom the conversation between his friend and the woman stopped abruptly. As if transformed, her sullen expression brightened to a false disturbed smile.

"Who is this nice young gentleman, Tom?" the woman asked clutching a small cloth bag in the strangest way. Her eyes were fixed on Ralph's and held him with a deep blankness. Her mouth quivered as she spoke. Her strangeness chilled Ralph.

"This is Ralph Higley," Tom said as he flicked the fringe of his black hair to one side and added, "My friend."

The woman looked inquisitively at Ralph.

"Is he now? I always look forward to meeting new friends of Tom's. You know, I am sure we shall meet again." She turned to Tom and looked at him hard.

"I have to go. Don't forget what I told you, there's a good boy."

Tom nodded obediently, as though under a spell.

Ralph felt uneasy in her company and was glad when she left.

"Who is that old battleaxe?"

"That's Mrs Ridley," Tom said. "She was mother's land-lady before we moved here. She's always been around."

"Broomfield is full of weird stuff just now," Ralph said. "First I nearly caught a raven. Then Mr Gordon turns creepy."

"What's that about a raven?" Tom asked as he poked in the snow with a long stick.

"Never mind the raven. It's Mr Gordon we need to worry about. I saw him at his gate looking ashen white and his eyes were blank just like a zombie's." Ralph drew Tom closer and paused for dramatic effect before he revealed his terrible experience.

"You won't believe what I saw next!" he whispered. Tom's jaw dropped with anticipation and Ralph beckoned him even closer.

"Tell me then!" Tom said, after getting impatient with the dramatic pauses. He nudged Ralph with his stick to hurry him along.

"I saw a creepy black creature the size of two large fists on Mr Gordon's shoulder," Ralph exaggerated his eyes as big as saucers. "It's a living creature of some kind. I saw its eyes!"

Tom looked shocked and squealed with excitement.

"It's a rat. I bet they've got rats in their house."

"I know rats," Ralph said, disconcerted that his mystery had such a simple explanation. "It wasn't a rat. Oliver could have dealt with a rat, but I wouldn't risk him with this thing. I didn't like it."

Tom nervously drew a sad face in the snow with his stick.

"I don't want to hear any more. You're trying to freak me out."

Ralph gave a mocking smile. "Let's go to the park and watch the people all turn into zombies." Ralph then walked zombie like, his arms straight out in front and his legs strutted with a stiff stilted gait.

Tom gave Ralph a furious sideways look. He had seen that performance too often, and was not sure whether Ralph did it to mock him. Nevertheless Tom stuffed his hands in his pockets and followed Ralph towards the park.

At the Higley residence, Ralph's mum was busy in the kitchen checking her Sunday roast. Cooking wasn't one of her strong points. If she didn't burn the potatoes she would probably cremate the joint. But she was a martyr to her cause and come what may a meal of sorts always found its way to the table.

In the living room, Mr Higley had built a nice log fire. He had settled into his comfy chair and was reading his newspapers contentedly. Suddenly the doorbell rang and that set Oliver jumping and barking frantically. After putting his newspaper down, Mr Higley shut the dog in another room. He returned to the front door where through the spy-hole he saw Mrs Gordon.

Mrs Gordon was notorious, not only as a chatterbox but also for being a little batty. He took a deep breath and opened the door without any enthusiasm. The welcome was perhaps frostier than Mrs Gordon deserved, but she hadn't noticed. She was more distracted than usual. Clearly something was bothering her greatly.

Mrs Gordon wore a long bright blue coat over a heavy hand-knitted jumper and skirt. Her necklace was a strange design. Bright coloured beads contrasted sharply with the symbols of gold crescent moons that hung from them.

Her smile was unnerving. So was the way she blurted out her invitation for Ralph to come to tea that evening.

"I know this is short notice, Mr Higley, but Evan hasn't seen him of late. I do hope you will say yes."

Her eyes darted left and right as she spoke, as if to catch sight of Ralph. Mr Higley was pleased at Mrs Gordon's invitation. He thought Ralph could benefit from a little more socializing and if the Gordons were looking after his son he could get his newspapers read. Before he answered Ralph walked sheepishly up the path.

"You'd like to go to tea with Evan wouldn't you, Ralph?" Mr Higley said with a firm voice that invited no rejection.

What could Ralph have said? He could hardly refuse after upsetting his parents that morning. Normally he would jump at the chance of tea with his best friend, but not if that creature was lurking about. His mouth was dry and his voice barely able to croak yet he found the word "yes" flowed from his mouth like silk. He was appalled at himself for not saying "no!" He knew his father would not believe him about the shapeless creature. He hardly believed it himself.

Mrs Gordon beamed and told them both how pleased Evan would be. And they, she said, meaning Mr Gordon and her, would plan a little surprise for the two boys. On hearing that, Ralph felt a wave of great foreboding.

Teatime loomed and Ralph trudged through the snow towards Gloomstone Lodge. It was dark and cold. If he weren't in his fathers' bad books already he would have gone elsewhere. Even lessons at his school, Oswald's, would have been better, except there was no school on Sundays.

At the Gordons', Ralph was pleased it was Evan who opened the door. Evan was a small and tidy boy; capable of making his friends look dishevelled even when they were not. He wore his best woolly jumper and was as neat as neat could be. Ralph desperately wanted to speak to his friend alone to ask if there was anything strange about his father. But he didn't get the chance as Evan led him straight through to the living room.

The large room was decorated with all manner of Christmas trimmings. In one corner was a beautiful tree and in another a long table laded with a spread of mouth watering food. Mrs Gordon beamed as the back-to-normal Mr Gordon gave him a warm welcome and ushered the boys to the table.

"Ralph, you can sit over there next to Evan," Mrs Gordon said as she held a steaming dish of new potatoes. Ralph's mouth watered again. Then he noticed there were four settings at the table and not five as usual. Evan's older brother was missing. Ralph turned and whispered to Evan. "Is Colin not here for tea?"

"No. Dad says he's gone to visit his friend," whispered Evan, then excitedly changing the subject he asked, "Have you seen Tony Barker's new bike?" But Ralph's mind was elsewhere. He was nervously checking Mr Gordon's shoulder in case something nasty sat there.

"I don't think so," Ralph said distractedly.

"He didn't even have to wait until Christmas!" Evan continued in a huff.

"My bike has a flat tyre. I suppose I'll get round to fixing it one day," Ralph said as he made conversation.

Evan looked at his mother. "I haven't a bike," he grumbled.

Mr Gordon looked at him sharply.

"Now then, that's enough. You know I think bikes are too dangerous around here." He spoke in a flat, disinterested tone with a strange faraway look. After that rebuff, the atmosphere became tense.

Mrs Gordon passed around the plates and the boys tucked in. Curiously, neither parent was eating. Their total attention was on the two boys. Between mouthfuls of delicious food Ralph glanced at Mr Gordon's shoulder, fearing the strange black lump might reappear.

When Mr Gordon pointed to two silver boxes on the sideboard and announced that he had a present for each of the boys, his smile sent a chill down Ralph's spine.

"What's in the box, Dad? Is it a nice watch?" Evan asked, unable to contain his excitement. "You know I've always wanted a watch."

Ralph stared at the sideboard and wondered what the shiny cubes contained. He stopped chewing and swallowed hard. He had a terrible feeling about those boxes. He looked around the room ominously. He thought he saw the curtain move. He wasn't sure until it happened again.

"Mrs Gordon, your curtain twitched."

"You must be mistaken, Ralph. It is probably just a small draught from the window," Mrs Gordon replied casually.

But Ralph knew instantly that she was hiding something. He did not believe her.

"We need double glazing," Mr Gordon said smiling. But again the curtain moved.

Dark, spindly, spider-like fingers emerged from the edge of the curtain and the sight of them chilled Ralph to the very bone. He could do nothing as this creature slowly emerged and crept down the curtain effortlessly.

"It's on the curtain!" he shouted.

Evan looked, but saw nothing.

"What's on the curtain?" Evan screamed and climbed on his chair.

"How dare you, Ralph? You're scaring Evan," screeched Mrs Gordon. She clutched her napkin tightly and waved it frantically. Ralph was very scared and stood next to his chair.

"I am sorry, Mrs Gordon but...."

Ralph stopped in mid-sentence as the creature dropped from the curtain. It hopped and lolloped on the floor then leapt directly on to Mr Gordon's shoulder. Ralph was frozen with fear. With the thing at eye level Ralph saw every detail of the creature. Its hooked features were carbon black, gnarled and slimy. It had wings or, if not wings, then it wore a cloak Ralph couldn't tell for sure. The space around it was fuzzy and warped as though it smouldered.

"It's on your shoulder, Mr Gordon," Ralph cried. But Mr Gordon just shook his head from side to side and ignored him.

Ralph watched the creature whisper something into Mr Gordon's ear. It was just like the last time, when he saw Mr Gordon with the man.

Evan saw nothing on his father's shoulder, but now his father twitched and held his head slightly to one side. The odd behaviour made Evan cower trembling on the chair. He remembered seeing his mother behaving the same recently. He had thought nothing of it at the time but this memory was now terrifying.

"What's Ralph talking about, Dad? I can't see anything. Mum, what's wrong with Dad?" Evan screamed.

Mrs Gordon pretended to hear nothing. Her eyes had become fixed and glazed too. It seemed only Ralph saw the creature as it clung onto the shoulder of Evan's father. An inane grin swelled the face of Mr Gordon as slowly his mouth opened to speak.

"Evan, it's time to meet my little friend!"

The creature, still invisible to Evan, was about twenty centimetres high. Its gaze was fixed on Ralph as if he were the prey rather than Evan. At that precise moment Ralph knew why rabbits froze when caught in bright light. He was transfixed. The monster's cold, beady and bloodshot eyes with their warning hue of yellow were mesmerising. Ralph knew instinctively that the creature had no fear and that he was in mortal danger. All means of escape closed. He was trapped.

The creature's body flexed to pounce on Ralph but the distance between them was too great. The monster bounded to the middle of the table, where it hissed and grunted at Ralph.

Terrified, Evan screamed again. He couldn't see the creature but he heard it. He climbed from his chair in tears and sought refuge behind it.

Mr Gordon seized one of the silver boxes from the sideboard and sprung its lid open like a trap. Mrs Gordon snatched the other one and stood ready with it open.

"Put him in the box, Croucher. Put him in the box," Evan's father shouted at the fiendish creature.

Ralph realised in one terrifying moment that both Evan's parents were in league with this monster they called Croucher. They were helping it.

Croucher leapt again, this time directly at Ralph, who ducked quickly. The creature soared over his head. Ralph watched in alarm as it landed on Evan. Cloak and claws thrashed madly. He saw razor-sharp talons sink deep into the flesh of his poor friend. He tried to look away but he couldn't.

Ralph expected Evan to cry out with pain but he didn't. Croucher seemed to have an extraordinary power that restrained Evan. Then he saw the terrible desperation in his friend's eyes, the same desperation he felt when he needed Evan's help. But now it was his turn and he was powerless.

There was more horror. The excited Mr Gordon raced forward with the silver box in his left hand, and with his right hand tossed a pinch of yellow dust over Evan. Then he leapt back as the dust formed a yellow sulphurous cloud. Evan cowered with both hands over his head. The yellow cloud encased him as he froze like a statue.

Ralph saw Evan gradually shrink inside the sulphurous cloud. It was beyond belief. His friend was shrinking like a deflated balloon. A terrible wail came from the monster as he seized Evan now about eight centimetres tall and flipped him high in the air. Mrs Gordon shrieked with delight. "Put him in here. Be quick, be quick!" And she held up the silver box to receive her son.

Croucher, with the agility of an acrobat, tossed Evan into the tiny silver prison. The box snapped shut and Ralph knew that he was next. He charged for the door but Mr Gordon blocked his only escape route. Mr Gordon glared menacingly at Ralph and forced him back into the room.

Ralph had lost sight of Croucher but he knew the monster was ready to swoop on him at any moment.

He was determined to escape. But after that failed attempt he was struggling to come up with another idea. Without warning, a tall figure appeared in the doorway. The man stood like an apparition behind Mr Gordon. He held a curious silvery object and aimed it directly at Evan's unsuspecting father. It was oval in shape with tiny fragments of blue glass attached to its surface. There was a blinding light and Mr Gordon crumpled to the ground. Like a stage magician the stranger used a sleight of hand and the device vanished from sight.

This stranger looked familiar and Ralph stared at the man for wearing some very odd spectacles. On each side of a heavy brass frame tiny clockwork cogs moved two pairs of blue crystalline lenses in and out. These became luminous as they snapped into focus. Ralph was puzzled. They looked antiquated but at the same time they seemed very advanced. This tall stranger could be a secret agent. But working for whom? Ralph needed to know whether that man could be trusted.

The stranger yelled at Ralph.

"Leave, leave!"

Ralph recovered from his daze and ran for the door. Mrs Gordon pulled her husband to his feet and together they stood motionless in a trance. Ralph knew instinctively that Croucher controlled them but he could not fathom the power the creature was using to command them.

Ralph ran from the room.

The tall stranger focused on the black shape that squatted at the feet of Mr Gordon.

"So! There you are. Now I see you. I know exactly what you are," the man declared as he looked through his special imaging glasses.

The creature shifted its body, preparing to pounce. There was no expression in its eyes. It stared at the man. Recognition dawned on its craggy face. In distorted, warped, barely intelligible syllables the jet-black fiend spoke to the man.

"Greystone. I see you. I know you. I am Croucher. Let me bring you to Ragna Doom. You will always find room as a guest at my castle, the Devils Hunch. Come, accept my invitation, dear friend."

"Hell can freeze over if ever I become your friend, Croucher!" the tall stranger said defiantly.

If Greystone showed even the slightest weakness Croucher would strike, swift and deadly.

The Gordons slipped furtively from the room clutching their silver boxes one with Evan still inside. Greystone sensed grave danger as he faced the creature alone. He must leave quickly. He took a small glass sphere from his pocket and threw it close to the creature. As it broke, a cloud of green smoke billowed out, through which no one saw. He turned and quickly advanced through the hallway. Croucher's gravelly voice shouted in rage.

"There will be no escape, Greystone. I will triumph!"

Ralph, already through the front door, heard everything, including Croucher's menacing curse. Ralph was acutely aware of how evil that tiny creature was. He waited until he could follow the tall stranger and then unburdened himself.

"They've taken Evan. I so want him back," he cried. He was so breathless he could barely continue. "You wouldn't believe what they did? I couldn't help him."

"Ralph, there is nothing you could have done," the stranger told him.

"Who are you?" Ralph asked wondering how the man knew his name and everything that happened.

The man took off his strange spectacles and folded them into his top pocket.

"My name is Greystone," he said. "You have had a close escape, my boy. That creature would trap you too in a silver box if he could, helped by unwitting and deluded people. You would have been whisked away. As for who I am, I am a scholar and a master of mysterious things."

Immensely relieved Ralph couldn't stop asking questions.

"Why did the Gordons help that creature? Why did they do that to their own son? Evan shrank smaller than my hand. He looked so helpless. His own father did it and put him in the tiny box! Was it magic?"

"There was no magic," Mr Greystone interrupted Ralph. "But tell me, do you mean you actually saw the creature? Well, bless my soul. I wondered about it. I felt sure you could. These creatures can make themselves invisible so we need special equipment to see them."

Ralph realised he could see them and this scholar and master of the uncanny considered this special.

"How many of these creatures are there?" Ralph asked concerned.

Greystone's face contracted a little, as if reminded of something painful.

"A few. Yes, there are certainly a few. But we can talk about that later, you and I. First we'd better get you away from here."

Now worried and very tired Ralph leant against the huge trunk of an old tree. He told Greystone that the Gordons knew where he lived. Greystone smiled.

"Don't be concerned. The Gordons will be far away by now. That foul fiend has brainwashed them!"

Still gripped by fear Ralph asked, "Mr Greystone please tell me what that thing is? It moved fast and so ferociously."

Calmly, Greystone spoke.

"I am sure that little creature is a Snarg. That particular one calls himself Croucher. Snargs are an ancient species, nasty but highly intelligent. Over the years we have gathered information on them but as yet our records reveal very little. We know they can make themselves invisible, and doing this makes it easy for them to brainwash their victims. Brainwashing can take the snargs days and days, driving their victims to the edge of madness until they become only too willing to please. As to why they are here, I don't yet know. They shouldn't be here at all!"

Ralph stood up from the tree and brushed the bark dust from his sleeve as he listened to Greystone. He felt relieved knowing someone like Greystone was opposing these monsters.

"Where do these snargs come from?" Ralph asked, "and what are your strange glasses for?"

A smile flickered across Greystone's face. "Glasses! I call them gonoculars. They see all kinds of strange things that have found their way into our world. Invisible things. Things that shouldn't be here at all. Such as Snargs."

Greystone gestured for Ralph to follow.

"I think it is time you and I went on a little journey," he continued.

"There are certain matters you have to know. To begin with there is the reason you see snargs without the aid of Gonoculars. However, we must press on."

After a short distance they came to Wattle Alley. The dimly lit street had high walls on either side, and in one there was a large wooden door, aged and worn. Greystone stopped in front of it.

"This is no ordinary door," he said. "And beyond it lies another equally special door. Very few people in our world can use these doors. To most they are invisible. Those of us who know call them "Ghost Doors." They lead us to another dimension of existence.

"They are the greatest and best-kept secret of our world. What lies beyond is extraordinary. Another world where the rules of nature have been rewritten! Once you go through one of these doors you become bound by an oath to never reveal anything about them. This binding oath makes you one of us, part of the guild we call the Binders. Now listen to what I say: sticks and stones may break your bones but nothing must make you break this oath! Do I have your word?"

Ralph nodded. "Yes," he said.

Greystone struck the door three times. The door was pulled ajar by a short, squat man with a bald head.

"Yeah?" he said brusquely.

Greystone spoke firmly to him.

"The Oaks are bare but the heart is strong."

The little man slowly opened the wide door and bid them to enter. As he sloped into the murkiness the man muttered his response.

"May your journey be just?"

Ralph guessed those exchanges were passwords but the little man puzzled him.

"Who is that?" he asked.

"He is a Gate Keeper," was all Greystone said.

The door clanged shut behind them. Ralph sensed something menacing would happen. He wanted to know more but there was no time to ask.

Loud noises boomed and encircled them like a big storm. Stretched ahead like a long tunnel Ralph saw light swirl into a vortex. The wind roared from the vortex and hit them full in the face. Ralph wanted to turn back. He hesitated.

"Come on," Greystone yelled above the noise. "This is a cross-over between what you think is real and what becomes real. Once you experience this, your perception of reality will change."

Ralph didn't know what Greystone meant but the words struck a chord inside him and he nodded.

"Where are we going?" Ralph shouted.

"To Wychen. To another world, my boy," Greystone cried.

The tall, grey haired man marched resolutely into the howling vortex and was gone.

Fearing he would be stranded, Ralph quickly plunged after Greystone. His heart was in his mouth. He saw light and dark crash together. He was dragged forward. A huge rush of energy and heat struck him as if a giant oven door had opened. Then, in a blink of an eye, he arrived by Greystone's side.

four: sir john's book

Ralph was no longer in Wattle Alley. He was a million miles from anywhere he had ever known.

"Never will you have seen a place like this," Greystone said with a huge smile. Ralph was too astounded to answer.

Greystone spoke firmly as he gave instructions to Ralph.

"When you find the right doors, Wychen becomes a never-ending place. In the guild we say a Ghost Door is like a flower: a thing of beauty but which only opens for those with the right key. Those who are the butterflies and bees of the world. Ghost Doors open only for special people. The believers!"

Greystone had more to explain.

"Each new door discovered is recorded and mapped by a group of explorers. I am one of them. We form a secret guild known only to ourselves. We are the Binders."

Ralph was torn between looking around this extraordinary new world and listening to Greystone. It was all like a dream. The narrow path meandered through lush pastureland and led serenely to a small brook crossed by a tiny wooden bridge. To their right a huge boulder protruded strangely from the ground. Ralph ran to the boulder almost in a trance and climbed up it. He could see far into the distance.

"Everything is so green," Ralph said. "It's warm and summery but we have just come from winter. I can see grassy hills and huge woods." He paused. Something was missing. "I can't see any gates or hedges! Why is that?"

"Why? That's simple," Greystone said. "Animals are not kept prisoner in Wychen!"

Ralph looked concerned. "You mean they roam about like wild animals?"

This amused Greystone.

"Wychen has rules," he said and explained further. "It does not always conform to the ordinary laws of physics as you know them. I wouldn't say the creatures are wild. Most go about their business properly although some may be hunters and meat eaters. It has to be said that most don't have a taste for humans, since they don't meet many of us, but the odd one will think of trying us. You will begin to know when this happens because their expression changes as they start counting in their heads how many mouthfuls you would make. But this is rare. Very rare. Mostly they prefer to eat things from their own world."

Ralph struggled with this concept.

"While I'm here," he said, "I think I'm going to be a vegetarian. Just to be safe!"

"Hum," Greystone said, "I see you're a lad who might learn quickly. One more thing, Ghost doors somehow change the structure of our being, but only while we are here. There is a sacred nature to Wychen which is beyond our abilities to fathom."

"I can follow that," Ralph said thoughtfully. "Just."

As Ralph jumped from the rock he felt full of energy. He was not in the least tired, despite all the events in Bloomfield. He pointed northwards up the path.

"Where does that lead to?"

Greystone again gave a strange wrinkle of his face, as though the way north displeased him.

"Oh, that's the way to Groan-Minster. There is one corner of Wychen where you can moan about everything and everyone. Odd, isn't it? And without exception every-one in Groan-Minster is happy to listen. Which reminds me you must not stay in Wychen too long. People who do turn into creatures that reflect their own bad nature. You probably know already that every human carries a tiny flaw. I have seen good Binders turn slowly into ogres and never to leave Wychen again. You might think a snarg is hideous. Wait till you meet an ogre."

Ralph though for a moment.

"A moaning ogre in Groan Minster. That sounds scary!"

Greystone smiled.

"Worse still, if these late-stayers return to our world they return as beasts!" he said.

Greystone advanced with determination along the path towards the south. Ralph followed eagerly and tried not to think of these consequences.

"Where are we going?" he asked politely.

"To Tinglebury. Everyone wants to go to Tinglebury and nobody wants to leave. All the most knowledgeable people go there. If you imagine Wychen as a perpetually revolving wheel then Tinglebury is the hub."

"Why are we going there?" Ralph asked.

"We are going to meet someone who has a present for you," Greystone said and halted briefly. "He has waited many lifetimes to give it!"

Greystone paused to let this sink in. Then he said something even stranger. "I should tell you now this person is a distant relative of yours from about 400 years ago. His name is Sir John Higley."

"Four hundred years!" Ralph looked at Greystone in disbelief. "You are taking me to see a dead person? I'm not good with dead people you know!"

Greystone was amused by the idea.

'Sir John is not dead. Far from it. He is just different from what you might expect in a relative of yours and as this is your first time in Wychen I don't want to shock you too much."

"He hasn't got six arms or two heads, has he?" Ralph joked.

"No, nothing quite so dramatic," Greystone said. "Your distant relative has become a stoat!"

"Did you say stoat? As in weasel?" Ralph asked. Then he laughed at that picture in his head. But Greystone was serious.

'Sir John comes from a long line of Binders," he said. "Poor Sir John was the first to make the mistake of staying too long. He became a stoat before he knew what was happening. He can still talk, though."

Ralph giggled. "This is going to be cool. I am going to see a 400-year-old relative and my first talking stoat!"

"Now, Ralph," warned Greystone, "no poking fun at Sir John. He has waited a long time to see one of his kin and give you this birthday present."

"But my birthday's not till Wednesday," Ralph said.

Greystone raised his eyebrows as though this was something he not had expected.

"All I know," he said thoughtfully, "is that since I told him that I had found you he has pestered me about this birthday present."

Ralph was so pleased about meeting Sir John he wasn't bothered about discrepancy in the dates.

They came to a wooden signpost for Tinglebury and saw the village nestled in the slight dip between two hills.

"Can you see those round houses with pointed roofs?" asked Greystone.

"Yes and…. wow, they all look crooked. Some larger buildings have smaller buildings sticking from their roofs and even smaller houses perched on top," Ralph replied with eyes that grew larger. From a distance Ralph could see villagers moving about. They looked like ordinary people but from that distance he couldn't be sure.

Greystone pointed.

"Just beyond the town and over to your right. The large structure with three turrets is Splinter Down Hall and that is where Sir John lives."

Ralph saw that the large building towered impressively.

"That's the biggest house in all the village," he said. "The longer you stay in Tinglebury, the larger your house becomes. They grow with time."

When they reached the hall Greystone insisted Ralph should knock on the door. The door was huge, and a black rim knocker hung on it. Inside this was a smaller one half the size. Ralph reached for the big knocker.

"Not that one! Use the small one," Greystone told him.

Wondering who could hear such a tiny knocker Ralph gave it an extra hard bang. But on the very first knock the building shook so hard a tile fell from the little house next door and smashed on the path.

"Whoops! Sorry," Ralph said in a whisper of embarrassment.

Then he heard the long creaking sound of a door, but the big door hadn't moved. Ralph was bewildered. Then down towards his feet a tiny door opened. Out stepped an angry stoat in chequered waistcoat and highly polished shoes.

"Who's trying to rearrange my furniture with all this knocking?" demanded the stoat.

Two large shadows loomed over him. He looked up and saw his visitors.

"Bless my soul, it's Mr Greystone. And this young man, I suppose, must be Ralph."

"It's nice to see you too, Sir John!" Greystone said gaily as he stooped and shook hands. Or more precisely, as he stooped and shook a stoat-like paw.

"Delighted, delighted," Sir John replied.

The little animal was so dapper that Ralph couldn't resist a comment.

"Look, he's wearing such nice neat little clothes," Ralph whispered to Greystone.

Greystone grimaced but was too late to answer. Sir John interrupted in a huffy voice.

"Good gracious, I am not hard of hearing, young man. Did you think I would walk around naked then?"

Ralph looked down into two spectacled eyes that watched him sternly.

"No, sir," he replied.

"Then try and learn some manners, even if you can't learn any sense," Sir John said brusquely. "Whispering is rude or it was in my day."

Sir John raised both paws above his head and looked at Greystone as if to say, 'What is it all coming to?'

"Ralph means no harm," Greystone said quickly. "This is his first day in Wychen."

But Sir John was not one to pull his punches.

"There will be others that will buck his ideas up if I don't!"

Ralph was mortified.

"I am so sorry, Sir John," Ralph said quickly. "It's just that your clothes make you the smartest stoat I have ever seen."

Flattery did the trick. Sir John grabbed Ralph by the hand and said, "That's good of you to say, lad. You stick with old John and he'll see you right! I'm glad you brought him, Mr Greystone. Now let's step inside."

Sir John slipped back through the small door. Greystone and Ralph followed through the larger one.

"It's really big in here," Ralph said. When he looked up to the ceiling he saw something truly staggering. The roof was a dome filled with a gigantic, ornate Planetarium.

"That is amazing, those large globes are revolving planets aren't they. Oh and that's the Sun and, oh, I can see little moons too!" he said excitingly.

Underneath the mechanical wizardry ran steps and platforms that allowed Sir John to make scientific adjustments.

"I have some grave news for you," Greystone said, and as he spoke a veil of great sadness descended over Sir John's face.

"In the past two or three weeks children have gone missing from Broomfield. Black-Bob and I are convinced the snargs are behind this. We believe the snargs are kidnapping the children and taking them to Wychen and down into the caverns of Ragna Doom."

Sir John shuffled uneasily, deep in thought. At last he looked over his spectacles at Greystone.

"Impossible," he said. "Snargs have never been seen outside Ragna Doom since the time of Judge Majestic!"

Greystone raised a hand. He had to disagree on this. He needed to convince Sir John.

"I know, like you, that snargs cannot pass through the Great Seal," Greystone said in a commanding voice, "but I have seen them in our human world. What if they have found a way through the Great Seal? Much time has passed. Much may have happened that we do not know. They may have found another way out of Ragna Doom. What if they have a new type of projection system, to transport themselves directly into our world and Wychen's?

"We have discovered that they can transport children by shrinking them and stabilizing them in a tiny silver box. This may be part of a projection system to take the children straight to Ragna Doom. And if that were not enough, we think Jack Thorn is back at work and involved in all this!"

Sir John snarled through his tiny gritted teeth.

"If this is true then it is bad. Very bad," Sir John said softly. "I know what snargs can do. I'll bet that the snargs will be using those poor children as slaves to stoke the boilers of their cruel machine. And if Jack is back you can be sure his filthy hands will be in it, whether snargs are there or not. If I could leave Wychen I'd get half way up Thorn's trouser leg and shake all the snargs out of him, I swear I would."

Ralph chuckled with excitement but when he spoke it was all serious.

"I'll help you stop him, Sir John."

Greystone was appalled at Ralph's presumption and gave him a stern stare.

"Ralph, I despair of you. You don't know enough. You are no match for Thorn. He is a predator. He sticks with his own kind, just as the Snargs do. Cross his path in any shape or form and he'll put you in a silver box!"

"I survived the snarg attack at the Gordons, didn't I?" Ralph piped up proudly.

"He's a fighter, Mr Greystone. You must give him that," Sir John said with gusto.

"Sir John, this is not about strength, or even about courage," Greystone said, berating them both. "Stealth is a precious art. Knowing when to strike is even a greater one."

"All right, all right," said Sir John as he placated Greystone. "Let us then change the subject to one we can manage."

Suddenly, a set of alarm bells sounded loudly, sending Sir John into wild shouts of "Hooray. Hooray!"

He scrambled up the metal staircase into the workings of the Planetarium. There he examined the positions of all the spheres. He leant over and shouted with exuberance, "It's a conjunction. It's the Alphecca. A regal king and a lowly beggar. Who would have thought it? What can it mean? Is one of them in Wychen and the other in Ragna Doom? But which is which and when and where is anyone's guess. There are many good omens here."

Greystone and Ralph watched as Sir John bounded down the winding steps and shouted, "Perhaps it's time to throw the dice!"

Sir John looked back up at the Planetarium.

"There is so much work still to do!" he sighed. "Now where was I? Oh yes, I remember. A few centuries ago I had a chance encounter with an imp called Nimlet. I discovered he was a booksmith!"

"What's a booksmith?" Ralph asked. Sir John tapped the side of his furry snout as a signal to the impetuous Ralph and smiled to reveal sharp little teeth.

"Booksmiths are at the cutting edge of all the imp technology. Very clever, these imps."

Suddenly Sir John seemed to have a problem with his pointy stoat ears. Gently he scratched behind his left one then behind his right, in a very stoatish way. He then continued with his story.

"Imps don't have friendships they make bargains. But you must think wisely before you swear an oath on a deal with an Imp! There will be no get-out clauses and they always collect their dues. They have no compassion for oath breakers.

"Now, back to Nimlet. He agreed to craft a book for me. It was to contain copies of handwritten scrolls belonging to the very first binder, Judge Majestic. These scrolls tell of his encounter with snargs!"

Sir John moistened his lips and paused for a moment. "In return I had to keep something safe for him." Again he stopped, grinned and tapped the side of his nose. He then ambled over to a large bookcase and continued to tell his story.

"I see nothing of Nimlet and then out of the blue he arrives at my door clutching the book. Such beautiful workmanship, the cover reads 'Raven's Wood' and is embellished in ornate gold leaf. It tells of the legendary place that is lost in a maze of ghost doors, which has become an enigma, a kind of Holy Grail for us binders to find. Unfortunately, Judge Majestic was the only one who knew its location and he took its secret to the grave."

At last Sir John pointed to a small book on the top shelf. Almost jumping for joy he asked the tall Greystone if he would fetch it down for him. Greystone obliged. The book looked precious. It was the first time Greystone had seen it and the image of a black raven on the cover drew his attention. Sir John held out both paws. Politely Greystone handed the book over.

Although the book was pocketsize it was almost too heavy for Sir John. Straining not to drop it he handed it to Ralph.

"I want you to have this book. It is of no further service to me," Sir John panted.

Open-mouthed Ralph carefully took it.

"Thank you," he said graciously

Sir John gave a big sigh when the book left his hands, as though he was sad at the loss.

"There is one condition, though," Sir John said with a smile.

"Only one?" Ralph said happily.

"Before you take it away," Sir John said with great meaning, "I would like you to read me the opening chapter."

"I'll be only too pleased," Ralph said. He carefully opened it. The pages were old but not crumbly like the paper should be. Ralph rubbed a page between his fingers. It felt cold, but it was not like any paper Ralph had seen before. Sir John saw Ralph was puzzled by the texture.

"This is the finest paper imps can make. We have no idea how they do it. It has a most unusual property. It will not burn."

Astounded, Ralph turned to the opening chapter. He took a deep breath and began.

'This testament is from Judge Majestic, of the Brewham Hundred, written in his own hand in 1496 AD.

Heed my warning for I shall say it long and true: none may enter Raven's Wood unless forsworn. Repent and be forsworn or face the folly of greed and ignorance.

A key I found, one simple key that's all. Nothing special to look at but a snarg key, dull looking and odd of shape. I dragged it from the marshes.

Its appearance was like a twig of a monkey-puzzle tree. I was able to twist the stem of it. Three times I turned this devil's knot, three times sun-wise, and a lock of locks was cast open.

When the owl hooted high above the gloomy moot I heard a sound deep below the earthy ground. I heard rocks cracking, rocks breaking, and a lonely wind roar. A watery chasm was breached unto another world and a mighty gateway hurled wide open.

There in a subterranean world sat hordes of snargs. Where wheel upon wheel turns the devil's work. Small and squat I knew they would come scurrying with their dark ugly faces.

What foolishness to have seized that key?

It was a counterfeit imp key reworked by Smelter, a master of the snarg forge. He turned this Imp craftsmanship into a much more sinister object. This key belongs to a snarg lord known as Croucher and among the snargs it had a name.

They spoke of it. "Where's our Shine, the Shine?" These grim snarg spectres leapt upon my back screaming like banshees. They hung there day after day. Invisible. Unshakeable. Upon my shoulder the bony things sat, whispering evil words in my ear. Riches and treasures they promised. The worst was Croucher, the ugliest and grimmest of all, who never stopped his temptations to me. To rid myself of his deadly poison, I succumbed.

They gave me wealth, that nice feeling of gold in purse. I gave them back their "Shine", their trinket. I gave them freedom.

Stealth gave them passage to the hovels, the dwellings of the Hundred. Slyly they entered these simple places.

From every man and woman they stole a child.

What had I done? It was I who gave them this freedom. The suffering was mine as I watched village after village turn into stores of misery. To atone for my guilt I pursued them.

Finally one night I caught Ragnag. He was a brother of Croucher. So I shook this wriggling snarg and his squawking brought more of them. I held Ragnag tight and would not let him go.

"Give us Ragnag," they shouted. I heeded them not.

"Give me the Shine," I demanded, "and I will release Ragnag."

I heard them mutter and groan as they squabbled amongst themselves.

The worst of these smouldering devils held something aloft. It was black and twisted like their tongues. This foulest of creatures, Lord Croucher, held the Shine. Wicked beyond wickedness and treacherous to all outside his kin, he would not let me harm his brother. He flung the Shine angrily at my feet. And they all screeched and snarled curses.

Only when I freed Ragnag did their babbling fade.

Now these devils wanted their trinket back. Again I became their prey.

I took flight and eluded them, slipping behind trees and stooping low under bracken.

I was at their mercy. Their howling was torment until I sought sanctuary with a priest and with great lamentation relinquished the Shine to him. Now I was free and the snargs departed into their halls where those vast wheels whirl and whirl. At last I found peace. The word snarg is one I wish never to hear again.

So say I, servant of the realm, Judge Majestic, founder of the binders.

At the bottom of the page Ralph saw the Judge's signature. Below was a pictogram of a snake drawn in the shape of a figure eight, like a snake tied in a knot. Ralph wondered how easy it would be to tie a snake and not get bitten. He pushed that thought from his mind. Ralph closed the book.

"What happened to the Judge after he found his freedom?" Ralph asked.

Sir John jumped on the table and lightly touched the book. Although it was no longer his, he still wanted to handle it.

"For a long time the Judge was a troubled man," Sir John said with sadness as he neared the story's end.

"He was a walker between the two worlds. He returned to Raven's Wood and while he was there he made an oath to the Great Oaks. They are almost as old as the rocks. These Oaks are lawgivers, even for the Raven King, a mighty ruler. The Oaks warmed to Majestic's spirit and he to their wisdom. The Oaks passed a judgement on the snargs and commanded the imps to forge a great metal seal to imprison the snargs in their own world. And in their wisdom the Oaks turned the snargs' power against them by using the corrupted imp key they called the Shine to lock them in. And so it was closed, incarcerating all the snargs in Wychen's underground caverns of Ragna Doom."

Sir John paused to scratch his ear then held the book tightly. He sighed loudly and continued.

"Let me tell you more about the key. Originally it was stolen from an Imp called Rimgorn, who designed and made it. This caused bad feeling between the snargs and the imps. Ultimately, this theft leads to the Great Snarg War. Croucher stole it when still a young snarg. Even when he was young he was a nasty upstart.

Shrewdly he commissioned Smelter, a snarg black-smith to give the key darker qualities. They called it the Shine but it was a hideous thing. The snargs used it to steal happiness from people. It made Croucher stronger and invincible. He became a Lord of the Snargs. But his strength lasted only as long as the Shine was in his possession.

The imps had been very clever when they made the great door so that it could be locked and unlocked only from the outside. Wychen rock is hard so the snargs could never mine their way through; and no imp would ever let them out.

"But the Oaks can read the future. They foresaw a time when the snargs would become strong again. So the Oaks built a highly fortified keep and hid the Shine beyond the Snargs reach. No one has ever found it, or its whereabouts," Sir John paused to catch his breath before continuing,

"Others of the subterranean races, such as imps and some solitary creatures, were allowed to leave Ragna Doom before the seal was closed and most did, leaving the snargs and their evil allies locked deep underground. Judge Majestic's mark was used inside the seal as a warning. Eventually the illustrious Judge left Raven's Wood, never to return, and took to a hermit's cell in a monastery. What happened after is just legend."

Sir John solemnly stepped down. Ralph slipped the book into his pocket. Greystone sighed and said softly, "Ralph, I think we should go."

As they were leaving, Sir John called Ralph back.

"I want to tell you one last thing," he said. Then he beckoned Ralph lower and whispered in his ear.

"Keep the book close to you. When the clock strikes midnight on your 13th birthday you will see the real treasure and, when you do, tell no one!" He gave Ralph a sly wink of his eye. Standing in the doorway, Greystone heard and saw none of this. As they walked from the hall Ralph was deep in thought and remained quiet.

five: gloomstone lodge

Greystone led the way along a twisted stony path back towards the centre of Tinglebury. Ralph noticed some small creatures that ran back and forth across the narrow path. They looked odd. Two darted into the boughs of a large tree and hid there like squirrels. Ralph would have asked Greystone about them but his attention was elsewhere. As they passed a row of crooked little houses, two people came out and headed straight towards them. Once closer Greystone recognized the man as Black-Bob and greeted him warmly.

"Good day, Black-Bob, well met. Is this the new student I have heard so much about?"

"Indeed, Greystone, this is Rebecca Harwood, my understudy." Black-Bob spoke proudly. Greystone nodded and Ralph gave a shy, awkward smile. He was never at ease with girls. They were a question mark to him and he couldn't always find the words to answer! But things were different with Rebecca. Ralph seemed compelled to make an effort. He was spellbound.

He couldn't put his finger on it but there was something familiar about her. Then it came to him.

"Are you in Mrs Deacon's class?" Ralph asked, realising they were at the same school.

"Why yes!" Rebecca said and smiled. Long strawberry-blonde hair swished past her shoulders.

"I'm in Mr Hewitt's form," Ralph told her.

"That's a year below me," Rebecca said, as she remembered him. "Don't you hang out with that scruffy lad? Tom someone or other!"

"Only when I have nothing else to do," Ralph said defensively.

Rebecca looked brightly around and with a hand on her hip she asked what he thought of Tinglebury.

"Really cool," Ralph said. "I have never been to a place like this!"

Ralph spoke enthusiastically, although he wondered if that was an understatement. For Rebecca it was already a quaint old-fashioned place. She had seen and learnt of far more exciting places in that strange land. But Wychen was her passion and wild horses would not stop her enthusiasm.

"If you think Tinglebury is cool you should see the waterfalls at Hansfar. It's heart-stopping. There's eeriness all around and the cascading water makes no sound at all. The light is so bright even the carp in the pool wear sun goggles. And best of all, the ghost door is a bit of a giggle. You'll never guess what road back in Broomfield it's in?"

"No" Ralph replied, sure that he couldn't.

"Water Tap Lane! I laugh out loud every time I think of it. The Ghost Door is at the end of the lane in the little hollow of the hedge. The binders have nicknamed it the Plug Hole. But you have to be careful going through that one. It's what they call viper-tongued."

Ralph was captivated. Everything seemed to explode from her. As he listened his smile grew broader and broader.

"The Plug Hole is forked like a snake's tongue, with one entrance and two exits. As you enter, you have to lean to one side or the other for whichever exit you want. Lean the wrong way and you end up in the wrong place. It's that simple," she laughed.

"It sounds fantastic," Ralph said. "The only excitement I've had is coming face to face with a snarg." Ralph was trying to be more interesting.

Rebecca gasped. "You've seen snargs? Now that is scary! In my creature studies they say that no one has seen snargs for hundreds of years, not since they were locked in the fabled Ragna Doom. Do you know they can make themselves invisible? Except if moonlight falls on them."

"I saw them by daylight and by night," Ralph said. "They took over a family in my road. I had to fight one off and it nearly killed me!" Ralph was exaggerating but only a little. "Now I'm worried for my best friend, Evan. His parents helped the snarg capture him."

Rebecca's eyes widened with alarm.

"Wow, it must have been terrifying. I've read how nasty these creatures can be. I also read about the odd way they breed." Rebecca giggled and leant over and whispered in his ear. "They spawn just like frogs do!"

Ralph raised his eyebrows. "You've got to be joking?"

"It's true." Rebecca was adamant. "I saw it in Black-Bob's copy of the Binder's Almanac. There's a small section in the back of volume three all about Ragna Doom. There's a copy of the Almanac in the Scriptorium."

Ralph listened intently. Everything Rebecca said was new and exciting, even if he had no idea where or what a Scriptorium was. She was so bright and intense that Ralph felt out of his depth. But he wasn't going to show it.

"This is great stuff," Ralph said. "Maybe we could meet at break time at school. I will look out for you!"

Rebecca had lit a fire within him. As he waited for to her answer the momentary pause seemed an eternity.

"OK," she said.

Ralph managed to blurt out "Great" before Greystone who had finished his conversation with Black-Bob ushered him away.

As they walked away Ralph realised that Greystone was agitated. Ralph couldn't guess why. Gradually this agitation passed as Greystone spoke.

"It's time to get you home, Ralph. We can visit Wychen again if you like. In fact, I'd like you to become my understudy. Will you consider it?" Greystone said as the last of his agitation dropped away.

"Will I have to do exams?" Ralph asked apprehensively. He hated exams.

"Not exams, as such, but you do have to absorb what I teach you. Travelling in these worlds is fraught with danger. Our binder code demands us not to lose a student, on pain of being thrown out of the guild. That has happened only once during my lifetime."

There was a pause.

"Alright, I'll do it," Ralph said.

Greystone beamed and took a letter out of his pocket.

"Good lad. Now, take this letter to your headmaster Mr Brack. He is a binder and will take good care of you. He'll show you how to enter and use the binder laboratories. You will love the gimbals. It's a great place. It's where adventures begin."

Ralph was stunned to hear that Mr Brack was a binder. It seemed the once ordinary headmaster and a grey-suited bore might well be more exciting the he looked. Ralph carefully took the letter and slipped it into his pocket.

Greystone and Ralph strolled slowly from Tinglebury until they were back the way they had entered. Here Greystone gave instructions on how to return home.

"Going back through a Ghost Door is easy. That's because when you enter Wychen through a Ghost Door you leave a tiny trace of yourself behind, and when you approach that same spot on the Wychen side you trigger a trace element in the Ghost Door and it re-opens. Also, there are no Gate Keepers on the Wychen side."

As Greystone finished, Ralph heard the roaring wind and the door opened with a swirl of light.

"And hey presto," Greystone said with an enigmatic smile, "we should be at the oak door in Wattle Alley."

This time Ralph didn't hesitate and Greystone was right, they were back.

"It's a little late," Greystone said apologetically, and glancing at his watch. "Time you went straight home."

Ralph's own watch showed ten past ten. They were back in the grip of winter, where all was cold and dark.

"We've been gone hours," Ralph said worried. "I must get home before Mum and Dad."

"There is one more thing," Greystone said. "Don't mention anything of what has happened. Not to anyone. Not even your parents! The Gordons will have gone to ground by now so we must leave the task of tracing them to Black-Bob. We don't want anyone in that house destroying clues. We want Black-Bob to find them."

"My lips are sealed," Ralph whispered with a secret-agent smile.

Once they reached the end of the alley, Ralph made his way home alone. He felt a tinge of fear as he passed the Gordons' house and crossed to the opposite pavement. The house was abandoned and in darkness. But every shadow Ralph saw moved and danced in his mind. He tried not to fear the unseen, even though he felt if bad things lurked around every corner. Then, just when he thought he was safe, he glimpsed a light flicker in an upstairs room. Ralph froze. Should he run or stand fast? This ethereal light looked strange. Was it a ghost or a snarg or something even more sinister?

If just when he thought he wouldn't be more scared, he heard sounds of scraping and grunting from the dark prickly hedge next to him. Ralph had had enough; all he wanted was to be home snug and warm in bed. He was tired of being frightened out of his wits by weird things that swooped and jumped and grunted.

The next few steps took strength. But one after another and they quickened into a run. From the darkness behind him he felt black claws that tried to grab him. Were they real or just in his mind? Fear made him run faster and after the Gordons house he didn't stop until he reached his own gate.

Back on home territory he felt safe. But as he reached for the handle of his front door other things came to mind that didn't seem so good. His parents! Would he find them waiting angrily for him? At least they couldn't be as frightening as the snargs?

His hand hovered nervously on the handle. Its achingly slow turn made his spine shiver. If the door locked was locked then he was home before his parents. But if the door was unlocked he would have a lot of explaining to do. He held his breath and gave the door an irresolute push. It was locked. Ralph sighed with relief. In his pocket he fumbled for a key. His fingers sifted carefully through all the discarded sweet wrappers.

Out came the key with sticky wrappers attached which took a few frustrating moments to remove. The struggle to insert the key into the lock was a torment until finally the door was opened. Once inside he felt calmer. With the door closed firmly behind Ralph groped blindly for the light switch.

Oliver, who was asleep by the front door, suddenly scrambled up on all fours to dodge Ralph's clumsy feet. When the light came on he looked up and wagged his tail. Ralph comforted the dog with a few strokes and rubbed his ear. Excitedly Oliver jumped and licked his face.

"Lie down, there's a good boy!" Ralph whispered, trying to settle him.

Ralph clambered up the winding staircase to his bedroom glad that his late homecoming was undetected. Once in bed he reached for Sir John's book. He hadn't until then given it much attention. But he now realized it was peculiar. It was much heavier than expected for a book of that size. He took a similar sized one from his bookcase, weighing it in his hand against Raven's Wood. Sir John's book was twice as heavy.

Ralph pored over the book, pondering on what Sir John's last words about "real treasure" meant. Ralph sighed and yawned. Then he remembered Evan. He felt bad. How had he, despite everything, thought of treasure rather than his missing friend? Full of sadness, Ralph closed the book. His sleepy eyes fixed on the image of the Raven on the cover. Its black pearl eyes were mesmerising. Ralph pushed the book under his pillow and drifted to sleep. He later didn't hear his bedroom door open. It was his mother checking all was well on their return home.

By midnight, Twizzle Street was the quietest place in the neighbourhood. The temperature was well below freezing and the snow, which had turned mushy during the day, was solid again and crunchy underfoot. As Ralph slept warm and snug in bed, a strange lone visitor arrived at the icy and deserted Gloomstone Lodge. It was the man with the large floppy brimmed hat and long coat.

He paused quietly to make sure he wasn't being watched. Then without any ado he vaulted the high garden wall; his dark coat billowed and flapped in the air. A muffled thud marked his landing on the other side. A master of stealth he stole into the inky shadows. Who was he waiting for?

Moments later at the other end of the street Black-Bob appeared and was soon joined by Mr Greystone. Little was said between the pair before they arrived at the Gordons house.

"Will anyone come tonight?" Greystone asked.

Black-Bob was confident.

"We could still be lucky," he whispered, "even though the Gordons plans went badly awry! Our man will still show if he thinks his collection is on schedule."

Quietly they tried to open the Gordons gate.

"It's locked!" Greystone said in a hushed voice.

"I'll climb the gate," Black-Bob muttered. "You watch the street."

Greystone concealed himself in the gateway as Black-Bob climbed nimbly into the garden of the lodge. Neither had any notion they were being watched a short distance away. Greystone stood guard as Black-Bob stepped lightly and quickly across the lawn to the Lodge's side. Then he vanished from view behind the rear of the house.

It was eerily silence. Then, after a few minutes, Greystone heard muffled voices and feet scuff on loose gravel. He peered over the gate and saw a man sprinting towards him. Black-Bob staggered behind and shouted, "Stop him, Greystone. Whatever you do, stop him!"

Greystone watched in alarm, trying to determine where this dark figure was headed. The man saw Greystone at the gate and changed direction. He then charged toward the high wall.

Like a gazelle he was up and over but landed awkwardly on the street below. His balance regained he took to his heels. Desperate to gain on the man, Greystone powered his muscles into a sprint. But the stranger had greater speed, leaving Greystone further behind.

As they rounded the corner, the man was already twenty yards in front. Slowly, Greystone was losing heart.

The stranger followed the long tall privet hedge that ended at the gravel drive to an old Victorian house. He turned sharply onto the drive and hidden from view, pulled a shiny object from inside his coat. It looked like a round metal bar.

Then he disappeared.

Seconds later, Greystone rounded the corner. No one was there! Where was the man? He was perplexed. Greystone was too close for the man to have found a hiding place. When Black-Bob caught up he saw his friend's mystified look.

"Were did he go?" Black-Bob asked.

"I have no idea," Greystone puffed, trying to catch his breath. Black-Bob had an astute look in his eye.

"Perhaps he jumped through a Ghost Door," said Black-Bob. Then he paused for a moment. "Which would mean we missed one some how."

Greystone looked thoughtfully at Black-Bob. He felt stressed.

"That will be a first. But I can't believe it, especially right under our noses. Let us check," Greystone said and pulled his gonoculars from his pocket. He slipped them on and carefully powered them up. They made a whirring sound as they began to glow. Greystone meticulously scanned the whole area, in the hope of a Ghost Door. But there was nothing. And yet, invisible even to the gonoculars, the stranger was still there, right in front of Greystone. He watched their every move. Neither Greystone nor Black-Bob saw him, for he was sandwiched between two dimensions of space.

"I knew this was pointless," Greystone said with a disappointed sigh. He adjusted his gonoculars and fell silent. Had he seen something?

Greystone stretched out his hand in the hope of touching something solid. In the gonoculars' field of vision he thought he saw a thin shadowy form. It was there for only a second before it evaporated like fingers of fog. Greystone groaned in frustration. There was no trace of a Ghost Door and none of the man either.

"You recognized him, didn't you?" Black-Bob asked.

"I did, I'm ashamed to say," Greystone said in a low voice, grimacing.

"It was Jack, Jack Thorn. I don't want to talk about him just now, nor the evil trade he plies, though I fear he will be back. My guess is that he has not yet collected his precious cube from the Gordons."

"It seems the rogue has learnt much," Black-Bob said with heavy emphasis. "He must be dealt with. This has to stop!"

Black-Bob was frustrated but also annoyed by what he regarded as Greystone's bungle in letting Thorn slip free. Greystone hung his head in the knowledge Black-Bob was close to the truth.

"Jack will come to a sticky end one day, of that I am sure," was all Greystone said.

"There is a lot we don't know about Jack," Black-Bob said, a deep frown on his face. "I heard talk of him murdering a man after he went off the rails, and that he got away with it. The man has lost all his conscience. But it seems the luck of the devil rides with him. Neither of us should tackle him alone."

With this sombre thought, they returned to the Lodge. The cold chilled their very bones as they kept watch until dawn. But every second of discomfort was worthwhile if they had caught their man and saved more children.

Ralph's alarm went off at seven in the morning. He flung out an arm and turned the horrid thing off, and lay thinking what strange things he had dreamt that night. He rolled to the side of the bed to get out. Something strangely lumpy was under his pillow. The Book! Those dreams weren't dreams. They really had happened. He had some serious questions to think about. Not least…how was he to stop his mother finding the book?

He needed a hiding place. He looked around his room and the only place that seemed right was the large chest at the end of his bed. Still in his pyjamas he climbed out of bed and slid the book gently under a jumper at the bottom of the chest. "That will do for now," he thought, closing the lid. There would be time to study the book properly once he was home.

Ralph dressed quickly and went downstairs to have breakfast. He made some porridge using plenty of milk. By the time his mother was up, Ralph had already finished and his empty bowl was in the sink. They both said their good mornings, just as Ralph noticed his mother casting a critical eye over him.

"Have you brushed your hair yet?" she asked firmly.

"I have," he confirmed.

"Cleaned your teeth?" his mother asked.

Ralph was used to the routine. It was part of a check-list his mother went through every morning.

He gave his mother his standard answer: "Yes, Mum."

"You're supposed to clean them after breakfast, not before," his mother grumbled.

"Yes, Mum," he repeated.

"Ralph, I'm going to write a thank-you note for Mrs Gordon. Could you drop it through her letter box on your way home from school," she said.

Ralph was going to say there wasn't any point, as the Gordons weren't there any more, but thought better of it, saying only, "Yes, Mum." He wasn't always so compliant but at that moment he didn't want any distractions.

He went back up to his room and packed for school while his mother wrote the thank-you letter. He glanced out of his frosty window at the church clock and couldn't believe how time had flown. He had wanted to be away early. He grabbed his things and dashed down the stairs shouting, "Bye, Mum. I'm off to school now."

"Don't forget my letter," his mother called.

Ralph stopped in his tracks. His mother's letter had suddenly reminded him of the one Greystone gave him for Mr Brack. Ralph raced back up stairs, wishing he wasn't so stupid and forgetful.

With both letters in his bag he charged out of the house, slammed the front door in a whirlwind, and sent Oliver into his usual fit of barking. And that always made his mother cross. She would shout at him but he would be out of earshot.

Ralph had pulled on his coat by the time he reached the gate. In the night an untouched blanket of fresh snow had fallen.

As he passed the Gordons front gate he was nervous and curious. The gate was broken, as if something had hit it really hard during the night. Wide open, it hung limp. What had broken it, he wondered? Wood splinters were scattered across the snow. He paused and briefly looked to see if anyone was about. The gate puzzled him, but not to know Evan's fate troubled him more. But that answer had to wait. He turned on his heels and hurried towards Oswald's, his school.

Tom was coming up the street so Ralph waited by the newsagents. But Tom walked slowly, reluctant to meet his friend.

"Are you all right, Tom?" Ralph asked, concerned. "You look a bit pale this morning."

Tom was off colour but that wasn't all. For a few moments he stared at Ralph as if he had seen a ghost. That look from made Ralph uneasy.

"Its nothing," Tom said. "I had boiled eggs for breakfast and I must have eaten them too fast."

But his voice was so strained that Ralph wasn't convinced. Could it be Tom hadn't expected him to be at school and that meant he knew the Gordons had more than tea planned yesterday? Ralph decided not to mention anything about Evan.

As he went through the school gates he wanted to see Evan, but it was not a morning for miracles.

Ralph's form room was number thirty-four in the north block. Tom followed along the corridor. It bustled with pupils, all jostling in different directions. A group of the bigger lads were slouched against the wall and jeered at the younger boys football team for playing like cissies. "We saw you get thrashed by Haddon School. The girls' hockey team could have played better." The younger boys were having none of it. Although seethed with anger they kept their cool until they were far enough away and they yelled back "Rubbish" and "Get lost." By the time the older boys gave chase the younger ones were long gone.

Ralph was halfway along the corridor, lost in thought, before he remembered the letter for Mr Brack. He stopped so abruptly that Tom carried on without noticing.

"I'll catch up with you later," Ralph shouted.

Tom shrugged, as Ralph turned back.

"Oi, Higley, you're going the wrong way," someone shouted, but Ralph was too preoccupied. He was wholly focused on reaching the Headmaster's Study.

six: the headmaster

Finally Ralph arrived at the headmaster's dark oak door. He stood and dug in his pockets for Mr Greystone's letter.

Eventually he pulled the envelope from his jacket. It was badly creased. Ralph looked in dismay.

"Oh no, I can't give it to him like that," he thought.

Down on one knee, Ralph used his other leg and with the flat of his hand smoothed out the creases. It was a marginal improvement but it would never look pristine. Ralph took a deep breath and knocked softly on the door. He heard a stern instruction to enter.

Ralph opened the door gingerly, hovering nervously in the doorway. The Mr Brack sat reading letters at a very large desk. He wore a dark suit and black-rimmed glasses. He spoke without looking up.

"Come in and close the door properly," he said. Ralph did. Mr Brack had put his letters into a neat pile before he gave the boy his full attention, after that he forced a smile to put Ralph at ease.

"Good morning, sir," Ralph said.

What Mr Brack saw before him was a slightly untidy pupil. When he noticed Ralph's tie was crooked he showed disapproval and muttered, "Hum." Mr Brack liked tidiness. Things that were not in the right place irritated him immensely.

"And you are?" Mr Brack asked with forced kindness.

"Ralph Higley, sir," Ralph said, before he broke into a childish smile.

"I have heard that name before, Higley," Mr Brack said as he slowly interlaced his fingers. "And what can I do for you?"

Ralph held out the crinkled envelope.

"I was told to give you this, sir."

Mr Brack took the letter in a whimsical fashion and laid it on his desktop like a flower he wished was less wilted.

"It's from Mr Greystone," Ralph continued.

"I see his mark," Mr Brack said, suddenly looking at Ralph with more interest. He quickly slit the envelope with a paperknife, whipping the letter out with practiced speed. Silence fell as he read.

The silence grew long and heavy, which added to the stifling effect Ralph felt. The room was dim and musty. Ceiling-high shelves filled with old books stretched along each wall. Ralph was relieved when Mr Brack finished and looked up from the letter.

"You have made an impression on Mr Greystone," Mr Brack said, as his eyes narrowed and darkened. "He asks that you attend the binder classes in the Gimbals."

Mr Brack gave a heavy sigh, clearly unimpressed by the dishevelled student.

"No doubt you will be another of Greystone's prodigal flops," he said.

"Can't you put your tie on straight? To become a Binder you must sharpen your appearance as well as your mind."

Ralph nodded obediently, adjusting his tie as he did so.

"Yes, sir." he said. "Please, sir, what are the Gimbals?"

Mr Brack liked an enquiring mind and began to warm to the lad. He pulled his glasses down his nose and peered over them.

"A good question," Mr Brack said with surprise. "This must be all so new to you!"

He then explained.

"Below the town there is a vast network of secret tunnels called the Gimbals. Some link the old houses and important buildings together. All lead to huge vaulted rooms. One is the Scriptorium, while the others have been turned into specialised laboratories. Collectively, these form the Binder headquarters for Broomfield."

Mr Brack held the letter in both hands and crumpled it into a tight ball. He then handed it back to Ralph. What stunned Ralph more was the Headmaster told him to pop the paper into a strange-looking teapot that was sitting on a small side table. Ralph was stunned. Nervously, he stepped over to the table too astonished to question the orders.

It was an odd teapot. Potbellied in shape with tiny rectangular metal panels held together with rivets, it looked heavy. The lid was domed like a car hubcap, with small flat fins that radiated from a small cylindrical handle that protruded from the top. The spout reminded Ralph of a miniature cannon. It looked lethal.

Mr Brack nodded with a dark grin. Rare in a man who seldom smiles.

Ralph lifted the lid and dropped the paper into the pot. He closed the lid, edging away from the table quickly. For a while, nothing happened. Then the cylindrical handle moved up and down like a piston. The lid rose up and spun. But that was just the beginning. Two telescopic legs sprouted from the bottom of the pot and lifted it five inches from the table. The lid spun like a gyroscope and kept the body of the teapot stable while it balanced on small legs. The whole thing seemed alive, as it wandered about like a headless chicken. It came to an abrupt halt perilously close to the table's edge and there it seesawed backwards and forwards as if in perpetual motion.

Mr Brack saw Ralph was perturbed.

"It's alright, Ralph. All you have to do is put your hand in front of it!"

Ralph wanted none of it. If that spout was a cannon he feared he would be stung, shot, burnt, or suffer pain in some other odd way. He gritted his teeth and with heart-pounding effort stepped forward with an outstretched hand. The lid began to spin faster and faster. Then the whole pot started to shake. Ralph was terrified it would explode.

He braced himself and waited for the worst. He heard something rattle inside and the sound grew louder and louder until at last something shot out. Whatever it was, it flew straight and fast into his palm but landed with a gentle touch.

Ralph looked closer and saw a wonderful disc of deep blue crystal the size of a large coin. He stared into its depths and couldn't believe his eyes. Curled around a golden letter B he saw the tiniest of creatures. It was a dragon, he was sure. He had seen pictures of creatures like this in books, although they always seemed huge. This one was exquisitely small. The dragon blinked its eyes and looked at him. Ralph saw it was alive and very, very real.

"This really is a dragon, isn't it?" he said as he turned to Mr Brack. His eyes widened with astonishment. "I can't believe it's real. It is real, isn't it, sir?"

"Yes," Mr Brack said. He sat calm, elbows on his desk and fingers clasped together he watched Ralph closely.

"These dragons come from deep caves high in the Glenowan Mountains in a faraway region of Wychen. And that crystal object," he said, "is known as a binder shield."

Ralph was so captivated by the dragon he didn't once look up.

"There is much to learn about your dragon," Mr Brack said, "Dragons can live for a 1,000 years and even longer. You have a male dragon. His name is Synge. He is around six hundred years old and you are his ninth keeper. Now I shall teach you how to let him out."

Mr Brack made a twisting motion with his fingers to indicate what Ralph had to do.

"Turn the shield bezel anticlockwise to open the top but don't shake him out. You must wait until he jumps."

Ralph turned the bezel and it sprung open. It was a strange moment, as he waited for the dragon to pop out. Then everything happened quickly. The tiny dragon jumped and the moment it landed it was the size of a pony. The dragon kept low with its flowing tail swirled in an arc around Ralph, his new keeper.

The colours reflected in the dragon's wings captivated Ralph. He watched them fold and unfold like a peacock's tail. "He's mine, my very own dragon!" he giggled. The dragon snorted like a bull around his feet, while Ralph did his best to remain composed.

He then summoned up the courage to call out his name: "Synge." The dragon stopped circling and with bright eyes swished his tail like a dog. Ralph noticed a curious smell, like a smouldering candle.

"They don't really breathe fire do they?" he asked Mr Brack.

"Oh yes!" said the headmaster. "Pull their tails or get them angry or too excited and they can spew out fire intense enough to smelt steel. You must beware. Dragons are very emotional creatures. The essence of good dragonkeeping is, to be calming and not to let it get out of control. We don't encourage binder students to feed dragons on the school premises. In the past, some students were careless and fed their dragons indoors at home, only to have their houses burn down. And don't bother to ask your parents if their house insurance covers them for dragon fires. It won't!"

Ralph felt bewildered. He ran through the important questions.

"What do I feed Synge? Are dragons easy to feed?"

He saw a sardonic grin return to Mr Brack's face.

"Almost as easy as feeding a fish," Mr Brack said. "Dragon appetites relate to their original size, which means they eat very little. A few houseflies, perhaps or black beetles. They need fresh food so it's best that you feed them live insects. If you feed them too much or more than once a day you will make them hyperactive and trouble-some and reluctant to return to the shield."

Mr Brack paused. He saw Ralph stroke Synge's head and knew they were perfectly matched.

"Stroking him is very good. It calms him," Mr Brack continued. There was much to tell this new dragon-keeper. "I have already fed him so you do not need to feed him today. Wait until tomorrow. You can keep Synge's supper in this empty matchbox. Synge will sleep a lot and should be left undisturbed most of the time. And now he should go back into the shield. This is what you must do. Put the shield close to the floor but still keep hold of it. Synge will understand and will jump in."

"Like this," said Ralph with the shield held an inch above the carpet. Synge scampered around the room, just like Ralph's dog Oliver. He made a frantic dash towards Ralph but stopped short as if something held him back.

"Yes, but quickly!" Mr Brack said. Then he saw the problem. "Make sure the bezel is fully open or you'll give poor Synge a headache!"

Ralph quickly pushed it wider. Immediately Synge leapt into the shield, shrinking back to a tiny size. Mr Brack again made the twisting motion with his fingers and Ralph screwed the bezel shut.

"Excellent, Ralph," said Mr Brack. Then he had a thought and said: "Mrs Pickles the school librarian holds a class for problem dragons on Thursdays. These classes are well worth attending. She tackles every aspect from their feeding habits to their health and happiness."

Ralph smiled and took the hint. He told Mr Brack that he would enrol with Mrs Pickles.

"Excellent," Mr Brack said.

As Ralph was putting the shield in his pocket, Mr Brack stopped him.

"No, not there. Binders usually wear shields under their jacket lapels, always hidden from view. You must be wearing your shield to gain entry to the Gimbals."

Ralph took his shield from his pocket and held it awkwardly, as he wondered how it attached. He saw a very thin spike on the back of the shield. He tried to pin this to his jacket when the spike seemed to take over. It pierced the material and without Ralph's help it twisted and knotted itself into the cloth. Ralph looked with doubt at Mr Brack but the headmaster reassured him.

"This pin is a locking mechanism. Only you can remove it without waking the dragon. It makes a superb anti-theft device. Not one shield has been stolen in the past 500 hundred years!"

Ralph looked distracted, so Mr Brack tapped the end of his pencil sharply on the desk and to regain his attention.

"Listen carefully. If you are ever in mortal danger, release the dragon. They will defend you to their death. They are tenacious and loyal. And now a word of warning; do not brag and do not show off, otherwise your dragon will get angry. He will know if you do this. Dragons can hear a whisper two miles away. So think twice before you do anything silly. Do you understand?"

Again Ralph nodded, but with so many rules he was tempted to ask if he could take the dragon on a week's trial. And if that didn't work he could send it back. He was about to suggest this when the headmaster ordered a return to his classroom. There he would soon be called to his binder's lesson.

Back in class, Ralph made his way to a seat near the front. The goons always sat at the back of the room where they made the most noise. Sometimes Tom sat with them.

But that morning Tom was not his usual self. He sat miserable and clutching his bag tightly. At one point he opened his bag, as if to check something was safe. Ralph thought he saw something in his bag that was silver and it made him curious. Ralph was ready to slide across and sit with him. He wanted another glimpse in the bag, but class tutor Mr Hewitt stormed in.

"KEEP THE NOISE DOWN!" he bellowed.

When extremely annoyed Mr Hewitt's voice raised two octaves above normal. Not one pupil dared to snicker even though it sounded funny. No one crossed Mr Hewitt. Hearing the sound of his voice, everyone stopped mid-sentence and a deadly silence filled the room.

"Do you know," Mr Hewitt said as he looked around the room with a theatrical air of disappointment. "I just came past one of the lower forms on my way here and guess what I could hear? You, Ralph Higley, what do you think I could hear?"

Ralph had not been paying attention. He had been deep in thought worrying about Evan. Mr Hewitt's question startled him and he was jolted back to the class.

"Don't know, sir," Ralph replied. It was a truth of sorts… he hadn't even heard the question.

"Nothing, Higley," Mr Hewitt said. "Absolutely nothing. You lot are turning into a mindless rabble. In three or more years you'll be out on the street looking for jobs and who will want mindless chatterboxes? No one."

He shook his head, dismayed and called the register. When nothing was said about Evan's absence, Ralph decided to ask.

He waited for the pupils to pile out of the classroom as Mr Hewitt shouted after them, as he did usually, "Quiet in the corridors. I do not want to come after anyone. You have been warned."

"Yes, Higley, what is it now?" Mr Hewitt asked, as he closed the register and clipped a pen into his top pocket.

"Please sir, do you know if Evan Gordon is coming to school?"

Mr Hewitt looked at Ralph with some concern.

"I had a note this morning from the headmaster," Mr Hewitt said as he lifted his black briefcase from the floor. "There has been a death in the family. Evan has been excused school for a few days."

Ralph took the news with disbelief when the headmaster himself arrived and told Mr Hewitt he wanted a word with Ralph. Mr Brack must have heard the conversation and noticed Ralph's anxiety. He waited until Mr Hewitt had left and then gave Ralph some advice.

"What happened to your friend is now binder business. It does not concern an understudy like you. And on no account should a fribbler, like Mr Hewitt be involved. Mark what I say: with binder secrets come responsibilities."

"Yes sir," Ralph said submissively. "Why is Mr Hewitt a fibber, sir?" Ralph asked.

"I didn't say fibber." The headmaster looked at Ralph with exasperation. "I said fribb-ler. Fribblers are non-believers, the ordinary people. Anyone who is not a binder."

It crossed Mr Brack's mind that his first impression of Ralph had been correct. Time would tell.

"Your first timetabled lesson is geography," he said, with a hint of urgency, "but you will not be attending. Your new assignment is in the binder labs. Go to the library and ask Mrs Pickles, the librarian, to recommend you a book. She is expecting a new student for the Gimbals and has instructions."

Ralph's eyes lit up. This was good news. He couldn't wait to visit the Gimbals and see what was hidden below his feet.

seven: the gimbals

The library, once the town's old corn exchange, was some distance from the main classrooms. Gothic arches ran on three sides of a quadrangle with the exchange building in the centre. Ralph opened the large wooden door quietly. It was iron bound and worn with age. He had been in the library a few times, and to his mind some of the books might be even older than the door. The main room of the library had a high ceiling and massive stained glass windows that filled the upper walls. The clunk of the latch as the door closed echoed through the ever-silent space. Mrs Pickles sat at her desk to the left of the door. She was prim and dainty but not to be underestimated. Large shelves stretched away behind her and contained every book imaginable. She was engrossed in a book, and chuckling to herself.

As he arrived at the desk a little brass bell on the desktop pinged three times all by itself.

"Good morning, can I help you?" asked Mrs Pickles, looking up.

"Can you recommend a book, please?" Ralph said, remembering what he had been told.

"Ah, the new student," she smiled. "Today's good read is The Wonderful World of Comets. I'll show you where to find it."

Ralph followed Mrs Pickles past shelf after shelf. Finally she stopped and asked: "Are you are wearing your BS?" Before Ralph can answer she corrected herself. "Of course you are. How silly of me. The bell rang, didn't it?"

"What's a BS?" Ralph asked, confused by the abbreviation.

"A BS is your binder shield, my dear," Mrs Pickles told him kindly, but her glance conveyed her concern that he might be a slow learner. Ralph nodded without speaking. It was one thing to be thought a fool; it is quite another to open one's mouth and confirm it.

At the back of the library, by a bookshelf far away from prying eyes, Mrs Pickles explained.

"On this bookshelf you will always find the right book. Don't forget your BS or this will not work. Now look for the book that I recommended."

Ralph scanned the titles until he found The Wonderful World of Comets. He reached to take it down but Mrs Pickles stopped him.

"No," she said. "Not like that. Push the book forward and keep pushing."

As he did so, all the books and the bookcase moved forward.

"Walk forward as you push," she urged him. As Ralph stepped forward so did Mrs Pickles. They entered a secret space. Behind them a false bookcase sprung up, concealing them.

As the floor lit up Ralph nervously asked, "What now?"

"Push the book again," she said with a laugh.

Ralph pushed. This time there was a jolt and the floor and books moved downwards.

They went down six storeys. When they stopped Ralph saw a long corridor that was brightly lit. It was made of red brick and had a curved roof. All the things that lay ahead excited Ralph.

"To get back to the library you return to this spot and pull that black lever. The platform will come down automatically and will take you back up," Mrs Pickles said as she carried on walking.

"This is the Gimbals and the cleanest parts are the Binder Labs," she told Ralph with an air of pride. "Some of the Gimbals are not so nice. In fact, parts are absolutely horrid. If you want to travel around down here I recommend you use the Imp-Tram system. There are tunnels that go for miles, usually dark and muddy and used by other creatures. We really don't know what else is down here but the Imp-Tram is safe."

She led Ralph down the corridor to a large vaulted hall where an enormous bronze statue stood in the middle. He couldn't take his eyes from it and nor could he recognise what kind of creature it was. He wandered closer for a better look. The creature had a round face, big eyes and ears that were too large and dangly for its head. It also wore strange clothes. It would have looked cute and charming except for teeth that gave it a meat grinder of a mouth.

Mrs Pickles was about to tell Ralph about the statue when a soft voice spoke from a seated alcove.

"That is Professor Pookabar, one of the greatest imps of all. He was a pioneer in the field in high mathematics. He died before his time when the snargs brutally murdered him in the Great Snarg War. This hall is the Pookabar Gallery. Of course, in real life, imps are only 60 centimetres high and not as fierce as they look."

Ralph turned and was surprised and pleased to see Rebecca although a familiar face reminded him of Evan.

"Evan never made it to school," he told her, his voice breaking with emotion. "I'm convinced the snargs took him. And his parents have done a bunk, so it means the snargs control them too. What can we do? Except keep an eye on our own parents in case the snargs try to take them."

Rebecca placed a comforting hand on his shoulder.

"The snargs won't get to our parents," she said, her soft voice more determined. "The binders will see to that. We'll get Evan back."

Rebecca's spirited words left a smile on Ralph's face.

"So that's what an imp looks like?" Ralph said and looked at the statue again. Rebecca nodded. She would have told him a lot more but Mrs Pickles interrupted.

"As you are both aware, Black-Bob is in charge of finding the Gordons'," she said firmly, "not you two. Now, Rebecca, you are in Tec One doing high maths. Ralph, if you follow me to the Green Lab I will introduce you to Professor Pumpkin."

Ralph shrugged his shoulders at Rebecca and followed Mrs Pickles to the middle door of three. A sign said GREEN LABORATORY and underneath NO UNAUTHORIZED PERSONS.

The laboratory was the size of a football pitch. Ralph saw colossal machines with dozens of crisscrossed gantries. Bizarre organic pipes like twisted vines ran everywhere. The sight was captivating.

As the door closed Mrs Pickles wrinkled her nose and looked around the vast array of machines.

"I hope the Professor will be near the Engraphiscope, otherwise it will take all day to find him."

While following Mrs Pickles, Ralph tried to examine the machines. Some machines resembled tree trunks and were inlaid with small slabs of rock. These slabs might well be control panels.

In the distance, they saw the figure of a man bent over a bizarre contraption. As they drew closer they saw this small, round and chubby man bob his head in and out of an open vent in the strange machine.

This was Professor Pumpkin, who was right inside the machine and was consequently in considerable discomfort.

"With you in a moment," the professor groaned. "If I can just move this ... ahh, blast it."

Sparks and smoke drifted around the vent he was blocking with his body. He groaned as he heaved himself out and slammed a cover shut.

"I hate static," he said with exasperation. "Too much and poof! Too little and nothing works." As he straightened he felt his hair stand up with a static charge. Ralph turned away for he couldn't help but smile.

"This is Ralph Higley," Mrs Pickles smiled, as she tried not to laugh at the professor's hair as it swayed in a static breeze. Reflected in the shiny surface of the machine the professor saw his own hair stood on end. His hand made comical movements in a futile attempt to flatten it. Ralph giggled as he greeted the professor and politely went to shake his hand. But as the professor's hand came within centimetres of Ralph's a blue flash of static burst between them, knocking Ralph to the floor.

"Sorry. I so hate static," the professor said, his hand still tingling. Exasperated by these antics Mrs Pickles rolled her eyes and left.

"I have something exciting for you this morning," the professor told Ralph. "Have you heard of changelings?"

"Like in fairy tales?" Ralph asked, his face contorted with deep thought.

The question delighted the Professor.

"Fairy tales, folk tales, nursery rhymes, sagas," he said. "Yes, these were once the mainstay of our education.

Traders and seafarers were treated like scholars in those olden times. That's how knowledge was passed down. But today I will show you the Engraphiscope, one of the great imp marvels."

As they zigzagged their way around the machines the Professor warned Ralph: "Nearly all of these machines are 'Imp Tec'. Don't touch!"

Nestled amongst the larger machines was a weird piece of apparatus. It was smaller with a raised circular platform with steps that led to it. Along the edge of the platform pipes formed a cage. At the top these curved downwards.

The Professor pushed a lever set in the platform.

"This is the Engraphiscope. Like many of these machines it is thousands of years old!" he gushed ahead with his explanation.

"In fairy tales, a changeling is a replacement child, a carbon copy, often a sickly child. When the binders acquired their own technology from the imps they discovered how to make changelings. These are bio-morphic replicas of a person. First, they scan a person in the Engraphiscope. This is done with an intelligent bio-chemical matrix fluid. Poured slowly over the person it remembers everything touched. This fluid is then pumped to a device called the Dupluxseator. Am I going too fast for you?"

Ralph shrugged and sighed. He was bewildered but thought it wise to ask an intelligent question.

"What's the point of a changeling, sir?"

The Professor pushed another lever. An eccentric grin filled his face.

"That's precisely why you're here. Before you go to Wychen a changeling copy of you is sent to take your place. When you return, the changeling goes back to the Gimbals and stores itself in the Pod Chamber. Since changelings are almost flawless and harmless, no one will miss you. No one can spot the difference, not those at school, nor your closest friends and above all, not your parents."

The Engraphiscope was ready but Ralph was too apprehensive to step into the cage and the Professor grew impatient. Ignoring his protest the Professor pushed him up the steps into the cage. The door was shut firmly. Ralph felt trapped.

"Don't panic," the Professor said optimistically. "It will only take five minutes."

"I don't want any filthy bio-stuff poured over my head," Ralph protested. "I don't want it on me!"

The Professor took no notice. He pushed another lever and told Ralph not to be such a baby.

Seconds later Ralph was caught in a gush of a sticky fluid that cascaded from the ends of the pipes. Unable to move, he screamed as he felt the green gunk trickle over his head and body. He was covered from head to toe and looked like some cartoon character. In a very short time, the slime oozed over his body and through the sieve-like floor. It seeped away without a trace and left him bone dry. It was all very bizarre.

"That's it," the Professor announced. "It's over!"

Ralph sighed with relief and asked, "Where does this stuff go now, sir?"

"In there," said the Professor and pointed to another outlandish machine. "In the Dupluxseator. Come on, let's take a look."

"Why does it look like a giant walnut?" Ralph asked. The Professor roared with amusement.

"I don't know," he said. "When we open it may be there's a nut inside!"

Ralph looked blank, after he failed to understand the Professor's humour. This amused the Professor more and he chuckled to himself as though there might really be one there.

"The thing you called a giant walnut is a kind of a Bio-Spheric Accelerator. The bio-morph or changeling is ready to emerge after an hour. Feel how hot it is," said the professor.

Ralph put his hand on the side. It was toasty warm.

"You see, Ralph," the Professor continued, his enthusiasm raised, "changelings are essentially plant life-forms, but there are drawbacks. For one, they are not very bright, which can cause problems. Secondly, if you leave them standing on soil too long, like on a lawn or a flowerbed, they take root. Digging them out can be a major task. When this happens we have to send in a special tactical team to uproot them. With changelings you must always expect the unexpected."

Ralph couldn't imagine what it was going to be like to have a double.

"We have nearly three quarters of an hour to wait, so why don't I give you a little tour of the Green Lab," Professor Pumpkin said and glanced at his watch. "When we return, the changeling should be ready."

High above ground, way above these underground secrets, was Nettle's End Cottage. This was once the home of May Singer, a sweet lady and an artist of international renown. But May died suddenly, and tragically, long before she should have, and in suspicious circumstances never explained. Her death happened shortly after her niece came to stay. Many in Broomfield thought the timing was suspicious but could prove nothing. Again fingers were pointed, when May's Will was read and, much to the family's resentment, the niece was the main beneficiary, inheriting most of Ms Singer's money as well as her cottage.

The niece, now wealthy, had become a pillar of respectability and well known in Broomfield. She still lived in Nettle's End Cottage, alone except for a mysterious white cat. Known as the lady with the bright red coat, her name was Mrs Ridley.

Recently there had been strange comings and goings at Nettle's End Cottage. The odd cat watched from the front window, as if to vet the people who called at peculiar hours. Today, on Monday morning, an ominously loud knock on the door sent the cat into a spin and alerted Mrs Ridley to an important visitor.

"It's alright, Cubitt," Mrs Ridley called to her cat as she went to the door. "I know who this might be."

Cubitt scratched frantically at the window frame hoping to be let out, but was ignored.

Jack Thorn stood at the cottage door, just as Mrs Ridley expected. Today she was the razor to his blunt knife, however devious Thorn thought he was.

Thorn's athletic frame filled the doorway, his right hand rested at the top of the doorpost. He was in a black mood. He tipped up the rim of his hat and his voice was gruff, as if he was holding back a torrent of anger.

"I went to Gloomstone Lodge," Thorn said, "just as you told me. After midnight. And what do you think?"

Mrs Ridley looked at Thorn firmly. She knew what had happened and was prepared to stand her ground.

"It all went wrong," Mrs Ridley said. "I had a note pushed under my door from the Gordons. Your old friend Greystone ruined the trap."

"I already know that," Thorn interrupted harshly. "I was there, remember?" he said with sarcasm. His face, contorted with rage, as if flayed by a hundred nasty devils.

"When I arrived I saw Greystone and that pet of his, Black-Bob, lying in wait. They are out of their league, but they don't know it. I will do for them both, I swear."

"At least we have one cube ready," Mrs Ridley said, her words sweetened to deflect Thorn's temper. "They boxed their son, Evan, in a silver cube. Croucher saw to that! But now it isn't possible for the Gordons to return. I suppose Croucher will see to that too!"

Mrs Ridley's face leered and for a split second her foul grin made her madness visible.

"But never mind," she continued in conciliatory tone, "I know the cube is safe. The Gordons gave it to little Tom Moffat and when school finishes today I will be seeing him. He is a good boy, Tom. He is my little runner and most amenable. "

"I have promised our snarg friends I will deliver to-night," Thorn said. "But I warn you. If you fail me this time it will be your head Croucher has, not mine."

And with that he swaggered down the narrow path to the gate.

"Did you hear what he said," Mrs Ridley snapped at Cubitt unnerved. "That pig threatened me!"

Cautiously, Cubitt showed his support and lightly tore at a chair cushion in defiance of Thorn. The collar around his neck had a tiny cube-shaped bell made of silver that jangled and sparkled with light.

Mrs Ridley watched as Thorn left. Her smile had faded. As Thorn vanished into thin air a shiver of fear ran down her spine. She slammed the front door as if to shut out a ghost, then picked up her cat.

"That man walks with the devil," she whispered bitterly to Cubitt. The cat held a frightened stare and purred as if his life depended on it.

Deep down in the Green Lab, Ralph marvelled at the scale and complexity of the machines. No matter how many he saw there was always another.

"It's time to return to the Dupluxseator," the Professor said noticing the hour was over. Ralph was reluctant to turn back. He was only centimetres away from yet another fascinating machine.

The Dupluxseator made a loud pounding noise; clouds of wispy steam rose from it. The Professor dashed to the controls.

"It's reached critical mass already," he cried, clearly in distress. "We must get the changeling out or it will come out as big as a sumo wrestler."

The Professor pulled and pushed on a row of long levers like those in old railway signal boxes. The Dupluxseator opened like segment petals of a huge water lily. White jets of steam billowed between the segments and a strange figure emerged. As the steam cleared Ralph saw the changeling, his supposed doppelganger.

"Oh my," he gasped open-mouthed. "It has a huge turnip for its head!"

"A small setback," the Professor said brightly, to cover up his disappointment. "Don't worry. It will be fine and shrink to normal size if we don't water it for the next three hours."

But Ralph was worried. And there was worse to come. The changeling's skin had turned distinctly green and a strong smell of cabbage wafted towards him.

"Sir," he moaned with disgust as he pinched his nose with his fingers.

"It smells worse than school dinners."

The Professor couldn't smell the cabbage. The odour of many weird and ill-fated experiments had put an end to what was once his good nose.

"Don't worry," he stammered, as he tried to think of an excuse. "It's only superficial. That colouring will soon be gone. The smell isn't bad. I barely sense it."

But something else happened. The professor noticed movement in the changeling and watched closely.

"Yes," he said, after he observed something important, "the three-hour protocol will make our changeling a normal size and shape."

Suddenly the changeling moved again. It opened and closed its mouth with a yawn. The Professor was so pleased he jumped for joy.

"That is good, very good," he said jubilantly. "It's waking up! And for the time being, Ralph, you must stand here quietly, don't talk to it just yet. And when you do speak to it on no account say it's fat! In these early hours they're highly sensitive. Remarks like that can kill them."

Ralph nodded. He was happy to keep his distance.

The new changeling opened its eyes, stretched out its arms and looked from the Professor to Ralph.

"What's for breakfast? I'm thirsty."

The Professor ignored the changeling's question. He stepped onto the platform and with a friendly smile supported his wobbly creation.

"Let me introduce you to your new master," the Professor said, taking a green hand to coax the creature from the platform. The Dupluxseator sphere closed behind the changeling with a resounding double clunk and a prolonged satisfied hiss of air.

"This is Ralph Higley. He is your new master. You must serve him well."

The Professor seemed contented with the changeling but Ralph was uneasy. He couldn't envisage that freaky bio-morph would be turned into his exact double in three hours time. There was no similarity. They had identical clothes but they fitted much too tight on the Changeling. Ralph shook a green hand gingerly.

"Hello, I'm Ralph Higley. What's your name?" Ralph asked and felt foolish.

"The same as you, of course," the changeling laughed. "I'm Ralph Higley. But you can call me Ralph Postor. I am imp-made so you could say I'm an imp-postor!"

Ralph smiled weakly.

"I thought you said they weren't very bright," he whispered to the Professor.

"They're a bit like humans," the Professor replied. "Their capacity for learning is greatest when young. They learn quickly for the first day or two, reach their full potential and learn very little after that."

The Professor took a large magnifying glass and examined the changeling's eyes.

Suddenly the changeling's face went from happy to sad. It looked as if it had been abandoned. It refused to speak to Ralph or the Professor and slumped on the floor slowly like a heavy sack of potatoes.

"What's wrong with it now," Ralph asked. He could see endless problems with the temperamental doppelganger.

"It's gone into the doldrums," the Professor told Ralph. "Changelings are prone to melancholy although I think this one is suffering from being too long in the Dupluxseator. Don't worry. In three hours it will be fine and dandy."

"It doesn't look like or sound in the least like me," Ralph said.

"Don't worry," the professor said. "They are outstanding mimics. With their vocal range they can sound like anybody!" The Professor held his tatty old clipboard and read notes to jog his memory on the qualities of changelings.

Mr Greystone arrived clearly out of breath and greeted Ralph and the Professor warmly. But the Professor wasn't happy at Greystone's arrival. He looked bemused and furtive, as though inconvenienced, and turned his body to block Greystone's view.

"How are things here, Pumpkin?" Greystone asked, "is Master Higley's changeling completed?"

"Oh yes, it is an excellent copy," the Professor said and braced himself. "Ralph Poster, as we shall call him, is raring to go."

"He is just a bit green though, isn't he, Professor. And a bit…" but the real Ralph was interrupted by the Professor.

"Nothing to worry about, Greystone," the professor said. "Just a little enzyme excess, it will go away."

Greystone was not impressed. This wasn't the first time he had been told of the little enzyme excess.

"We must do better, Pumpkin," Greystone said. "I have clearance from Binder Operations for a field mission in the New Forest. A new Ghost Door has been discovered and I am taking my understudy, but yet again I find my work jeopardised by your Green Lab curse!"

"Well, I'd hardly say jeopardised, dear Greystone," the professor said sharply. He felt aggrieved by the attack on his professionalism. "After the obligatory five hours I have for processing and facilitating, this changeling will be ready for duty, I assure you. You will have Ralph Poster before the school gates close."

"I hope so, Pumpkin," Greystone said in a reprimand. "I don't want changeling disorders ending in binder mishap!"

When Greystone turned to Ralph his surly tone evaporated.

"Tonight you must meet me outside the library doors at the stroke of ten. Take care not to be seen. Come via the Gimbals. Rebecca Harwood is waiting to give you the Gimbals tour and to show you where your Changeling exchange will take place. Listen to her. She is an excellent student and may soon graduate to being a binder."

To be going on a trip so soon! Ralph hardly opened his mouth and said yes.

Greystone smiled at Ralph and gave the professor a stern look before he disappeared into the maze of gadgetry. Disgruntled the professor looked at his watch in horror. There was no time to spare if the changeling was to be ready.

"Our lesson is over," he told Ralph. "I think you will find Miss Harwood waiting in the Gallery. See yourself out. Goodbye."

Ralph recognised a bad mood when he saw one and didn't dare ask the reason. He just thanked him and left.

eight: the imp tram

Rebecca was sitting high on the plinth of the Pookabar statue, a folder on her lap, deeply engrossed in her work.

Ralph called to her.

Rebecca gave him a forced smile and then in high dudgeon berated him. "I have given up half my high maths lesson for this tour. I love high maths as every lesson reveals a hidden secret of a number!"

Ralph saw intenseness in her eyes that could ignite the hall.

"I doubt that you know, but studying imp mathematics is like being right inside the numbers. Professor Pookabar says, the art is not just understanding the equations but feeling the fire when finding the answers."

Ralph hadn't a clue what Rebecca was talking about.

"The only thing I know is I'm cold," he said blankly.

That infuriated Rebecca.

"Listen to yourself," she rebuked him. "I can't imagine why Mr Greystone wants you as an understudy. You can't even manage to throw off your old fribbler thoughts."

Ralph didn't like being called a Fribbler. He had aspirations far beyond that.

"Just because I'm not an expert in high mathematics shouldn't mean you think I'm a fribbler," Ralph defended himself.

Rebecca laughed, pleased to have provoked a response.

"Come on," she called as she jumped from the statue and headed for the elevator. "It's time to start your tour of the Gimbals. The Imp Tram system is just the craziest thing."

For a moment, Ralph was tempted to be stubborn and not go. Rebecca's temperament was so mercurial he found it confusing. He deliberately followed Rebecca indolently but she either hadn't noticed his childish stubbornness or was ignoring it. She pulled a lever.

The elevator summoned, steel ropes clattered as counterbalance weights pulled up the small cage. It stopped with a judder at their level. The next stop was the trams. Rebecca stepped into the cage and grinned as Ralph hesitated.

"You're not a scaredy cat, are you?" she mocked. Even in the dim light she saw his annoyance.

"I was making sure it was going to stop," Ralph said sharply, all too aware this was the second time she had put him on the defensive.

Rebecca felt the wicked urge to play games with Ralph. He was still the new boy.

She thought to herself, "I bet I can make him scream. Let's make the elevator go fast." Then, without a smile, or any perceptible emotion she said: "Push that lever all the way, Ralph."

He did and the lift plummeted into the gloom. Then it suddenly jolted to a stomach-churning halt. Ralph hadn't screamed, but he was slightly woozy. Rebecca was secretly impressed. Calmly, she stepped from the elevator, followed closely by Ralph, who was determined not to show his wooziness. He stayed half a step behind as she led the way down a short murky corridor. Then something caught his eye. He stopped and pulled out the matchbox he had been given by the headmaster. Rebecca turned and saw Ralph stoop to grub about the floor.

"What are you doing?" she asked.

"Beetles." Ralph beamed with joy. "I've found some nice fat black beetles!"

"I'm amazed you can see black beetles in this gloom," she said and squinted into the dimness. "Especially without a torch!"

"I saw something shiny moving about. There's a tiny bit of light bouncing off their backs. Come here yer little devil," he puffed as he caught the last one.

"It's cruel to keep big beetles in a box that small. They should be kept in something bigger, like a jam jar, and with some holes punched in the top!" Rebecca looked annoyed at Ralph. "Does that matchbox even have holes in it?"

Ralph stared at her blank and guiltily. "I'll put them in a jar when I get home!" he said.

Exasperated Rebecca snatched the matchbox and from her flowing hair took a hairpin, stabbed holes in the box then handed it back.

"I hope you haven't killed them," Ralph whinged.

"Don't be so silly," she said and looked at him sharply. "You're the one who's killing them."

Ralph said nothing. He knew he had lost the argument. He slipped the box and its beetles into his pocket and they set off, this time in thoughtful silence.

The tunnel took them to a brightly lit area that looked like a little Victorian railway platform. To the uninformed observer no one could have guessed that a tramline ran in those tunnels. Ralph was surprised too. He looked down at the tunnel floor and saw no tram rails. "This is absurd," he thought.

He nearly asked Rebecca about it, when a tall thin man came onto the platform. He wore a dark suit and carried a leather briefcase like all nerds that stalked the corridors of power. Rebecca gave Ralph a hearty nudge.

"Not a word," she whispered. "That is Mr Moynton."

Ralph shrugged his shoulders, mystified.

"Moynton, the Privy Chamberlain, a very high-ranking binder," she continued with a muted voice. "They say he has ears like a bat. Black-Bob says Moynton collects rumours and weaves them into his web of conspiracy. He detests Moynton."

Rebecca stopped talking as Moynton turned to look in her direction. Then he adjusted his jacket and casually glanced at his watch. After fearing she was overheard Rebecca sighed with relief.

Moynton was unusual in the binder's world. On the surface he appeared a sociable, organised and practical man. But underneath he was a schemer, ambitious and obsequious, ready to be fraudulent when it furthered his goals. He suffered unpredictable black moods that made him aggressive and cruel, and in those moods he misused his power of position.

Like an undertaker, Moynton shuffled impatiently on the platform.

"Will he be on the same tram as us?" Ralph asked Rebecca.

"I hope not!" she whispered.

A red light flashed above the arch of the tunnel and a bell rang loudly. In the dark of the tunnel Ralph saw a bright light, the outline of a tram approached. But what mesmerised him was the strange blue-white light that ran at full speed ahead of the tram. It arced and danced like an electrical storm. Suddenly the mystery of why there were no rails was solved. With each burst of light a new section of track appeared and raced ahead of the tram.

"So that's how it is done," Ralph thought, smiling with admiration. As the tram glided into the station Ralph saw that the tracks behind the tram disappeared as easily as they appeared in the front.

The tram made a hasty stop, its doors were flung open and a small voice from inside bellowed, "Point twelve, point twelve, if you're on, get off; and if you're off, get on!" Ralph looked at Rebecca. Was it on or off for them?

"On!" she said smartly and quick as a flash they both leapt through the doors.

Onboard the tram Ralph saw that the voice came from a tiny man at the front window next to a strange array of controls. Ralph looked closer and saw this man wasn't human. After they sat in their seats he tapped Rebecca on the arm and pointed to the driver.

"He's an imp," Rebecca said in a matter-of-fact, hushed voice. She could have said more but Moynton had boarded the same tram and was making his way past them. He wished them a good morning in his unpleasant smarmy voice.

Anxious dry throats fractured their good mornings to Moynton.

Before the Privy Chamberlain took a seat he flicked it over with a handkerchief. Once the dust cloud had settled and the seat was clean, he sat and waited the trams departure.

There were two short dings of a bell. The tram lurched forward and accelerated at great speed. Ralph sat transfixed as rough-hewn walls of the dark tunnel race by.

They were barely into their journey when Ralph saw the unmistakable bright spotlight head their way.

He tried not to panic and turned to Rebecca.

"That's another tram heading towards us!" His voice was shaky.

Rebecca beamed a large grin.

"I told you this tram system is crazy. Just watch!"

Ralph looked at Rebecca in a manner that pleaded, "Tell me it's not..." but she didn't.

The light was almost on them. Ralph saw no room for another tram in the tunnel. He held his seat with a white-knuckle grip and steadied himself for impact. He saw the front of the other tram. He saw a smile on the other imp driver. He saw the imp hand wave in languid greeting. Everything was in slow motion. But it all happened in the craziest split second, he saw the oncoming tram flip onto the tunnel ceiling and it passed overhead in an instant. "Aaaaaah," escaped from his lips with a long breath as the impending disaster receded.

Rebecca shook her head at Ralph.

"You didn't think we were going to crash did you?" she remarked calmly. "Imps are much too clever for that!"

Ralph slumped in his seat as the tram sped on. It plummeted through the blackness as the tunnel twisted and turned. Then suddenly it screeched to a halt. The little imp voice shouted, "Point thirteen, point thirteen: if you're on, get off; and if you're off, get on!"

"Quick, we're getting off," Rebecca said with a raised whisper.

The short wooden platform was dusty and dimly lit, although compared to the dark surroundings it was an oasis of light. Ralph glanced back towards the tram and saw Moynton looking at them through the window with unconcealed interest. As the tram sped away Ralph thought no more of it.

His attention turned to three large steel doors. These were old and solid, held together with heavy steel rivets.

Above one door the sign read, "To the Old Post Office." On the one next to it he saw: "To Longsdale."

"That's where I live!" Ralph said. He went to open the door but there was no handle.

"How do we get this open?" he asked, frantically waving his arms. Rebecca gave him a withering look.

"It's not motion-sensitive, so you can stop waving your arms like a windmill," she said. "Try showing your binder shield."

She held up her own shield. Two tiny glass eyes appeared in the middle of the door. They blinked at her.

"Is that door alive?" Ralph asked.

"Who knows?" Rebecca whispered cautiously, in case someone was listening. "These doors are probably as old as the tunnels. Even the binders don't know how half this stuff works!"

The big steel door swung open. Rebecca pushed Ralph inside and quickly secured her shield to her jacket.

"We can't hang about," she told him. "The door will close by itself in 30 seconds."

The tunnel, dimly lit like the others, went steeply up with a wobbly incline. Ralph led the way up the stone steps. He looked at Rebecca for these it seemed went on for ever.

"Not far now," she gasped as Ralph groaned. At the very top they found an ordinary wooden door with a plain old-fashioned door handle. Rebecca recognised where they were.

"That door opens directly into your cellar. This is where your changeling will be waiting. It is your responsibility to do the exchange on time."

Ralph opened the door carefully. It had part of a brick wall stuck to its back, which was unusual for any door.

Even in dim light he recognised the cellar belonged to his family. The dusty bits of old furniture were familiar. How many times had he been in that cellar and not known a tunnel existed. In one corner he saw the steps that led to the rest of the house. Ralph went to move towards them but Rebecca pulled him back.

"The tour's over," she said unsympathetically. "Don't even think about it."

"I only wanted a peek into the house," he pleaded.

"We're not here," she told him. "We're at school."

She pulled him back into the tunnel and closed the door.

"We aren't here to play games," she said. "And it could wake your dragon."

Ralph saw her point, even if she was a killjoy. Their return journey to school was just as enjoyable even though uneventful.

nine: tom

That morning Ralph's first lesson was painfully slow after the excitement of the Gimbals. Lunchtime proved awkward. There was little time for Ralph to think or talk to anyone. Tom was moody and avoided Ralph, as he safeguarded his bag like a clucking mother hen with her clutch of eggs. The bell ended Ralph's free time.

His first afternoon class was maths with Mr Hewitt. He crossed the yard at the back of the school and headed for his lesson. On his way he saw Rebecca amongst the other pupils.

"Becky," he called. She walked on, her arms full of books. Ralph called again a little louder.

"My name is Rebecca," she complained as she swung round, "not Becky. I hate Becky."

Her fierce reply stopped him in his tracks. He raised his hands defensively.

"I won't call you that again, I promise!"

"Mind you don't, things like that put me in a bad mood." she told him. "It's bad manners and bad manners drive me mad. What's up with you?"

"I need to talk to you," he said. "There is something fishy about Tom and I can't work it out?"

"Your bad-boy friends are no business of mine," she snorted.

"It is your business," he said. "You and I are the only ones who know about snargs and why Evan's not at school. And Tom's been acting funny with his bag all day."

"You should tell Greystone," she remarked.

"He already knows. He saved me from the Gordons. But this isn't just about Evan. How about that little girl Alice? She went missing too. And Tom's my friend and I don't want Black-Bob after him. I could lose a friend and end up looking silly if there's nothing to it."

Rebecca was still reluctant to be involved.

"Bad boys are bad vibes," she said then paused. "But maybe it's lucky for you that Rule One of the binder code says; do not to turn your back on fellow believers. I want to be the first girl from Broomfield to become a Binder, so I will have to help you."

Rebecca wasn't so frosty and a sparkle of fun had returned to her eye.

"We need to do some snooping," she told him as she took charge. "Let's meet in the park after school."

"Great," Ralph smiled with relief.

When school finished, Ralph was the first out. The snow looked and felt like it would last weeks. By the time Rebecca reached the park, he was sat waiting on a swing.

"I don't think I am dressed for cold weather," she grumbled.

"There isn't time to go home and change," Ralph said. "We need to follow Tom and find where he goes."

As they crunched in the snow towards the park they saw a group of kids snowball fighting but Tom wasn't among them. Then Rebecca spotted him along Foundry Walk.

"There he is," she said and dragged Ralph by the sleeve as she hurried after him. They came within a hundred meters, hung back and watched him.

"This isn't Tom's way home. Where's he going?" Ralph said mystified.

A tall woman in a blood red coat stopped Tom and they begun to talk. Ralph recognised the woman and a cold fear descended. Tom looked around warily. Rebecca sensed their cover was about to be blown and pushed Ralph into the large snow-covered hedge and went in after him. They both winced at the prickly foliage.

"Did they see us?" Rebecca whispered.

Ralph spat snow and twigs from his mouth.

"No," he whispered. "But I know that woman in the red coat. She's Mrs Ridley and I don't like her."

"Could be interesting", muttered Rebecca.

From their hiding place, they watched like vigilant hawks. When Tom reached into his bag Ralph strained for a closer look. He saw Tom remove an unmistakeable, gleaming silver cube from his satchel and slip it into the woman's bag. She covered it with her red and purple scarf. Neither Tom nor the woman spoke again and they went their separate ways.

Ralph flared up. He looked at Tom through a red mist of anger. How could he be involved, he was supposed to be his friend.

"I hate him. He's a traitor," he said with gritted teeth.

They watched while Tom skulked down a narrow alley towards his home. Retribution would have to wait. They had to follow Mrs Ridley. She had Evan.

She turned and continued along Foundry walk, just as Ralph and Rebecca climbed awkwardly from the hedge. At that very moment, Mrs Ridley glanced back along the road. Stopping in her tracks, her icy stare fell on them like daggers.

Rebecca looked up and their eyes met.

"Run for it," she yelled. Ralph stopped brushing and juddered into action. Mrs Ridley gave chase but was no match on slippery snow. Seeing the children getting away, she screamed a bitter warning. "Come here, or I will cut your ears off!"

Ralph and Rebecca didn't stop until they reached the corner.

"Well, we're safe but you heard what she said. She's vile," said Rebecca, leaning on a lamppost while she caught her breath.

"Yes." Ralph panted. "And I think she meant every word. Did you see the silver box?"

"I did," she said, "but no one would believe Evan was in there!"

Ralph grew pale with worry.

"What if she's cut his ears off?" he asked anxiously.

"We'll get him back," Rebecca said, to boost his confidence. "But we need to catch up with that old witch."

As she strode off Ralph scowled with anger and followed.

They caught up with Mrs Ridley further along Foundry Walk. It was a road full of old industrial buildings and tall chimneystacks of the old iron foundry. Halfway along she passed through a slightly opened pair of large gates.

Moments later, Ralph and Rebecca peered through into the huge scrapyard. They saw old cars piled high, twisted steel, buckled bicycles and even the broken cockpit of a jet fighter. Tilted forward the aircraft's nose cone looked like part of a crash site. Everything was snow-covered, giving a clinical, cold dimension to the general rustiness.

Mrs Ridley knocked on the door of a solitary brick building. She looked tense, huddled in the small porch under the icicles that hung like slippery glass daggers.

She waited and knocked again. A tall man answered but even with the door wide open he made no attempt to invite her in.

Neither Ralph nor Rebecca heard the conversation between the pair. And neither saw Mrs Ridley pull out the colourful scarf that wrapped the silver box. She passed the bundle to Thorn with both hands.

"Evan," she said through wrinkled, pinched lips. "I said little Tom was a willing boy you could trust."

Thorn's dark eyes pierced deep into hers.

"We are all trusty servants, Mrs Ridley," he said with weary conviction. "Our snarg friends see to it."

"How are your snarg friends at dealing with meddlers, Mr Thorn?" she asked in her wheedling voice, glancing over her shoulder.

"Meddlers, Mrs Ridley. What do mean?" Thorn asked.

"On my way here I came upon a couple of nosey kids. They ran off before I could catch them. I know one of them, a boy called Ralph Higley. Tom told me about him, he's been asking questions. I don't know the other one. A brazen girl with strawberry-blonde hair."

"They're just kids, Mrs Ridley," Thorn snarled. "You deal with them! Don't bring trouble to my door. The only kids I want to know about are here," he said shaking the bundle he held tightly.

Back at the gate, Ralph was deep in thought. "Do you know who that is, with the floppy hat?"

"Yes, the clothes are a dead giveaway," Rebecca replied with a hushed voice.

"Guy Fawkes?" Ralph joked badly.

"Jack Thorn," she said. "Haven't you heard the name?"

"No. I mean yes. Greystone says he's trouble."

"You won't hear much from Greystone about Thorn," Rebecca told him. "There is too much hurt between them. Thorn was Greystone's first understudy and being the first Greystone treated Thorn like a son. There was an accident of some sort and Thorn was thrown out of the Guild."

Ralph's eyes darted about the scrapyard.

"What should we do now?" he mumbled nervously.

"We need to sneak in and hide until Mrs Ridley leaves. Then, when Thorn is out of the way we'll slip into that building and grab the box," answered Rebecca.

"Oh, I don't know," Ralph whispered, hesitantly. "Greystone says Thorn is dangerous."

"I didn't have you down as faint-hearted, Ralph," Rebecca said as her wide eyes twinkled. "Where's your sense of adventure?"

Ralph's fear melted. He wanted to say she how pretty she was, but he was afraid she would laugh at him.

"You think I'm chicken?" he said. Then with no mood for an answer he slipped inside the gates and was gone.

"Wait Ralph, wait," she snapped faintly.

Rebecca was quick but already Ralph was out of sight. She dashed in and hid behind some old tin drums. As she looked around she knew this yard was full of dangers.

With no sign of Ralph, she softly called his name, but there was no reply.

She went down a gangway between the piles of junk. She saw a small figure near a large tower of scrap. It was Ralph.

"What's he doing?" she wondered to herself.

Inside the jet fighter cockpit Ralph was in a world of his own. He was about to climb out when a voice made him jump.

"What are you playing at?" Rebecca hissed. "You'll get us caught if you start mucking about. Let's do what we came for."

Feeling foolish, Ralph clambered down.

"I'm sorry," he muttered. "It's just that I always wanted to be close to the controls of a jet."

Rebecca wondered if she'd been too harsh.

"That's OK. Let's get over near that building, so we can see what's going on," she said gently. Immediately, Ralph grew serious.

As they made their way, something moved up ahead. Ralph grabbed her by the arm and pulled her back. Rebecca froze.

"What is it?" she asked.

"Something's by that old red car!" he said.

Rebecca stared hard. Her eyes focused on a curious metal object about the size of a washing machine. It was dirty black with jagged curling pipes that encircled the whole of its framework.

"It looks like an old milking machine or something?" Rebecca guessed.

Ralph didn't think she was right, but was starting to feel as if they were being watched.

Rebecca thought it odd the object hadn't any snow on it. None at all!

From the object's dome-shaped hood a red light started to flash. It turned into a focused beam and pulsed rhythmically. Pencil sharp and steady laser beams radiated from a thin slit in all directions. As the hood rotated, Rebecca was petrified. So was Ralph.

"I think it's scanning movement!" Ralph told Rebecca, his voice trembling.

There was a loud whirring sound and all the curled and jagged pipes unfolded. The contraption took shape and finally it stood on four angular legs as tall as a man. Its two long arms were multi-jointed like a flexible hose.

Ralph shivered with fear and cold. This thing was lethal.

"It's a Guardian, said Rebecca. "The snargs designed them to capture intruders. But sometimes Guardians get re-programmed to kill outright."

"Will it kill us?" Ralph asked.

"We'll soon find out," she answered.

"Maybe we could out-run it?" he asked with a desire to flee.

"All I know, Guardians hunt like lions. How you out-smart one I have no idea. I suppose this one might be restricted to the scrapyard. We could be lucky, if we can just make it through those gates?" said Rebecca shivering.

The Guardian continued its search for intruders, the beams sweeping from side to side.

As Ralph and Rebecca ran for the gates the criss-crossing beams ensnared them. They had been found.

"We're in trouble now," Ralph said desperately. "Run!!"

Instinctively, they fled in opposite directions to make the Guardian's job harder. It lunged for Ralph and gained on him. The ground shook the thud of robot feet. Ralph heard clunking and felt the metal arms swipe behind him. The Guardian was close but so was the distance to the gate. As his muscles ached and adrenaline pumped, he threw himself through the narrow gap of the gates and burst to freedom. At the gates the Guardian stopped and swivelled in a sharp ninety-degree turn. It had failed its mission.

Ralph limped on a twisted ankle and scanned Foundry Walk for Rebecca. She was still inside. He took cover behind a nearby lamppost and waited.

It wasn't long before Mrs Ridley left the yard and walked off down the road. Ralph saw her bag was much lighter and knew Thorn had the silver box. And there it had to stay until they could find a way through the Guardian.

Winter nights came quick and daylight faded with no sign of Rebecca. The streetlight flickered on and spotlighted Ralph for the whole world. He had to go back for her.

Cautiously Ralph walked towards the gate, aware he was almost blind in the gloom. As he reached the gate, a figure dashed from the darkness. Ralph jumped back in pure terror.

"I didn't scare you did I?" a welcome voice said.

"Rebecca!" His heart thumped like a drum.

"Where have you been?" he moaned, almost lost for words. Then he saw her face and sniggered with nervous relief. Her face was plastered in black oil.

After she saw the oil slick on her fingers she knew what a very dank and grimy place she chose to hide.

"Camouflage," she said gathering her wits to glamorise her state.

"Dirty waste oil muddled the Guardian's optic scan!" she said with sophistication. Hoping Ralph thought her skilled and controlled at all times.

Ralph was impressed by her coolness.

But as she stepped into the streetlight Ralph's mouth dropped. Her school clothes! It wasn't just her face that was filthy.

"You are going to be in such trouble when your mum sees what you've done," he told her. Rebecca looked down at her clothes. "A good Binder is always prepared for the worst," she smiled awkwardly.

"You mean washing them?" he replied.

"Well, sort of! I have another set of clothes for school. So I will stash these until I can get them to the Binder's Lab. They have a machine that can restore cloth to look like new!" she said with a shrug of her shoulders.

"That's cool," remarked Ralph. But then he became more serious, "What can we do for Evan?"

Rebecca, who usually had an answer, had none.

They walked glumly to the end of the lane, where Ralph remembered his news.

"I'm meeting Greystone at ten," he said. "I'm going on my first field trip. That is, if my changeling is ready. I have no idea what this is all going to be like."

"You can tell me all about it tomorrow, if you like," Rebecca smiled.

As they went their separate ways, Ralph felt a little more optimistic. He slipped and slid all along Ingot Street as he raced home. And once home his only thought was tea.

ten: to the emerald wood

After nine that evening Ralph tiptoed from his bedroom down to the cellar. It was dark there. He switched on his torch and looked for the secret door. It was so cold it appeared every exhaled breath was like a jet of steam.

His torchlight lit the pile of old furniture he saw when the door was opened from the tunnel side. He was certain of the door's location but when he shone the torch on the wall there was no sign of one.

Ralph's big mistake was not asking Rebecca how it opened from the other side. He examined the brickwork and ran his fingers between the gaps in the bricks. Nothing. He shone his torch into the corners of the cellar in the hope there was a remote lever or a secret trigger. There was just dirt and dust.

Ralph slumped on to an old rug rolled up on the floor. It smelt musty and damp but he didn't care. Alone, with no possible way out, he felt like a prisoner of war. He looked at his watch as the minutes ticked away and felt worse.

Anxiety turned into a feeling of fury. He thought about moving all the furniture but in the darkness it would take too long and the noise might bring his parents down to investigate. Ralph stamped his foot hard with frustration and groaned.

He sat quietly and stared at the wall. He noticed the faint remains of graffiti. People over the years must have scribbled and drawn there with chalk. One showed a cat drinking from a saucer. Another was a stick figure that skipped over a rope. One drawing, more faded than the rest, showed a bee flying to a flower with the words 'buzz, buzz'.

"Well," he grumbled, "someone had fun down here. I wish I could. What a load of buzz."

He knew he was wasting time. So with nothing to lose he moved a couple of the broken chairs and was about to pick up a wonky hat-stand when he suddenly had a revelation. His mouth dropped open.

"Buzz," he thought and shone the torch on the wall again. "Buzz! How can I have missed it?" The bee that stared him in the face couldn't have been a simpler clue. This was a child-like allusion to the letter "B" and was surely a pointer to the binders. Ralph's revelation had been to connect Mr Greystone's analogy of flowers to Ghost Doors, for flowers always open for the butterflies and bees of the world. He looked at the drawing and had another brainwave about why it was more faded than the others. He reasoned over time someone had kept touching that part of the wall. So on that very spot he pushed until the brick moved with a click and the secret door revealed itself.

Ralph shined his torch into a dark grimy tunnel, but was startled when something crept up those stairs. He stepped backwards and nearly tripped over his own feet. He calmed only when he realised it was the changeling. The lone figure staggered into the light of his torch and Ralph gasped with shock.

"This is just unbelievable, it's like looking in a mirror" Ralph stuttered.

The Changeling stood and grinned at Ralph as he stared back. He was smartly dressed in school uniform. Ralph wondered how long it would stay that way.

As a greeting, the changeling held his hand out. Automatically Ralph shook it.

"Ow-aa!" Ralph yelled, recoiling with pain. A strange surge of energy had been dragged from his hand.

"What's that about?" he asked angrily. His arm sore, it felt heavy and limp.

"I should have warned you," the changeling said. "I was a little lost and needed to pick your brains. Anyway, now I know where my bed and the bathroom is."

"You mean my bed, don't you?" Ralph said with a worried insight into what it meant to have a double.

"It's my bed till I'm called back," the changeling argued.

Ralph looked the changeling in the eye.

"Get this straight," he said firmly. "You can wear my clothes, eat my food and sleep in my bed, but you keep your hands off my books, games and everything else in my room. There is only one exception," Ralph said, as he nearly missed a trick, "My schoolbooks. You can use them in class. And don't forget to do my homework."

The changeling flinched, intimidated by Ralph's resentment.

"I don't feel well," the changeling groaned.

Ralph remembered changelings were gentle creatures that could easily slide into depression when confronted or confused. He felt guilty and tried an apology to revive the changeling's spirits.

"I'm sorry. We both have to get used to this situation. I'm a private person and find it hard to share my things. Anyway, I can't call you Ralph. That's weird. You're such an absolute copy of me that I just want to say 'Snap' when I see you. So if it's OK with you I'm going to call you Snap from now on."

"Snap," the changeling said. "That's good." A smile beamed from his face.

"I am so tired. I need sleep," Snap yawned, stretching out his arms. Ralph couldn't help but yawn and stretch too. Bizarrely he watched as Snap walked sleepily up the cellar steps. So that was how he looked to other people! It was surreal and unnerving.

Ralph glanced at his watch. He'd better hurry if he was to make it to the library by ten. As Snap climbed the stairs from the cellar and headed for bed, Ralph made the mad dash into the Gimbals' gloom.

After a ten-minute tram ride Ralph stepped out into the inner sanctum of the library. Mrs Pickles was vexed that he had cut it fine for Mr Greystone's field trip. She unlocked the library door and led him out into the starry cold night. She then muttered so he clearly heard: "Only minutes to spare. I don't know what students think these days. They have no concept of time, wasting so much of it."

He shivered in the cold and wondered what on earth she was talking about.

"I'm sorry, Mrs Pickles," he said hastily, and then spoke more sharply than intended. "If I had any spare time I would put some in a jar and use it when I'm going to be late, like fairy dust."

"Suffice to say, Ralph Higley, that even a mountain of fairy dust is unlikely to cover your failings. More effort and less cheek is all that is needed, don't you agree?" She stood sternly in the open doorway and waited for the apology.

"Yes, Mrs Pickles, sorry I was late," Ralph said reprimanded. She gave him one last stern look and closed the door behind him. He was familiar with that courtyard by day, but under a canopy of twinkling stars it looked spooky.

The church clock struck and made him jump.

On the final stroke of ten Ralph heard a strange distant sound, hollow and metallic. It clattered louder and louder, until from nowhere, a large horse-drawn carriage appeared. The huge horse shone silver and gold. It looked as if it was made of metal. Ralph stared flabbergasted. He'd seen nothing like it before. The carriage was silver and gold, with small black windows on its side. It had no wheels. It was suspended in mid air, two feet above the ground. Two golden shafts, serpent shaped, connected the carriage to the horse. A low hum of power came from inside the carriage.

Stopping in front of Ralph, he could see a round lion's head doorknob rotate three times and click with each turn. The door opened with a hiss. A set of small steps unfolded smoothly. Ralph saw a figure in the dimly light interior of the carriage.

"Mr Greystone?" he questioned.

"Hello, Ralph," Greystone said and stepped from the coach. "What do you think of Silver Lightning?"

Ralph walked its length as his eyes gleamed.

"This horse is incredible," he said with wonder.

"This is Nex," Greystone said with his hand rested on the horse's shoulder. "He is one of a kind. You can touch him if you like. Nex won't bite."

Ralph rubbed Nex's nose, just as he would a real horse's. The metal was warm, not cold as expected. And though it had the hardness of metal it was soft at the same time! Ralph pulled his hand away surprised, and then touched the horse again. Greystone smiled.

"There is a lot we find mysterious in imp technology. They are the true kings of metal smiths. The magma at the centre of their world is a strange element. They learnt to tame and shape it over thousands of years. Nex is one of the high points of their achievement."

At ease with Nex, Ralph warmed his cold hands on its nose.

"Come," Greystone said, "We must leave. It is a short journey to the Emerald Wood and then our expedition will begin."

Greystone climbed the steps into the carriage and held his hand out for Ralph. He paused then went up the steps eagerly.

Inside, the carriage was bathed in a green and orange light. The décor was curiously archaic, like from the days of steam locomotion. They sat on a red leather bench across the back of the carriage. A control panel was built into the front.

"Time to get Nex up to speed," Greystone said and told Ralph to close the door with a pull on the small lever. He then turned his attention to the cogs and dials on the control panel.

While Greystone concentrated on the strange controls he told Ralph about Emerald Wood. That it was a secret place in the New Forest only known to Binders. He paused as he struggled to turn a little cogwheel and muttered to himself to oil it later, "I don't want that seizing up when cloud-hopping."

Ralph looked around the interior with curiosity.

"I don't understand," Ralph said. "Why does the Silver Lightning look so old in here but from the outside so new? And anyway, wouldn't a helicopter be quicker?"

"She is old," Greystone frowned. "She was built in 1734."

"1734?" Ralph repeated with astonishment. "Twin rotors and jet propulsion, that's what we need."

"The imps built it with technology they had only just developed," Greystone said, as he felt obliged to explain why the Silver Lightning was superior to a helicopter.

"It came to the binders as a gift from the Imps and I inherited it thirty years ago when a binder Grand Master passed away. Silver Lightning is a work of art. It's an enigma to us. Machines like this should not be in our world."

Ralph fell silent, with much to think about. Greystone pushed and pulled levers and engaged elevation and propulsion. Ralph felt a jolt and a force pressed him into his seat. Through a window he caught a glimpse of his school roof. But it was passed and gone. He saw the streetlights and Christmas lights of the town, but they too were soon gone. They raced into the blackness.

After a few minutes, Ralph felt unwell.

Greystone saw the pale green tinge on Ralph's face and passed him a small paper bag.

"I should have warned you. The spinning lights in the floor can make you nauseous but the feeling should soon pass. It is just a little travel sickness and the paper bag just a precaution."

Greystone's words sounded reassuring but the glint in his eyes made Ralph wonder if he had deliberately delayed his warning. Perhaps as a reprimand for the comments he'd made about the Silver Lightning. He sat, bag in hand, and waited for the feeling to pass.

"You should be alright soon," Greystone said. "The instruments show it won't be long before we arrive!"

In Broomfield, Foundry Lane was in darkness except for the old oil lamp that burned in the red brick building of the scrapyard. Jack Thorn sat in a rickety wood chair with his floppy hat and long dark trench coat still on. In front of him the table was piled high with dusty books, discarded newspapers and rusty tins. A potbellied stove burned with coal and kept the place warm. A steaming teapot stood on its top. In his hand Thorn held an old tin mug half full of tea as he watched the door. He was waiting for someone.

From the corner of one eye Thorn saw a small silky grey mouse with long whiskers. It scurried across the room, tempted in by the warmth of the stove. Thorn glared. He hated vermin with a vengeance. His eyes fixed on the mouse he stealthily reached for a knife. One that was always sharp and well polished.

"Stinking little vermin," he snarled and flung the knife. The blade whistled through the air and stuck fast into an old rickety cupboard made of wood. The mouse escaped with its life, but lost three whiskers.

"By a whisker," Thorn laughed without humour.

Thorn slowly sipped his tea and stared around the room each time he heard a noise. The oil lamp burned fitfully and threw shadowy movements where nothing truly moved, and corners were left dark and vague.

He was uneasy. The room was growing darker minute by minute as if something stole the little light he had. He heard the thud he had long expected. In a dark corner, a small wraith of a figure crawled over discarded hessian sacks full of unwanted items. The creature was invisible to fortunate folk, but not to Thorn. He caught its outline in a shimmer of light. A snarg.

Jack Thorn was not the only person enslaved by snargs. Since being enslaved he saw their forms clearly. Tonight it was seen the instant he heard the thud. He watched with bulging eyes as it picked its way over the sacks towards him. It scratched and crawled like a bat up a table leg. The filthy creature stood arrogantly on piled up newspapers. Thorn scrabbled to his feet. The old chair was thrown back on its four legs.

Thorn's mind spun like an empty windmill that echoed with the question of how did it get in. The snarg raised a long finger, pointed to the roof and croaked gruffly, "Under the eaves we come, through cracks we make our way."

Thorn was transparent to them, his mind an open book. The snarg fixed him with a stare from pin-sharp eyes, out of a blackened grey face. Thorn could almost felt its greed and smell its lust.

"Where's the child?" the snarg asked with icy tones.

Thorn was little more than a pawn in the presence of a snarg, as they break even the strongest of men. He reached into a rusty tin and pulled out a silver cube. He held it tight with his right hand. The highly polished box reflected the light and everything in that room. And in that box was the ultimate prize for a snarg: a human child!

"I want what's owed," Thorn grubbed, true to his debased form.

The snarg barely moved as a gleaming gold ingot dropped from its hand on to the filth-encrusted table. It was a handsome payment. The box rolled from Thorn's hand on to the table, where it lay next to the gold ingot. Thorn snatched the gold, his only concern, and held it belligerently. His grimace shined back at him from the brightly burnished ingot. The gold was his and that was all he wanted, for the time being.

The snarg leant over and rubbed a strange mark inscribed on the cube. The box smouldered and shrunk until it was no bigger than a thimble and the snarg gripped it with his spindly hand. Then like a conjurer, the beast tucked the tiny box beneath a swirl of blackness that resembled a cloak.

Thorn's job that night was done but there was one last thing he told his master before he disappeared.

"Croucher boxed that one himself," Thorn said. "So be careful with it. It's the young Gordon boy. I reckon he'll be a good worker and no trouble for you."

The snarg dropped to the floor and then bounded high into the rafters. It dashed from one roof joist to another before it silently slithered through a tiny crack in the roof.

And if someone somewhere had been counting, the world missed another child that night.

Down and down the Silver Lightning plummeted in the dark night. Ralph saw great torrents of snow swirl against the snow-laden treetops. Nex thundered through the air with its hooves, as its head lurched back and forth in rhythmic motion. The power and agility of Nex was extraordinary. Ralph reached new heights of excitement for he knew Nex, was unconquerable.

Open-mouthed Ralph looked at Greystone. Who smiled then briefly laughed. "Do you still want a helicopter?" he said.

"No, sir," was all Ralph said.

Once through the pine trees they came to a smooth stop.

"Here we are," Greystone announced. "The Emerald Wood."

Greystone turned dials and moved levers and the hum of the Silver Lightning faded as the generator shut down carefully. Out stepped the pair into untouched snow. Ralph had many questions for Greystone but one was topmost.

"Did anyone see us?" Ralph asked.

Greystone looked at him with raised eyebrows and explained, "Imagine sunlight striking a pane of glass. It passes straight through. So to the outside world we are invisible!"

He waved a hand in front of the lion-shaped door handle and the door made a low hiss as it shut. Ralph was then plunged into darkness until Greystone shone a torch.

"Not much emerald in this Emerald Wood," Ralph joked, excited and happy to be on the trip. "They should have called it the White Wood!" He was relaxed and confident with Greystone.

Greystone however was in a serious frame of mind and having felt the burden of command in the field, he ignored Ralph's flippancy. He set off, and followed a footpath covered in snow.

"Where is this door?" Ralph asked.

"It can't be far," Greystone muttered. He handed Ralph the torch as he fumbled with cold fingers and placed the gonoculars on his head. He took the torch and swept its beam from side to side. In the middle of the clearing was a large thicket.

"There it is," Greystone said, relieved and clearly delighted. "Goodness me, I think this one is in a Golden Bower."

Greystone was so taken with his find that he plunged towards the thicket and forgot Ralph who floundered a few yards behind. Ralph saw Greystone well enough, illuminated by his torch, but he couldn't see where to walk. Suddenly he stumbled into something wet and very cold.

"Oh, no! Look what's happened," he snapped, clearly blaming Greystone.

Greystone shone his torch. Ralph had trodden in a half-frozen puddle covered with snow. His right foot was muddy, sodden and icy cold. That was all part of life in the field Ralph had still to learn.

"Never mind, it'll soon dry out," Greystone said. "Come and look at this," he continued as he tried to distract Ralph's mind from the soggy shoe.

Ralph squelched over to Greystone where, without a word, he looked sulky and uninterested.

Greystone shone his torch on the thicket and quietly announced, "I have never seen a Golden Bower in this country before. The only one I know is in Germany."

"What's so different about this one?" Ralph grumbled, now barely interested.

"The thicket is a semi-circular bower," Greystone said, as his torch lit the dark underbelly of the thicket. "And look! You see the large opening at the bottom of the briars?" Ralph nodded as he responded to Greystone's animation.

"Well, that's the Ghost Door," Greystone said with triumph. "And when you go through this configuration you go deeper and further than you do with other doors."

"Come closer and tell me what you see," he continued.

Ralph shuffled forward and bent down to peer at the hole.

"All I can see are two half frozen snails," Ralph said disparagingly. "One on one side and one on the other."

Greystone was shaken and surprised. Perhaps he had misjudged the boy and Ralph was not a twister after all. Perhaps Ralph also needed gonoculars to see what Greystone could.

A sudden thought struck him. Perhaps the problem was again torchlight. He flicked the light off and asked Ralph what he could see.

For a moment Ralph was blind in the pitch-black but the deep dark slowly gave way to a new brighter stranger world. Ralph was overwhelmed. He struggled to describe it.

"Wow," he said in awe. "It's fantastic. Look at how many colours there are against the snow. Do you see how they send light in all directions? It's beautiful. And those snails! They're not snails at all. They are knights in suits of armour, each with a gleaming crown of gold. Why a crown of gold? Are they kings?"

Greystone wafted his hand across the entrance and the light streams moved for Ralph. Through his gonoculars, Greystone saw the light around his fingers dance.

"Not kings," Greystone said, "not kings at all. They are Gate Keepers. They see things we cannot. They see into our souls. They let good souls pass and leave the door shut for others. Their gold crowns mean this bower is extremely important."

"The light flows like water," Ralph said for he didn't need gonoculars. "Why does it do that, Mr Greystone?"

Greystone explained that the light was a dimensional flux that allowed elements to change. "For example, solid matter in our dimension can pour like water in another dimension".

Ralph stirred the light streams and they ran from one hand to the other. Both were silent, as they shared the experience of another world.

"Watch the Gate Keepers," Greystone said, "and follow me. They will open the door to our good hearts, I'm sure" and with that he plunged into the river of light.

Ralph saw the Gate Keepers as they shone brighter and a flood of light swallowed them like the flames of a fire. A tide pulled him deep inside the door and swept him up into a hall of light. The Gate Keepers soared ahead and shimmered on light beams as if they rode white stallions.

eleven: terror awaits

The journey through that Ghost Door was not the same as the previous one. Ralph plummeted down and down, faster and faster, then spiralled as if he were on a roller-coaster corkscrew. Then, the two Gate Keepers turned their light beams away from each other suddenly. He watched in astonishment as they changed direction a second time and hurtled back towards each other.

An explosion bathed everything in brilliant white light that faded slowly as Ralph's eyes were able to readjust. The night and the snow had gone. They were still in a forest, but this one had strange huge trees twice the size. It was like a forest from the Jurassic era 200 million years ago. Massive trees stretched as far as one saw.

They were on a well-worn path that twisted round a half-rotted fallen tree covered in a violet-sea green moss. It then gently meandered away into a darker part of the forest. A warm breeze pleasantly fell across Ralph's cheeks. This brought him memories of summer and adventures with Evan. He listened as branches swayed and creaked in an ageless song, drumming secrets in their soft wooden tap-tap way.

Ralph felt uneasy. He looked over at Greystone stooped low on the ground. He was examining something close and intently. When Greystone straightened up his face was anxious. He silently beckoned Ralph, a finger to his lips made sure the boy understood. When Ralph was close he whispered to him: "Cats. Many cats have passed this way."

"But, Mr Greystone," Ralph said, puzzled by his serious look, "I like cats."

The worry on Greystone's forehead deepened.

"These aren't the nice furry friends you keep at home. Look at their paw prints. These are big cats."

Ralph starred at the jumble of prints in the dust and begun to make out individual paw prints. They were the size of a man's hand. Now he was worried too.

"I wonder how many tins of cat food they eat in a day?" Ralph murmured, trying to relax himself.

Greystone frowned at Ralph's flippancy.

"Just the one, I would think," he said sternly. "One tin about your size."

Horror-struck, Ralph realized these were dangerous animals and nothing to joke about.

"Stay close," Greystone said in quiet command, "and don't lag behind. Tell me if you see anything but do it quietly. Shout only if absolutely necessary."

Ralph understood.

Greystone, like an experienced tracker, used his senses to collect information. His eyes searched the undergrowth. He strained his ears for every creak, crack and rustle of forest sounds. Once he assessed the dangers he moved swiftly and stealthily along the path. Ralph followed quietly, determined to stay close.

There were strange sounds from within the forest. Unseen creatures shook branches high in the canopy and their movements cast weird shadows. At ground level the movement and rustle of leaves reached Ralph's strained senses. He stepped over a fallen branch on the path and caught the flash of two green eyes.

Uneasy and alarmed Ralph tugged at Greystone's coat.

"I know! We are being watched," whispered Greystone.

Ralph heard the soft pad, pad of feet that barely made a noise. Through a gap in the foliage he saw the jet-black fur of a large cat. It glistened as the creature snaked parallel to them. Then Ralph saw another cat with black fur that tracked to their right. Greystone was forced onwards. Ralph heard another cat and glanced behind but only saw movement in the leaves.

Greystone seized and pulled Ralph ahead to where he would be safe. Further on the path widened into a clearing. This was where cats could attack. In a jumbled ruin large stone blocks offered a refuge.

"Run for your life!" Greystone shouted and pushed Ralph. "Run."

Ralph's heart was thumping. He heard Greystone shout something about boulders. His lungs were bursting. He didn't hear for all the noise inside him. He looked back to see if Greystone had kept up. Greystone thundered on Ralph's heels.

"Don't look round, just run," Greystone yelled frantically. Ralph was impressed, for an old guy he really shifted. In the clearing both ran flat out through the tall wispy grass. Just ahead were the ruins of giant stone blocks. The black cats kept pace, as their backs undulated, and their tails thrashed.

Those ruined stones towered over Ralph. He had no idea how to climb them.

"I need a ladder!" he shouted over his shoulder in desperation.

"This is the best ladder I have," Greystone grunted, as he grabbed Ralph's belt and foot and flung him five or six feet in the air with gargantuan strength. Every ounce of effort went into that throw. "Grab the top."

Ralph grasped the top and with his last energy scrambled up. Now he looked down to where Greystone had no choice but turn and face the cats. These snarled to each other and slowly moved forward for the kill. Ralph instinctively reached down to give Greystone a hand up the boulders but it was a futile gesture.

Greystone stood tall and brave. He waited for their attack, but instead of pouncing the cats suddenly stopped and pressed themselves to the ground in concealment.

Ralph heard a distant buzz like something he heard earlier echoed through the forest. The buzz had grown louder and its low pitch resonated. It sounded like the beat of wings in the air. At that height Ralph saw far across the forest canopy where curious dark shapes skimmed the treetops. They moved fast and were headed straight towards them. Greystone heard the sound too. As he looked up he saw six strange creatures swoop over the trees and into the clearing.

"Dragonflies," Ralph called out. "Look! Huge dragonflies." He recognised them but couldn't believe their size. Even Greystone was astounded.

"Hawkers," Greystone called out, "dragonflies that hunt." He told Ralph to keep down but Ralph only heard the roar of beating wings. Ralph stood up and gazed around oblivious to his own safety.

The dragonflies flew low over the wispy grass and criss-crossed in a precise pattern as they searched for prey. One of the creatures broke formation and made directly for Ralph. About four feet away it hovered perhaps to study him. At that distance the dragonfly was enormous, bigger than a fully size horse. Its body shone iridescent green. Its double set of wings, equally proportioned, spanned at least 9 meters. These made a huge downdraft and beat so fast they became a blur.

With great foreboding Ralph watched as the creature slowly opened its huge mandibles. He dived for cover as the dragonfly soared over his head and dropped to the ground. It grabbed something in its jaws. It was one of the cats, and it screeched with pain, as it was lifted vertical by the powerful dragonfly. Two other dragonflies thudded down in the long grass and each rose vertically with screaming black cats in their jaws. The few surviving cats then vanished into the trees, back to safety.

As the dragonflies departed, the forest came alive again with a symphony of daily chatter.

As Greystone helped Ralph from the boulder, Greystone realized it wasn't natural stone, but were cut blocks. He was surprised by this discovery.

"Why does everything in this forest have such nasty teeth?" Ralph asked, wholly preoccupied with recent events. "I thought you said there was no eating in Wychen?"

"I didn't say that," Greystone said, "I said creatures from Wychen don't usually want to eat us. I don't know why those cats are acting like that. But I am concerned by another puzzle. These stone blocks could be an old watchtower, but a lookout for what I wonder? We need to investigate."

They followed a path behind the stone blocks until they saw a tree-lined rampart and the start of a vast city.

They entered warily through a gate in the rampart and walked down a narrow street enclosed by towering high walls. The street opened into a series of squares and courtyards. Some buildings had enormous statues set in the walls. The statues portrayed great and strange creatures that were tall and slender with kind eyes. Some statues had smiles so beautiful on their carved features, that they made Ralph smile back.

"Are these the people who built this city?" Ralph asked.

"Maybe," Greystone replied, "but I have no idea who they are and why this place is deserted?" Greystone was more perplexed than usual.

Strange things were happening. From a long way off Greystone heard a faint intermittent hum like electric surges of a large transformer. These faded on the returning breeze.

"Can you hear something?" Greystone asked. "Stay close and we'll check it out."

In the courtyard was a tall bell tower, not the tallest tower there but high enough for a wide view across the city. Greystone found the tower's polished granite door hard to open, as though it was geared for stronger creatures. As they went in Ralph pushed it too, unable to resist a feel of its weight. The square tower was empty except for a grand staircase that wound around its outer walls, wide enough for them to climb side by side.

In a distant courtyard they saw movement and the source of the mysterious hum. A large machine. Greystone didn't recognise its design or purpose nor had he any idea where it came from, but one thing he was sure of, it didn't belong there.

Another smaller machine moved out of the shadows. A shaft of light fell onto glistening metal. Both Greystone and Ralph recognised it as a Guardian. Ralph's face took on a look of dread as Greystone grunted with growing anger and concern.

"That Guardian means that big machine is Snarg." Greystone whispered.

The Guardian moved in a familiar mechanized lurching way. It swung on its axis and juddered to a halt next to the big Snarg machine.

The humming grew louder as steam poured from a web of pipes around the Snarg machine's outer structure. A strange wheel with four evenly spaced nozzles protruded from the front of the machine. Suddenly the wheel turned until it reached an incredible speed.

As the humming noise peaked the nozzles expelled a huge cloud of spinning gas.

Greystone and Ralph watched with astonishment as a portal opened in the centre of the cloud. Blackened shapes slowly emerged. Snargs! Two flaccid shapes dropped like wet dishrags on to the courtyard floor, then squelched to the side of the machine where they made adjustments. Snarg mechanics! They made the centre of the vortex stretch into an elongated shape, the colour and texture of whirled soot. More dark shapes emerged. Greystone and Ralph didn't move for fear. Seven snargs swooped out of the soot like flying demons. On small green rings they flew, one to each clawed foot. Green putrid slime dripped from each ring that pulsated and glowed.

"That's all we need. Snargs that can fly!" Ralph snapped with fright.

Greystone leaned closer to the wall and remained concealed from the snargs.

"This is bad, these are gogaknights," Greystone said with a deep breath. "They are Croucher's elite guard. They have speed enough to bring down a running wolf."

Ralph saw that Greystone didn't need his gonoculars in Wychen. Snargs must be visible to all the creatures in here.

Suddenly, the gogaknights shoot skywards. Ralph observed them carefully, admiring their aerobatic skills but little else. Their sharp shiny claws were like handfuls of razor blades, capable of ripping an animal to shreds within seconds. The gogaknights twisted and turned in midair, then disappeared imperiously into the distance. They were on a mission.

"Even though they're gone," Greystone said despondently, "I don't think we'll get near that machine with its Guardian watching."

He thought for a while.

"I'm sure all this strange behaviour is to do with that confounded machine. But now we know how the snargs are leaving Ragna Doom."

Ralph was only half listening. Most of his attention was given to watching the sky in case the gogaknights returned. Greystone tried to reassure him but Ralph was lost in doubt.

Finally Greystone acknowledged they must leave the wood but he told Ralph he would call a meeting of the Binders Council as soon as they were back.

"These snarg's evil business must be stopped at all costs."

"Horrible smelly forest. Not coming back here in a million years. I hate this place." Ralph muttered angrily to bolster his spirits but his chattering infuriated Greystone as it prevented him hearing a distant noise.

"Be quiet," he growled. The noise was a faint crackle, the sort heard when gogaknights ride their green rings. He was also aware they were not armed well enough to keep them at bay.

When they reached the clearing of stone blocks it was peaceful, but Greystone still felt uneasy. He checked over his shoulder and saw on the far edge of the clearing a rapid zigzag movement through the trees. He had no doubts now. Gogaknights were hurtling towards them. They had only one hope. The Ghost Door.

The gogaknights released a bloodcurdling scream. They had spotted their prey and flew faster. The gap was closing by the second.

Greystone and Ralph thrashed the air with their arms, beating back branches that slowed them as Gogaknights gained fatal ground. Ralph's senses spun with fear.

But Ralph saw what Greystone could not. "The Door, it's opening. This way!" he shouted. He saw the dimensional flux, as it streamed in front of them along the branches and leaves. Some distance ahead the Ghost Door re-opened. But would they win their desperate race? Already the gogaknights mobbed them in a deafened screaming madness of murder. Ralph plunged for the Door. It was his only hope. Branches and claws ripped at his ears. They were both losing ground. Then everything merged into a dark ringing numbness.

Returned to consciousness, Ralph was aware he was shrouded in a cold darkness. He realised someone stood next to him but the numbing coldness made thoughts impossible. A light from a torch fell on him and a soft voice asked, "Are you alright, Ralph?"

He squinted into the light and strained to see.

"Is that you, Mr Greystone?" Ralph asked with uncertainty.

"Yes, I'm here," he replied.

"Where are we?" Ralph asked woozily.

"Back in Emerald Wood," Greystone said, his voice relieved and elated. "We made it home!"

As Ralph rose to his feet he felt Greystone's steady hand. It was then he saw Greystone was injured.

"Your arm, it's bleeding. Are you alright?" he asked sympathetically.

Greystone saw his sleeve had been torn to shreds and his arm underneath was bloody and raw. But the injury didn't look life threatening.

"From the look of my arm, Ralph, we escaped through the Door just in time. In another second those gogaknights would have ripped us to death."

Greystone spoke with real anxiety, paced a few feet from the briars and flourished his torch. He spoke to Ralph from the semi-darkness.

"It'll soon be morning. It's time to get you home."

With his torch Greystone summoned Silver Lightning, which re-appeared from nowhere. Nursing his arm, he climbed into the carriage and pulled Ralph to safety. The door closed. Nex took the harness under strain and under his immense power the Silver Lightning shot skywards.

Riding cloudless skies below the twinkling stars they were soon back in Broomfield and landed in the library quadrangle.

Greystone told Ralph to take a sleeping cabin in the Green Lab and rest there. He had no need to hurry home and it made the changeling exchange less complicated. Ralph gave a small groan as he considered his Changeling.

Greystone took Ralph to find his cabin before climbing into the Silver Lightning and once again streaking across the night sky.

Ralph struggled to find sleep. There were strange noises that came through a high window in his cabin and reflections of mysterious lights danced on the ceiling. His mind raced with terrifying images of gogaknights. But eventually sleep found him.

At the Higley house, morning came and Snap was up much too early. He made a terrible din on the landing by clomping about.

"What is wrong with that boy?" Mrs Higley muttered as she was forced out of bed. Sleepily she saw Snap bounce down the stairs, so she followed him.

In the kitchen, Snap was drawn to a dirty saucepan Mrs Higley had left soaking. And its soapy water looked good. For an ever-thirsty vegetable plant like Snap water was water, soapy or not. Snap stuck his head in the pan and took long gulps of water just as Mrs Higley came through the door.

"Ralph, what are you doing?" she yelled in shock.

Snap lifted his face of dirty soapsuds.

"I'm thirsty!" Snap bubbled. He was too young to know that soapy water made changelings act peculiar.

"Don't drink from the sink. You'll be sick," Mrs Higley insisted, her face held the horror. She ushered Snap from the sink.

"I think I'm a little hungry," Snap moaned in a way Ralph never had. A rare look of maternal sympathy flitted across Mrs Higley's face.

"My poor boy. You sit down and let me make you some nice porridge," she said still puzzled. Snap sat at the table and grinned with expectation, as the changeling never had porridge before. As Mrs Higley fetched the oats from the cupboard Snap began to talk.

"Do you know, my great-great-grandfather was a swede," the Changeling said in a matter-of-fact voice.

Mrs Higley was lost for a moment. This was puzzling, even by Ralph's standards.

"No, dear, he was definitely English," she said confidently, "As we all are."

But Snap was not listening. He watched Mrs Higley pour oats into a blue saucepan and a look of terror welled up.

"Whatever is the matter?" Mrs Higley asked, alarmed at the expression on her son's face.

"Someone has ground up my nephews and nieces and now you're going to make me eat them!" Snap cried.

"What are you talking about? Are you ill, Ralph? I'm going to fetch your father. Perhaps he can make any sense of you," she said with a sense of panic.

But Snap hadn't finished.

"You can't make me eat them," he screamed. "I won't, I won't! I am going to school." Snap rushed from the kitchen and paused only long enough to grab a coat. Mrs Higley yelled after the changeling but too late. She heard the front door slam.

twelve: midnight looms

Just as pupils were piling into Oswald's, in wandered Snap thoroughly disorientated. All changelings received strict instructions on where to go and when to do it in school. But Snap was inebriated on soapy water and his behaviour was badly affected. He was meandering down a corridor until Mr Hewitt stopped him. Mr Hewitt was carrying a large stack of books.

"Ah, Higley, just the boy. Take these books to Mrs Deacon's room," Mr Hewitt called out happily.

"Ah, Higley," gurgled Snap as bubbles blew from his lips.

Mr Hewitt raised an eyebrow at Snap. This was strange behaviour for any boy.

Snap took the pile, shook them and listened. "Empty books!" he muttered and stomped off.

Mr Hewitt was perplexed and bellowed: "Science room; not the art room." Snap turned and gave Mr Hewitt a sickly leer. He then lurched awkwardly in the other direction before muttering: "Silly Snap, silly Ralph!"

Mr Hewitt wondered if he had chosen the wrong boy even for that simple task.

Ralph had just arrived at school after a restless night in the Green Lab. Heading for his form room, he was unaware that his changeling hadn't returned to the Gimbals and was oblivious to the consequence. Rounding the corner he came upon Mr Hewitt talking to another teacher.

Suddenly Mr Hewitt blurted out, "Good grief!" as he saw Ralph.

The conversation stopped abruptly.

"Higley, have you delivered my books?" he yelled, believing he hadn't done so.

About to enter the form room Ralph froze to the spot as he heard his form teacher's voice. He hadn't the slightest idea what Mr Hewitt was talking about. The pale, blank expression on Ralph's troubled face was all too familiar to Mr Hewitt. It was the tale-tale sign of boys that had mice nesting in their heads instead of brains. Mr Hewitt's face turned dark and menacing.

"Well, I'm waiting for an answer," Mr Hewitt said, as he rocked both heels off the ground.

Ralph's mind raced as he struggled to oblige. It then dawned on him that Mr Hewitt must be referring to Snap.

"Yes, sir," said Ralph and crossed his fingers behind his back. Mr Hewitt glanced at his watch.

"If I find you haven't, Higley, it will be the high jump for you!" Mr Hewitt said.

Ralph made a quick exit. What would he have to deal with next?

When Snap failed to show at the library Mrs Pickles felt compelled to notify Mr Brack. She mentioned that she may have seen Snap from a distance but couldn't be sure it wasn't the real Higley boy. Mr Brack led the hunt as they searched the corridors for the changeling. Suddenly he saw Snap enter the science room.

Mrs Deacon was sitting her study desk and took the register, her face as long as a fiddle. She looked up just as Snap entered looking confused.

"Can I help you?" she asked, in a sarcastic, unhelpful tone.

"Text books from Mr Hewitt. Empty," Snap gargled, as a stream of bubbles popped from his mouth. Two girls giggled as more bubbles popped out. Mrs Deacon, however, was suddenly concerned that the boy might choke.

"Are you all right?" she asked, looking at Snap's lips as she removed the textbooks from him.

Snap didn't dare say anything for fear of blowing more bubbles so he held his breath. But to his horror even larger bubbles now escaped though his ears. The sniggers from the pupils grew into roars of laughter. But when Mr Brack entered the raucous laughter turned to silence. Mr Brack saw the predicament instantly.

"Oh, Mr Brack, this boy is ill. Bubbles are coming from his ears!"

"Don't worry, Mrs Deacon, it is just some fad. It was worm eating last week. Five pupils went home sick. This week it must be soap eating", he said.

"Goodness", she replied and looked at her class for more signs the new fad. The headmaster ushered Snap away and off to the hidden confines of the Gimbals.

Ralph didn't see Rebecca until school ended when she walked out the main gate.

"Hi Ralph, how did it all go?" she smiled. Ralph couldn't help but recount his exploits, his tiredness forgotten.

"What's the matter?" Rebecca asked as Ralph's unfinished tale ground to a halt.

With sudden realisation he looked at her, his mouth opened. "I've just remembered something," he said. "Greystone mentioned he would let us know when a binders' meeting would be called. He said to listen for the knock, but I've no idea what that means."

"The knock," Rebecca said. "You've not had one yet? It's very clever. It's a secret message service. There will be a dull thud or knock, that is where you find the binder's note. It could be anywhere in the room. But read quickly for they don't last long, they just dissolve away. They are made from a kind of sparkly sugar paper. It's lovely to see, just watch!"

When Ralph arrived home Mr Higley was waiting, ready to quiz him about his behaviour that morning. But when his son failed to answer convincingly he grew angry. The way he protested his innocence didn't help. His father was furious at what he called Ralph's uncaring and ungrateful attitude towards his mother. So he sent the lad to his room to ponder this.

Ralph felt it was all Snap's fault, but he could hardly say that to his father. It was just one more thing to deal with snargs, dragons, changelings, and worst of all a missing friend. He didn't expect much support from his parents. They were both fribblers, after all.

Being confined in his little room had always been boring in the past but not now. He had his dragon and it was feeding time. Ralph unpinned his binder shield from his jacket and released Synge, forgetting he was pony sized and not a quiet controllable creature. The dragon pranced around the little room, his clumsy tail threatened to demolish the furniture.

"Sssh," Ralph pleaded as he tried to stop Synge banging his tail against the floor. But Synge was hunting his supper. When Ralph realised he rummaged for his jam jar under the bed.

Synge, excited by the thought of dinner, perched next to Ralph's desk in the corner and laid his head on the chair. But Ralph had no time to admire his pet. The bugs were running around the jar and evading his fingers. He needed a better idea. So he emptied the jar of four black beetles and green leaves in the middle of the room.

Three of the beetles were on their backs, wriggling to get up. The fourth was on its legs and made a dash for freedom under his bed. Synge's quick predatorily eyes spotted the scuttling beetle. In a flash Synge pounced and swallowed the beetle whole.

"Good boy, Synge," Ralph praised his dragon. But he gave his praises too soon. The bouncy creature careered into Ralph's bed. The humungous thump shook the bed and, so it seemed, the whole house.

"Well, that's torn it for me now," Ralph sighed but Synge wasn't listening. He was pouncing on the other three beetles that still wriggled on their backs.

Then his mother clumped up the stairs. No one must see his dragon. Synge slunk very low and tried to slide under the bed, but he became stuck. Ralph rushed and pushed on Synge's rear end as hard as he could. It was hard enough and the dragon squeezed under the bed. The door opened with a burst and in came his mother. Fortunately she couldn't see the tip of the dragon's troublesome tail stuck out the beds other side. Her mind was on what caused the banging until something else drew her attention.

"What is that awful smell?" she demanded sniffing the air. Synge pulled his tail quickly out of sight. She barely listened to Ralph's plea that there was no smell.

"What is that stuff doing in the middle of the floor?" she asked with great concern and pointed to the leaves and the old jam jar. She often complained about her son's untidy habits.

Ralph thought quickly.

"It's my science project," he told his mother. "They fell out when I dropped my jar. And now it's all ruined!"

"Never mind, dear," Mrs Higley said, still concerned about her son's curious sensitivities that morning. "I'm sure you can put it back together."

He was surprised and didn't expect sympathy.

"That experiment better not include burning matches," his mother said, as she noticed a sulphurous smell again. "I'll not have you burning the house down."

Out of the corner of his eye Ralph saw Synge's nose under the bed. He stepped over and anxiously blocked his mother's view.

"It must be those leaves smelling, mum," he said. "I'll put them back in the jar." With a devious kick delivered at lighting speed he covered the dragon's snout with the loose end of his bedspread. But his mother still wanted the last word.

"Mind you do," she said. "I don't want that smell through out my house!"

"Yes, mum," Ralph said dutifully as his mother finally closed the door.

With his mother gone he summoned Synge out. But the dragon was having none of it. He preferred the comfort of the dark. It was another half an hour before Ralph enticed him back into his shield.

"I'm glad I don't have to feed him three times a day," Ralph smiled to himself. "Once is enough!"

It was a little before midnight and Ralph's thirteenth birthday. That meant it was time for Sir John's book. Carefully

Ralph pulled the book from the old trunk. The gold lettering of "Raven's Wood" shimmered in the pale light. It seemed heavier than before. He examined the book and even shook it to see if anything heavy dropped out. Nothing did. It was a mystery. So he opened the book and read.

Soon the church clock was showing a few minutes to midnight. It was also only minutes before he turned thirteen, the time when Sir John said to look for the real treasure.

He placed the book on the trunk and waited for something to happen. Then just as the clock struck midnight the book began to smoulder. Ralph jerked upright in alarm.

By the last stroke of midnight the book was ablaze. Ralph was on the verge of panic and about to fetch some water to stop the house burning down when he noticed how strange the flames were. They were not burning upwards like normal fire. They were burning downwards and outside in!

Ralph laughed nervously as gradually the book was consumed but the flames touched nothing else. Finally all that remained was a pile of ash. He stopped laughing when he realized the book was gone. Bewildered he looked at the ash. What would he do? He dreaded what Sir John would say. Ralph touched the ash as if the book would come back, like a mythical phoenix. But within the ash he felt hard cold metal and he pulled it out. There in his hand was an object about 7.5 centimetres in diameter and 5 centimetres deep. It looked like a small round tin.

But it was gold, solid gold. He lifted it close to his face and was bathed in reflected gold light. Why was it stone cold just after it had been ravaged by fire, he wondered?

It was as heavy as a small paperweight and had a pointer on top with a round dial inscribed with strange markings.

Ralph turned the dial. Nothing happened. He looked at the round ruby jewel in the middle of the dial. It was like a button. Ralph pushed it and the round ruby popped up. The device whirred noisily. Frightened, he placed it on the wooden trunk. The whirring stopped while a hissing begun. The object opened and split into two halves. These were joined together by three telescopic legs. Between was suspended a huge jewel, like a cut diamond. Nothing supported it. The gem floated in mid air. No matter what angle the device was viewed, it resembled an old oil lamp.

For the next half hour Ralph examined the object in the hope of discovering its use. But he grew ever more frustrated at not solving this question and muttered: "What are you for?"

Suddenly the glittering jewel spun wildly and directly beneath, a small aperture opened in the base. From that a pencil sharp green light shone vertically in a beam, straight into the cut jewel. Green shafts of light were thrown all over the bedroom wall. Slowly alphabet letters formed and were easily read.

"I am the Illuminatus, the Illuminator of secrets and hidden things."

"Now this," Ralph thought, "is going to be very useful."

He had an inspired idea. What his hungry stomach mostly wanted right now was a biscuit.

"Tell me a secret," Ralph said and licked his lips with anticipation. "Tell me where mum hides the biscuit tin?"

He waited but there was no reply. The golden artefact remained idle and silent.

"It's like everything I've had," Ralph grumbled to himself. "Faulty the minute I use it!"

Ever the optimist he asked the question again: "Illuminatus, please, tell me a secret. Where does my mother hide the biscuit tin?"

At once the machine whirred into life and again words appeared. Perhaps because he had said please? Ralph quickly read the answer.

"This tin of which you ask

Is by an old grey flask.

But you must stop and think

What it's hidden under rhymes with Wychen stink!"

Ralph contorted his face as he puzzled the meaning of the strange rhyme. But it didn't take him long.

"That's clever. It's the kitchen sink! It's under there, that's the one place mum knows I would never look."

He found the question easy and his mind flooded with others he'd like answered.

"Illuminatus, please tell me a secret. Where at school does Mr Hewitt keep his answer book?"

Again there was whirring and words appeared. But it wasn't the answer Ralph wanted. He read it aloud:

"I will reveal the truth but once a day;

After that I will say nay."

Disappointment filled Ralph's face.

"Well that takes the biscuit," he grumbled. "I don't even get three questions like three wishes if it was a Genie's lamp!"

In the coming week, Ralph learned to use the *Illuminatus* sparingly and so kept to the daily limit. He told himself when he desperately needed an answer he didn't want to be told: "Come back tomorrow!"

Also, he begun to understand Sir John when he said: "You will see the real treasure." It had nothing to do with the solid gold casing or the adornment of jewels. No. It was quite simply the knowledge it gave was priceless. And so Ralph kept the *Illuminatus* hidden at the bottom of his wooden trunk and told no one of its existence, not even Rebecca.

One night, when Ralph lay peacefully in bed on the verge of sleep, there was a dull knock. He sat bolt upright in his dark room. He listened intently and heard it again. He switched on his bedside light, rubbed his eyes and looked around the room. There was another knock and the wardrobe door shook. He slid out of bed and gingerly edged across to the wardrobe. He felt too nervous to open the door in case ghosts or snargs lurked there. He felt hot and cold at the same time. He wanted to run but it was too late. He had his hand on the latch of the door.

"One, two, three," Ralph counted and yanked hard. The door flew open. But instead of some fiend jumping out he saw an unusual post card. Bright sparkles of golden light streamed from it. It was a Binder's note, just as Rebecca described. The postcard was as light as a feather. Its texture reminded him of candyfloss. He felt a tingle in his palm and the card opened like a butterfly unfolds its wings. He saw his name and a message in bold print: "Ralph Higley is requested to attend an emergency meeting of Binders tomorrow at 4pm in the Grand Hall."

Moments later the card closed, crumbled to a sugary dust and was gone.

thirteen: the binders meeting

It was fast approaching four in the afternoon when down in the Gimbals Mr Lushington, clerk of the Binders, stood outside the Grand Hall's large door.

He was methodically checking people before they entered the hall against the official list in a large black book. Ralph arrived with only minutes to spare. He sat on the students' bench as the large doors banged shut.

Mr Lushington officiously closed his book and announced sonorously: "Council is now in session. All rise for our Master of the Chair, the Right Honourable Mr Goodwig."

Everyone stood as Mr Goodwig entered the hall from a side door. He was a stout little man. His black robe swished from side to side. He lowered himself magisterially into a large stately chair. It was certainly a magnificent chair, large and carved in the shape of a dragon. When Mr Goodwig sat everyone else followed suit. Next to

Mr Goodwig sat the Privy Chamberlain, the sinister Mr Moynton, who Ralph recognized from the Imp tram.

But Ralph was only half interested in Moynton. He was more curious about the very thin, pale and breathless boy that sat to his right. He had never seen him before. Ralph whispered: "Hello, I'm Ralph Higley." The boy jumped and grew more breathless. He fumbled in his pocket for an asthma inhaler. The inhaler made a strange rattle as the boy took a deep breath.

"I'm Simon," he said shyly. "Simon Mopley."

Unimpressed by all the chatter Rebecca leant forward and rebuked the boys sharply.

"I'm trying to listen. If you continue Mr Lushington will be over to put you out."

But that didn't faze Ralph. He was less respectful of pomp and ceremony than Rebecca, so he made a sarcastically apologetic face and sunk low into his chair. Simon, by contrast, was embarrassed. His face turned from pasty white to flush pink.

Greystone stood up from the seniors' bench and addressed the council. He demanded action over the recent mysterious loss of children from Bloomfield. His voice trembled with determination.

"We need to take note. I have no doubt this is snarg activity."

Moyton on Mr Goodwig's right hand stood and questioned Greystone about his evidence of snargs invading Broomfield.

"Mr Greystone, is it not true that Snargs have been confined to Ragna Doom for centuries?"

"Yes, it is true. But not anymore." Greystone replied without hesitation.

Moynton smirked sarcastically.

"Exactly what evidence do you have?" Moynton asked. He spoke offhandedly, as though dismissive of Greystone.

Greystone remained calm despite the disparaging line of questioning.

"There is a new Ghost Door in the Emerald Wood," he said. "Through this portal my understudy, Ralph Higley, and myself discovered the ruins of a large city. It should have been deserted except we saw a hidden machine there.

"It was a snarg contraption and it allowed them to come and go. Ragna Doom is no longer their prison. I believe from there they found a Dark Door and used it to access our world. I know these wild Ghost Doors with out gatekeepers are rare, but they do exist. And the snargs have had centuries to make plans."

His statement triggered a flood of whispers among the senior members until it filled the decorous hall with an unruly babble. Mr Goodwig banged his gavel on the table hard: "Order, order. I must have quiet!"

With a soured expression, Mr Goodwig looked directly at Greystone.

"I appreciate the gravity of your news," he said, "but we cannot and will not involve ourselves in Wychen business. You know as well as I that this has been part of the Binder code through all the centuries since we were founded. It is Judge Majestic's legacy. There you have it. Our hands are tied."

There was another rush of debate, which quietened only when Greystone spoke again.

"This isn't just about us," he said entreating the Binders. "What about the children of Broomfield. They are still missing. More will be taken. This is just the beginning, one day Ragna Doom will prepare for war!"

Mr Goodwig as chairman dismissed the plea in a most arrogant way.

"All through history children have gone missing. There are many reasons. It is a very big supposition to say this is due to a snarg invasion."

Next to him Moynton nodded dramatically in agreement and stared around the chamber as though threatening members to disagree.

"So," Greystone growled, sensing defeat, "are you telling me we are to do nothing?"

Mr Goodwig shuffled his papers while he prepared to leave. He paused and looked at Greystone thoughtfully.

"Not as such," he said. "This calls for careful monitoring and a further report. We must first make exhaustive searches here in Bloomfield, but not in Wychen!"

"But we need to act now," Greystone protested.

"This meeting is now at an end," Mr Goodwig announced and promptly left the hall.

"I cannot accept this," Greystone bellowed with rage. "I will take this to the High Council in London. They will listen."

Listening carefully already was Mr Moynton. His long spindly fingers flicked his greasy hair back arrogantly. He looked at Greystone in a devious manner.

"I shouldn't do that if I were you," he said. "Those instructions came from London. Try not to cause yourself further embarrassment!"

Greystone was clearly shocked and speechless. But two benches behind sat Black-Bob and he has had enough of the fiasco too. Jumping to his feet in support of Greystone. "If these children are not found, I will hold you responsible, Moynton," he shouted. "You are nothing but a meddler and I'm sick of it."

But Moynton was far beyond threats and accusations. He was not in the least concerned and left the chamber, leaving Lushington to deal with the furore that he and Goodwig caused. The room was in uproar.

Outside the hall, Ralph stood angry, as no one had asked him about Evan. How was that, when they said they wanted to hear the evidence? He would have screamed out loud if he hadn't felt a hand on his shoulder.

Rebecca stood with tears in her eyes. It was a moment where he wanted to cry too. But he couldn't for Evan's sake. He had to stay strong for his friends, especially the close ones.

Rebecca wiped away her tears.

"I am as sorry as you about the council's decision. I hate what it means for Evan. But Black-Bob and Greystone will not stop until this is resolved."

She then hugged Ralph, trying to comfort him. He almost succumbed to his emotions again. Trembling inwardly he hid them behind a sad smile.

Rebecca reciprocated and searched her thoughts for ways to give him hope.

"Binders never sort anything out in a day. They don't understand how hard this makes things for the new students."

Rebecca's words certainly had an effect. He realised it was time for action, not words.

"I shall go and get Evan back myself. I owe him so much. We've been friends for so long, I know he'd do the same for me. Nothing will stop me, not all the snargs of Ragna Doom!"

Rebecca looked away, not sure what more could be said. It was then she noticed Simon, breathless as he pushed his way through the Binders that remained. She nudged Ralph in warning.

"I'm glad I've caught up with you. I've only just heard the terrible rumour of Snargs taking your friend and..." but Simon was interrupted by Ralph.

"It's no rumour," he snapped, his face flushed with anger. "I was there. I saw the snarg who took him. I even have the snarg's name and address!" Ralph was shouting now, "And you can all have it: Mr Croucher, care of the Devil's Hunch, Ragna Doom. What more do they want?" he shouted angrily at no one in particular. Everyone had to know Evan was important and that he was ready for the fight.

Taken aback, Simon was inspired.

"Listen," he said. "I know you don't know me, be-cause I'm in lower form and we usually don't mix, but I would like to help."

"Good," Ralph replied his spirits lifted. He then looked at Rebecca and said, "You can join our team!"

Ralph's outburst brought Mr Lushington over and he had a face like thunder. But before Lushington reached them Rebecca and Simon dragged Ralph away.

They raced down the tunnel towards the Imp tram, unaware that Moynton had been watching from a high balcony. He had mastered gathering discarded letters and the art of blackmail but more importantly for Moynton, the art of eavesdropping.

When Moynton thought of making money his nose twitched unconsciously. After he watched those stu-dents, his nose was as busy as a rat that had smelt cheese.

After the meeting, Moynton travelled through Binder passages to meet someone in secret. He came to a squalid tavern in the Gallows, on the shabby side of town. It was not the kind of place he usually visited but the smell of money and the thought of making lots of it, had overcome his distaste.

The Smelters Arms stood at the end of a cobbled street. It was a magnet for villains and thieves.

Uneasy, Moynton stepped inside and looked carefully around the bar. A man sat alone at a round table, silhou-etted against the flames of a small log fire. He held an empty glass and stared morosely at the dancing flames. When he saw Moynton, the man grimaced.

"Charlie Moynton," he said sardonically and glanced back into his empty glass as though he preferred to brood. On the empty chair next to the man lay the distinctive floppy hat.

"It's Charles, not Charlie, if you please Jack," Moynton told the man.

"Oh, that will be when I please, Charlie!" the man said. Then with a look of menace he asked: "What on the earth are you doing here?"

Moynton looked at Jack Thorn cautiously.

"I came to warn you about a troublesome little Binder called Ralph Higley!"

Thorn interrupted Moynton; grabbed him viciously by the collar and pulled him close.

"We are not supposed to be seen together," Thorn snarled. "Not until this business is over."

Moynton looked around the room.

"I'm sorry," he croaked, as Thorn almost throttled him. "I'm sorry."

"I'm sorry," Thorn mocked. "You and your bellyaching makes me sick."

Moynton slumped onto the empty chair next to Thorn, and without realising knocked the wide brimmed hat under the table. Thorn didn't notice.

Like a scolded pup, Moynton wheezed as he spoke.

"Do you know who the little brat's mentor is?" he asked Thorn, with a smug ring to his words.

"Why should I care?" Thorn replied, sharp-tongued.

Moynton's eyes narrowed to a pinpoint. He slid closer and whispered his magic into Thorn's ear.

"You should care, Jack, because your dear old tutor Greystone has chosen this boy as his next prodigy. The old fool! And," laughed Moynton with an ugly pant. "If Greystone messes up once more he could be kicked out of the Binders. But there is more. Taking that boy Evan caused a big stir in the Binders' council. I personally had to obstruct their interest. But Greystone's little monkey kept poking his nose into our business. Jack, he has to be stopped."

Thorn gripped the edge of the table with a terrible clench that turned his knuckles bloodless white.

"What's the little brat's name again?" Thorn asked.

Moynton wetted his lips.

"Ralph Higley," Moynton said. "But what is curious about this boy is that he doesn't seem very bright. It makes me wonder why Greystone picked him."

Thorn rubbed his chin in deep thought.

"Ralph Higley, you say. Someone mentioned that name to me recently."

It was Moynton's turn to pass over the matter.

"Never mind that! If you dealt with the boy that would fix Greystone too!"

"So that's my pay off, is it?" Thorn snarled. "And what's in it for you?" he asked, without any loss of shrewdness.

"I only want to help," said Moynton, extremely versed in the ways of deceit. Then he moved his deception up a gear.

"But there is one little kindness you could do for me," Moynton said, while he hoped his polished slickness wasn't obvious. "You could put a good word in for me with Croucher. I would much appreciate that."

Once Moynton had a foothold in the snargs' camp he no longer needed Thorn. Then he would cease having to deal with Thorn's biting anger and his thinly veiled sarcasm.

"I have an associate," Thorn said. "A very great deceiver, a charlatan in the guise of a weak old lady. When she finds this Higley boy he will be done for."

"Do I know her?" Moynton asked as she sounded like a woman he would like to meet.

"Maybe," Thorn said. "She is notorious around Bloomfield. You might have seen my Mrs Ridley in a red coat, sometimes with her dark purple scarf, her Deadly Nightshade. Keep your enemies close is what I say."

Moynton shuddered at the name. He knew the gossip that concerned the mysterious death of May Singer and quickly he decided to avoid her. Turning to leave the tavern, he saw Thorn fumbling oddly under his table. Moynton thought, 'What a fool!' Smiling pompously, he closed the door.

By the time Ralph reached home he was calm but still determined on his quest. Quietly in his bedroom he prepared his plan to rescue Evan. The plan was simple; he would use the Illuminatus to locate the entrance of Ragna Doom and the castle of the fiendish snarg, Croucher.

He took his hidden instrument and laid it on the trunk. There was no book of instructions, so everything would be trial and error. But this was Ralph's way.

He turned the dial on top to another setting, one he hadn't used before. Then he pressed the red button and waited. The tripod appeared but then the Illuminatus shot out tiny bolts of lightning. Sparking and crackling like hundreds of white electric snakes they hit the bedroom wall. But Ralph wasn't prepared for this, the wall fizzled, melted and oozed away. After that, disbelief turned to horror as a huge hole appeared in the wall. The Illuminatus then snapped shut, its task completed.

Ralph scrambled to the hole. From there he saw the stars twinkle as a bitter cold mist drifted into his once warm bedroom. The outside wall hung down the side of the house like a melted apron of gooey, twisted bricks. Ralph was paralysed with fear at what he had done.

But there was more horror. Ralph's other neighbour Mr Newton stood in his backyard, with a rubbish bag poised above a dustbin. He stared up at Ralph with astonishment through the missing wall.

"Are you all right?" Mr Newton shouted in disbelief.

Stupidly, Ralph ducked behind his trunk and Mr Newton thought the young lad had collapsed.

Mr Newton leapt to the rescue and raised the alarm by banging on the Higley's front door. Behind the trunk Ralph groaned with despair knowing his father would soon come.

In desperation, Ralph seized the Illuminatus. He had to find a way to reverse the broken wall. But he panicked and dropped it on the table. This caused the Illuminatus to open in its tripod position. More white bolts of lighting shot from it. Suddenly the melted bricks rose up like a sheet of water until they all were back in place and the gaping hole filled.

Heavy footsteps pounded towards his bedroom door. He gasped with distress. In his hand the Illuminatus snapped shut. He turned to the damaged wall. It was in perfect shape and so was the wallpaper.

Suddenly, his door was hurled open and in dashed his father to rescue his son from certain catastrophic disaster.

Ralph watched his father's face change from panic to uncertainty. Where was the unconscious body of his son? Where was the collapsed wall? Ralph used that moment of confusion to slip the Illuminatus under his pillow.

"Thank goodness you're alright" Mr Higley said thoughtfully, his utter relief tinged with an unspeakable suspicion.

"Why shouldn't I be, Dad?" Ralph said as he recognised another figure. "Hello, Mr Newton. What are you doing up here?"

Mr Newton struggled to see anything wrong in the room.

"I don't understand," he said to Mr Higley. "I saw that wall crumble! I saw Ralph looking down at me in the yard. Am I going mad? I must be going mad!" Mr Newton trembled and was physically shaken. Mr Higley took his arm and kindly led him away.

As he did he called to Ralph, "Tea will soon be on the table." And considering what was nearly discovered Ralph was very grateful.

Ralph was determined the drama wouldn't delay his mission. Quickly he pulled the Illuminatus from under the pillow.

"No more experimenting," he thought. "Just press the button!"

A swirl of green letters appeared on the wall: "*What is your question*?"

At long last he thought.

"The lost Ghost Door to Raven's Wood," Ralph whispered. "How can I find it?"

Light glowed and twisted and flashed inside the machine. The message lit the wall:

"That which you ask
Lies buried in the past.
Only one remains who knows;
Listen to a foghorn that no one blows."

"Well, is that it?" Ralph fretted. "Is that all you can tell me? How can anyone hear a Foghorn if it's not blown? And, where will I even find one? This is silly!"

He couldn't face any more riddles, so he returned the Illuminatus to the trunk and went for his tea.

Over the next few days he frequently consulted the Illuminatus concerning the riddle. But the answer was always the same. Ralph was ready to admit defeat.

Then he remembered Rebecca; she was always solving riddles.

Windbury House, where Rebecca lived, was a large impressive house that overlooked the park. It's yellow stone drive swept smoothly up to the front door. Ralph walked briskly up and rang the bell. Rebecca's mother opened the door; she was a tall elegant lady with grey hair swept up into a tight bun.

"Can I help you," Mrs Harwood asked kindly.

Ralph knew to be on his best behaviour.

"Hello, I'm Ralph Higley. Is Rebecca in?" Ralph answered timidly.

Mrs Harwood knew who he was and took him through a very grand entrance hall into the large kitchen where Rebecca was eating at a long, heavy wood table in the middle of the room. Mrs Harwood left them and went about her business.

Rebecca smiled delighted to see him.

"This is a surprise! What brings you here?"

"I have a question to solve before I can find Ragna Doom," Ralph said with a serious look.

Rebecca was intrigued and asked what it was.

Finally he replied, "Well. What is a foghorn which no one blows and where can I find one?"

"I'll think," she said. "Would you like some bread and jam," and carved a thick slice of bread from a loaf. She buttered it before a thick layer of homemade jam was added.

Ralph chewed thoughtfully on the fresh bread and jam.

"Any ideas yet?" he asked.

"Not really!" she told him. "I'd be less confused and might be more help if I knew where your question came from."

Ralph wanted to keep the Illuminatus a secret. He played dumb and evaded her with an unsatisfactory, wishy-washy answer.

"I just know it will lead to Ragna Doom," he said. Rebecca rolled her eyes at this nonsense.

"You aren't helping," she said. "If we can't narrow the search we're not going to find it."

Then she had another idea.

"Let's go down to the Scriptorium in the Gimbals and ask the Sentinel to help. I am sure he will."

Ralph had never heard of the Sentinel, although clearly Rebecca thought he should.

"You need to spend more time studying," she said in a stern tone.

There was no reaction from Ralph as Rebecca walked over to the back door. But then a plump golden brown chicken strolled in.

"Meet little Greta," Rebecca announced and scooped up the cheerful clucking hen with both hands.

Ralph was surprised to see a chicken but was more astounded when Rebecca plonked Greta on the table. Ralph couldn't appear rude, so he stepped up to the table and spoke softly to the fine brown hen as it pecked up the breadcrumbs.

"It's really nice to meet you, Greta. So which part of Wychen do you come from?"

The brown hen ignored him and continued pecking but Rebecca was in a fit of giggles.

"I don't see what's funny?" Ralph said indignant.

"Greta doesn't talk," Rebecca said, "and she doesn't come from Wychen. She's just my little pet!"

"How am I supposed to know that?" Ralph complained. "Since you put her on the table I assumed she was a citizen of Wychen. Why else would anyone put a smelly brown chicken on a kitchen table?"

Rebecca's eyes widened with annoyance.

"Because Greta loves it on the table. It's a treat for her and she cleans the crumbs for me. And she's not smelly. My Greta is a very clean hen. Don't you give your daft dog Oliver a titbit?"

Ralph was indignant at the comparison.

"I don't put Oliver on the table," he said, seriously. "My mother would go spare!"

They glared, momentarily angry at one another, before erupting into laughter.

fourteen: the map room

The week was nearly over before Ralph and Rebecca could visit the Scriptorium. They descended in the Gimbals' elevator to the bottom level. The Scriptorium was a bizarre mix of ancient and modern, a large round building that looked like a Roman coliseum.

It stood by itself in the middle of a gigantic domed cavern cut into the rock. In the perimeter wall of the Scriptorium were large, round pylons of a shiny chrome-like metal. The circular wall was made of solid wooden blocks interlaced with strange tendrils, as though from a plant. From these sprouted large green luminous suckers that bound the wall into a solid timeless structure. The floor outside the Scriptorium was of black granite, shiny like polished glass. As they walked towards the tall entrance Ralph saw bright ghostly lights that floated in the floor just below its dark surface.

Ralph went to step on one.

"Don't do that," Rebecca yelled, but it was too late. The bright light was gone, extinguished.

"Now look what you've done!" she said with real venom. "Watch those clodhopping feet of yours and don't step on another one."

Ralph looked perplexed.

"This is no ordinary building," Rebecca told him furiously. "The Scriptorium was built by imps. It not only stores knowledge. It thinks. Those bright lights are big ideas, destined for some deserving person above. You have just snuffed one out. It might have been a fantastic invention but we'll never know now. That's it, lost for ever!"

Ralph apologised and with a sorry sigh stepped a little more carefully.

"And what are those little dull ones?" he asked, not wishing to do more damage.

"You know when you have an eureka moment completely out of the blue? You rush out to tell everyone. Only you can't remember the vital details? Well, those little dull lights are what will happen to the bright lights if we don't catch them. Bright ideas are invisible so we never see them normally. If they aren't used they will meander back here dull and rejected."

Entering the inner part of Scriptorium, Ralph saw millions of books around the circular wall stacked into cube-shaped shelves. These stretched to the roof and down to a floor made of thick solid glass. It was clear enough to see a continuation of bookshelves, circling endlessly down into the blackness.

They walked slowly over the small gantry that led from the entrance to a round glass island in the centre of the Scriptorium. The gantry had safety rails to stop anyone falling into the chasm. Ralph was curious.

"No one's ever been down there," Rebecca said. "The Sentinel won't allow it."

"Who or what is a sentinel?" he asked.

Rebecca pointed to the island and to the ominous figure sat at the apparatus that resembled a huge cathedral organ made of multi-coloured glass.

"He is the custodian of the Scriptorium. Nobody knows how many years he's been here, what he is, or why he always wears an eerie mask."

Ralph clearly saw the figure wore a dark purple robe with an odd shape mask that covered his face.

"May I help you?" the Sentinel asked in a rich, earthy voice.

"I do hope so," Rebecca said tentatively. "We have a question, but are not sure what it means. We are hoping to find a foghorn that no one blows. Can you help us?"

"A foghorn that no one blows," the Sentinel chuckled. "Oh my, that is very good! I certainly do know such a foghorn. No one blows dear old Jeremiah Foghorn. He's the unhappy binder who sadly disappeared. Let me see what more I can tell you."

Like a mad organist, the Sentinel pulled and pushed a number of glass knobs on the bewildering apparatus. This made the glass pipes behind light up in a symphony of colour. In the depths the shelves moved, sorting and sifting information on Jeremiah Foghorn. Suddenly the movement ceased with a 'ker-ching' and a small sign popped up.

"It appears the book Jeremiah wrote is on loan. I can request a return, but this can take time," the Sentinel said in an authoritative tone.

"I suppose we will have to wait," Ralph said disappointed.

"A Binder's note will be sent to you when the book's in," the Sentinel told them as he held out a hand.

Ralph searched his pockets for loose change but didn't have any.

"It's not money he wants," Rebecca said with irritation. "It's your binder's shield. Never mind, we can use mine."

Rebecca handed her badge to the Sentinel. He slotted it into the console, removing it again once a coloured pipe had changed from blue to pink. As the Sentinel handed the shield back he looked closely at her tiny dragon and asked her name.

"Ember!" said Rebecca.

"I wonder," the Sentinel asked with concern. "Have you been feeding Ember mealworms?"

"Some. But not many," Rebecca admitted.

"She looks a little bloated," the Sentinel advised. "A diet of mealworms will do that. Try an eye-drop of honey now and again."

Rebecca thanked the Sentinel for his advice but was hurt that anyone should doubt her care of Ember. She pushed Ralph out of the Scriptorium.

By the time Rebecca received the Binder's note it was spring. Almost frantic and with no time for a discussion, they dashed to the Scriptorium to collect Jeremiah's book. The Sentinel was expecting them.

"Welcome! Here is the book you requested."

Rebecca took the book and read its cover aloud: 'The Thirteen Deadly Secrets' by Jeremiah Foghorn.

"The answer must be in here?" she sighed.

"At least thirteen?" Ralph joked with a big smile. "I only need one."

They left the Scriptorium and returned to the school's library, where under the watchful eye of Mrs Pickles, they huddled at a small table in the corner and delved deeper into the old book.

They scanned each page for clues, looking for something that might lead to Raven's Wood and to Ragna Doom.

"Look what it says here," Rebecca whispered, brimming with excitement.

"Like many I undertook the ultimate quest, the search for the lost Ghost Door; the door that leads to Raven's Wood. My long search ended when I reached Dunton Abbey. I made enquiries about the abbey's history and asked if there was any connection with Judge Majestic. Locke, the Abbot, talked about the Abbey's history, but when it came to the Judge he denied any knowledge. When I asked if I could take a look at the Abbey Records he refused, saying: "They are treasured books, not to be

touched by any layperson." This made me suspicious. Over the coming months I returned from time to time to the Abbey.

Gradually I acquired the friendship of a Brother Comus. I asked him why the Abbot might have refused me sight of the records. His answer was unexpected: "Abbot Locke won't let anyone touch them, not since they revealed a beggar had given something to the first Abbot, Abbot Nostus. This artefact is now lost and Locke is worried that hoards will descend on the Abbey looking for it." I was puzzled and asked what a beggar could give an abbot that was so valuable?"

Rebecca was about to turn the page, when Mrs Pickles announced.

"The library is closing, so I'm afraid you both have to leave now."

Rebecca closed the book.

"Let's take it to my house and finish it there," Rebecca said after she carefully put the book in her satchel.

As they hurried from school, Rebecca sensed she was being watched.

"What's the matter?" Ralph asked but she said nothing.

At the park her fears grew when she saw an elderly woman loitering near an old van. Nervously she tugged at Ralph's arm.

"It's that old women, Mrs Ridley," Rebecca gasped and the alarmed pair quickened their step. So did Mrs Ridley.

"We mustn't let her catch us," he said. "I don't want either of us to have our ears cut off, or end up in a silver box."

They aimed for the safety of Rebecca's house, but their hopes were dashed when Tom, stepped out in front of them.

Tom, although small, looked mean and threatening. His unexpected appearance frightened Rebecca, who screamed, and startled Ralph.

"Where are you two going?" Tom snarled.

"Mind your own business," Ralph said hoping to appear braver than he felt.

Suddenly, Tom was callously shoved aside, as a hand came down and grasped Ralph's shoulder.

"Got you, you interfering little meddler," Mrs Ridley hissed. Tom laughed with bitter pleasure.

"Rough him up, Mrs Ridley!" he said. The old lady gave a ghastly smile and replied, "I intend to!" She then pinched Ralph's ear and made him squeal in pain.

"Better if we take them with us and lock them up for old Croucher. I will take their ears later," she sneered, but Rebecca was having none of that.

"Leave us alone, you old witch!" she yelled and swung her satchel wildly at Mrs Ridley knocking over both the old woman and Tom. But in the scuffle her satchel came undone and unnoticed Foghorn's precious book tumbled on to the pavement.

Rebecca called to Ralph to run and they took to their heels. However, the book on the pavement caught

Mrs Ridley's eye and she didn't give chase. Rebecca discovered her satchel was lighter and turned with horror. There she saw the old woman with Foghorn's book. Ralph and Rebecca had to abandon the book, for it was too dangerous to retrieve it.

Mrs Ridley straightened up and sensing its great importance secured the book in her bag. Then with her long bony finger she nudged Tom to march in front.

Ralph and Rebecca felt safe only when they reached Windbury. But with his ear throbbing, Ralph was livid.

"This is terrible! We need that book."

Rebecca was almost in tears and racked with guilt.

"It's my fault. I'm so sorry. Perhaps if Jeremiah is still alive we might find him!"

"What about getting that book back?" Ralph asked, as he considered how to find the lost Jeremiah.

"Well tackling Mrs Ridley is out. So, any ideas on how we can find Jeremiah?" she quizzed.

Ralph hesitated for he knew it was time he revealed his secret device.

"I might have a way," he said, and then told her his story of how he acquired the Illuminatus.

Rebecca was intrigued and impressed.

"Next time, bring it," she said, "I want to see how it works!"

Mrs Ridley sat in her floral patterned armchair at Nettles End Cottage. Already Cubitt, her white cat, was in hiding after she removed him brutally from her chair. On her lap she had Foghorn's book. Much of it was beyond her understanding but she jumped with recognition on reading the name Judge Majestic. She knew he was a Binder but not to his connection to nearby Dunton Abbey and the tower he paid to have built there.

"It's all here!" she muttered. "The snargs have searched centuries for their Shine, their nasty little key and now I know where it's hidden! This Foghorn tells us Dunton Abbey's tower holds the clue." Overjoyed, the old woman waltzed about, while her cat watched cautiously from beneath the table.

"What riches when I find their Shine," the old woman wailed. Cringing, Cubitt placed both front paws over his ears. He wanted to shut her out. When it was finally safe, he crept out and slowly strolled away. He was indeed a mysterious cat.

It was a warm sunny morning when Ralph hurried round to show Rebecca the Illuminatus. Mrs Harwood opened the door for Ralph and took him through to the living room where Rebecca sat on the sofa surrounded by old documents. She jumped up with enthusiasm, the strain of reading for hours dropping away as soon as Ralph leant on the armrest.

"I think I've nearly cracked it," she said. "When old Jeremiah had that book printed, it was 1849 and he broke the Binders' rule of confidentiality. The guild had no choice but to throw him out. Nothing was ever heard from him again, or so it seemed, until a letter dropped on the mat of the Grand Master, purporting to be from Jeremiah. This letter was dated September 1952 and it contained a warning that traitors were in their midst and no one was safe. But by then no one knew of Jeremiah and the letter was filed away as a hoax."

After scribbling in a notebook she looked up with excitement.

"So according to these records when Jeremiah disappeared he was about 50. That makes him around 150 when that letter was written. There is no way he could have lived that long, unless…." Rebecca paused as Ralph butted in.

"Unless he ended up like Sir John and stayed in Wychen!"

"Precisely," she replied.

"But Wychen has no records, said Ralph.

"So where has he disappeared to?"

Ralph looked at the mass of papers strewn on the sofa and floor.

"How on earth did you get all this?" he asked mystified.

"It wasn't so hard," Rebecca said. "Do you remember Simon, the boy at the council meeting? He spends hours down in the Gimbals, so he knows everything and where to find stuff. And I told Mum this was all a school project." Rebecca smiled, pleased at her cunning and initiative.

Ralph smiled too as he pulled the Illuminatus from his pocket.

"I think this will help," Ralph said and placed his precious object on the small table beside her.

Rebecca was astonished.

"Watch this!" Ralph told her as the device sprung to life.

"It's glitzy like a glitter ball," she squealed. "Show me more!"

"I'll let you ask the question," Ralph said generously, "because that's the clever bit. You must address it as 'Illuminatus' and say please. And think hard as you only get one chance a day."

Apprehensive, Rebecca hesitated.

"Illuminatus, please, where in Wychen will I find Jeremiah Foghorn?"

She heard whirring and words formed on the living room wall. Carefully she read them to Ralph, who scribbled the message on a note pad:

"Of Jeremiah Foghorn you may ask
But before you begin
You must find the dunnikin.
Then by the count of two
Make its occupant a badgers' brew.
With all asleep
The door won't keep.
Once you are through
Find a tree golden and blue.
There you will find your Foghorn anew!"

Realising the message was more than he understood he pushed it under Rebecca's nose.

Already she was sifting through an old almanac. She stopped and sighed.

"According to this a 'dunnikin' is a den. Possibly subterranean. So it could be telling us to look for a badger in his den or a Ghost Door guarded by a badger."

Ralph asked if she knew any Ghost Doors like that but she ignored his question.

"Can't we just ask the Illuminatus where the badger lives?" she asked.

Ralph looked disheartened and shook his head. He had tried that once before with another question.

"Listen, I've had another thought," she said enthusiastically. "We'll go down to Operations in the Gimbals and slip into the Map Room. That's where the location of every Ghost Door is logged, and we can search for one with a Badger!"

"That sounds terrific!" said Ralph as he slipped the Illuminatus into his pocket.

"But listen," he said. "The Illuminatus is our secret. No one else must know. Promise!"

"Cross my heart!" she replied very seriously. "Come on, it's time for the Gimbals."

She pushed him towards the patio doors and led him through a lovely walled garden.

"Windbury has its own secret passage but it's different to yours," she told him as they meandered down the little path to a half derelict brick shed. She pressed on the rusty latch and pushed the creaky door open. Ralph saw holes in the bottom of the door as if a large animal had gnawed it, and there were claw marks cut deep into the wood. Rebecca noticed what he saw.

"What do you think did that?" she teased him. Ralph looked anxious and shook his head.

"A big dog?" he suggested. Rebecca sniggered.

"You'd think so? It was rats but not a plague of them. Just three giant ones!"

Ralph was now seriously worried after his experience of the huge cats in Wychen. These must have been enormous rats.

As they entered, the dark dreary room was crowded with shadowy objects. Gradually his eyes became accustomed to the gloom and he saw old rusty tools and filthy bundles of junk scattered over the floor. The only light was from a dusty window.

At an old brick fireplace Rebecca pulled hard on two short chains hung either side. The ground beneath their feet rumbled. She stepped aside and Ralph caught a glimpse of the fire's sooty stonework. It slid away and revealed some small stone steps. Set in the chimney they rose steeply up into blackness.

Rebecca led the way up the tight staircase and disappeared. He heard her muffed voice telling him to mind the walls: "Some of the crevices still have soot in them."

He climbed up after her.

"Oh, Ralph," Rebecca called out, "I nearly forgot…," but she broke off when the cry of 'ouch' came from Ralph.

"It probably doesn't matter now," she said. "I was just going to warn you, about that stone beam." She looked down as Ralph rubbed his head.

"I'm fine," he grumbled. "Just keep going."

"I can't. You need to come up here."

Ralph clambered up and asked impatiently what was next.

"Just steady yourself," she told him excitedly.

Rebecca pushed hard on brickwork above her head. Then she stepped forward as the whole staircase suddenly tipped downwards. It was like standing on a giant seesaw and very unnerving. They went down another set of steps that stretched into the endlessly pitch black. When they reached the bottom, Ralph was pleased to see the flickering glow of an oil lamp. Now he recognised they were in an Imp Tram tunnel.

Soon a tram sped them into the heart of the Gimbals laboratories where they stood at the shiny black door of the map room. Unfortunately, a large note was pinned to the door. It read: "Closed for upgrade."

Ralph grasped the door handle and tried in vain to turn it. The door was locked. Rebecca, although disappointed, wondered how to find another way in. Then she saw a small familiar figure down a far off dimly lit corridor.

"Hello," she called. "Hello! Is that you, Simon?" Her voice echoed more than she wanted, and she looked around in case anyone else heard. The thin figure came closer: "Yes. Hi, Rebecca!"

Huddled like a trio of conspirators Rebecca told Simon their problem.

"There is a way to unlock that door with your binder shield," Simon grinned. "I know the trick."

Ralph's eyes sparkled with a madcap look of adventure.

"Do our dragons burn their way in?" he asked. Rebecca shook her head in dismay.

"Ralph, you have to stop this smash-up thinking all the time!" she remarked. Ralph folded his arms and said no more as Simon wheezed with excitement and unpinned his shield from his lapel.

"It isn't anything to do with your dragon," he said. "You just put your shield's pin into the keyhole. Like this!" He was full of himself although a little breathless. "Here is the clever bit. Not many binders know their shields are voice sensitive. You've got to hand it to Imps. They made them respond only in the Wychen tongue."

Simon held up his hand to silence them, gripped his shield tightly and then announced: "Oca knoca."

His shield pin twisted and flexed inside the lock until they heard a small click.

"That's done it," he said, repining his shield under his lapel.

The trio stepped into the map room, a large dark cavern. Suddenly, the door banged shut and startled them. It was all very eerie.

"I can't see anything, not even my hand now!" Rebecca cried in panic.

In the distance was a mysterious sound of running water. Then as if by magic, there was light.

"Who did that?" Ralph asked with surprise.

"No one," Simon said relieved. "I think it's the projectors starting up."

"Projectors! What are they for?" Rebecca said in amazement. Simon's face lit up.

"This is the first hydro-simulator made for the Binders. It's a virtual reality platform with projectors using free-flow bubble technology!"

Ralph wandered over to the edge of a large pool of water, while Simon and Rebecca examined a disc floating on the pool's edge. It was about disc about two metres in diameter, bronze and concave.

"I saw the drawings for this disc a couple of weeks ago," Simon told them. "I think it has only one command operator."

He then stepped confidently onto the disc. When the others joined him he gave the command: "Map up."

The bronze saucer moved slowly to the centre of the pool and stopped, held there by some unknown force. Then a strange metallic voice gave a loud warning: "SHIELD ACTIVATION IS IMMINENT. STAND READY. ACTIVATION IN FIVE, FOUR, THREE, TWO, ONE. ALL PROJECTORS WILL NOW ACTIVATE."

Suddenly huge quantities of water swirled and boiled up around them. This rose vertically like an enormous wave. The trio shut their eyes tight and took large breaths, expecting a tidal wave to drown them.

It didn't happen. They opened their eyes and found themselves in a large bubble. Above their heads were the thousands of gallons of water that reached the cavern's ceiling. The bubble was a force field, transparent and glowing. They looked pensively at each other as air blew through tiny vents around the rim of the bronze disc. Then another announcement: "HYDRO-SPHERE IS OPERATIONAL. THE MAP COORDINATOR WILL NOW BE ACTIVATED."

As they wondered what a map coordinator might be, water swirled strangely in front of them. A dark shape emerged and formed the face of a woman. She was elegant, three dimensional and looked truly solid. Simon was spooked and fell backwards. The face floated closer and pushed itself inside the bubble.

"I am Cavalla, the Map Coordinator," the woman smiled in a soft friendly voice. Rebecca smiled back and replied.

"I'm Rebecca and these are my friends, Ralph and…." But Cavalla interrupted.

"I know you all. I have spent much time with your changelings!"

Ralph pulled Simon to his feet as Rebecca asked the vital question.

"Cavalla, can you help us locate a Ghost Door? It is connected somehow with a badger!"

Cavalla's face slid higher to scrutinize their motives. After a moment Cavalla replied.

"I know many great Ghost Doors, but only one gate-keeper who is a badger. He is 'Brockus the Bold', long esteemed as a legend among the Saxons, Vikings and Danes." She shook her head. "None can pass Brockus without permission from the Binders."

Ralph was overflowing with ideas.

"That's the right place. Can you show us where to find it?"

Cavalla's retreated, as if offended.

"Of course I can," she said. "I am the Map Coordinator. That's what I do! Let me show you."

The water churned and bubbled as Cavalla faded. Only her voice echoed around them.

"The Ghost Door you seek is known as the Iron Gate. Let me show you," said the voice.

Slowly, minute bubbles that were of different colours appeared in the water. These formed into images and showed a most beautiful landscape. It was as though the world above was brought down into that water. The voice continued.

"Your journey to find the Iron Gate will start in the village of Wanty-Tump. You must take the lane called Pennyquick which you see across the common."

From inside their bubble the landscape rushed ahead. Then Cavalla spoke again.

"These are the Shire Stones and next to them is the stile. Go over the stile and follow the footpath down to the Shillings Brook."

The flight continued. Images changed and merged until a small stone bridge loomed in front of them.

"Look to your right," the voice said gently. "Not far from this bridge, beneath that large tree, you will find the Iron Gate. But note: you need special binder clearance to enter here, or Brockus will bar your way!"

Then the images of the countryside and the disembodied face of Cavalla dissolved away.

"How do we get passed Brockus without Binder clearance?" Simon asked.

Rebecca smiled.

"Kittens and hedgehogs like milk. Perhaps badgers are just the same."

Then the sphere lit up with an eerie green light and the metallic voice returned loudly: "WARNING. HYDROSPHERE WILL BE DEACTIVATED. STANDING DOWN IN FIVE, FOUR, THREE, TWO, ONE."

Suddenly the water cascaded down as if someone had removed a mighty plug. Slowly the cavern and pool returned to normal, the bronze disc jerked back to the edge of the pool. On the far side of the Map Room a loud clunking noise echoed.

"Look! Look!" Ralph called excitedly. "The door! The Map Room door is unlocked." Light from the Gimbals gallery pierced the gloom of the cavern.

The three children scrambled off the disk and raced across to the cavern door.

Ralph was first through, with Rebecca close behind. Breathless, Simon was last and escaped just as the door banged shut.

"That was close!" Ralph gasped. He lent on a wall, looked directly at his friends and asked:

"I don't suppose anybody knows how far Wanty-Tump is from here?"

Rebecca was stumped and shrugged her shoulders. Simon muttered something incoherent.

"We need to know!" Ralph said.

"It's fifteen miles!" Simon said quietly after he gained his breath. "We drove through Wanty-Tump when we visit my uncle."

"Oh no! We haven't the time to walk there, get through the Iron Gate and find Foghorn as well!" Rebecca said, disappointed.

"We could cycle," Simon suggested. But Ralph said his bike didn't work.

"Borrow one!" snapped Rebecca.

"From who? My best friend Evan, who's been snatched, or do you mean my other friend Tom, who's now my enemy? I bet neither of you has a spare bike!" Ralph grumbled miserably.

Then a bright idea lit up Rebecca's face.

"Why don't we take a look in the Binder Museum?"

"Good idea," Simon said excitedly.

"Will we find a bike in there?" Ralph asked.

"Oh, it's better than that," Simon said, full of glee. "It's full of old contraptions from Wychen. We could borrow something. Well, sort of borrow."

"What do you mean, 'sort of' borrow?" Ralph asked.

"He means it's not like borrowing from a library, but it's not like stealing either because we will put things back," Rebecca said quietly with a twinge of guilt.

"Isn't that against Binder rules?" Ralph questioned.

"To help Evan we're going to have to break rules. But we won't break them lightly." Rebecca answered, as her conscience cleared.

Ralph agreed. "I'm prepared do anything. We must get Evan home!"

Going along with Rebecca's idea they hurtled down a long twisty tunnel towards the museum.

fifteen: the binder museum

The three children stood outside the museum door, un-certain who should enter first.

"Rebecca should go first," Simon whispered. "After all, it was her idea,"

"If we stand here we'll be seen," Ralph said impatiently.

Suddenly footsteps from the tunnel grew louder, someone was coming. Rebecca turned the door handle and all stumbled through together. The door closed behind them.

Everything was fantastical. Display case after display case and each one, exhibited ancient artefacts. Large plinths held up huge contraptions and weird machines.

Running around on the floor were dozens of tiny ma-chines, bright and colourful like the toys of a small child.

"Cor, look at them go," Simon laughed.

"But what are they?" Ralph asked, amazed.

"They're called Environmentals," Rebecca answered.

"Yuk. They're eating dirt," Simon said disgusted.

"Dirt is good for their system. That's how they keep the place clean," Rebecca said knowledgeable of Environmentals. "Nothing gets damaged in here. They are self-sufficient and use dirt to power themselves. It's what they do, that's their purpose."

"Never mind them. Let's find what we came for," prompted Ralph.

Searching among the cabinets, it was Ralph who discovered something promising.

"Come and look at this," he called and tapped a glass cabinet. "These I think are weird boots."

Beneath a sign read: "One pair of Millipod boots. Designed by the great Imp inventor Rawcuss-Fawlcuss".

"It's a shame they don't have a paw-print design on them. That mucky green-brown does nothing for me," Rebecca said as she looked down at her feet.

Ralph glanced at her blankly.

"Look. What does this say?" he asked and pointed at a smaller notice. Then he read it to them: "Warning: high-speed use may cause dizziness!"

"These are no good unless there's a pair for each of us," Simon said. Ralph then turned on him sharply as though annoyed.

"Who says, you're coming?"

Simon looked hurt.

Rebecca rolled her eyes and shook her head. "Of course you can come," she said, "But we must find something useful soon or we'll be caught and then none of us will be going!"

Reluctantly Ralph conceded and wandered off to examine some objects. They were long and wrapped in black cloth. They rested neatly in a metal stand and looked familiar. He read the caption on the base: "Gamp's Travelator. As used by Old Mother Gamp. Not to be used indoors."

"Over here," he yelled excitedly.

To Simon they looked like umbrellas and he was not impressed. But Rebecca was intrigued and pulled one from its stand. She shook it to see if it would open.

Ralph leapt forward and shouted: "No, not in here! That's what it says."

Unfortunately, the Travelator slipped through Rebecca's fingers and the trio looked at one another.

As the handle hit the floor the Travelator sprung into life like a dervish. Then snapped open and hovered inches from the ground. Thin blades too fast to be seen spun around the central pole under its black canopy. Then out popped two sets of handles attached to the pole, one for feet and one for hands.

"I can fly this, these are easy," Rebecca told them, her eyes were bright with excitement.

"In here, are you sure?" Ralph called out.

Rebecca climbed aboard as the Travelator hovered. A metal guard fixed around her waist and secured her in the contraption as two levers appeared above her head. She smiled as her long hair blew in the downdraft.

For a moment she had control. Then it jerked backwards into a large mechanical exhibit. Metal pieces broke off and clattered to the floor.

"Now you've done it!" Ralph shouted frantically. "You'll wreck everything."

Simon quickly tidied the fallen metal and hid them from sight. Rebecca had better control now.

"This is easier than riding a bike," she yelled.

"I wouldn't let you ride my bike, the way you're flying," Ralph winced. Rebecca grinned and stuck out her wicked tongue.

"Oi, you up there," an angry voice called from the entrance. "What do you think you are doing?"

Rebecca stopped and hovered; confused she looked for an escape route.

"Hurry, grab a Travelator! Someone is coming," she yelled.

After a few seconds of meddling Ralph was hovering on his contraption. Simon was not so lucky. He fumbled, stumbled and in the end completely botched his takeoff. Still a little shaken he tried again. This time he was successful and his Travelator jerked ungainly upwards. He was airborne. It was then Rebecca saw a large opening, an old airshaft high in the roof.

"Follow me and be quick," she shouted.

As the burley figure of a man came into view they headed into the inky blackness of the shaft. Below them the broad shouldered man bellowed up with a gruff voice: "You won't get away with this. We'll find out who you all are."

Finally they emerged from an enormously tall chim-neystack into open sky. Straight ahead was the church clock and they flew round and round as it struck midday.

"We need to head for Wanty-Tump," shouted Ralph.

As Simon knew the way, Rebecca called on him to be Flight Leader.

A delighted Simon glided into the command position and shouted: "Tally ho."

In close formation, the three bobbed up and down across the skyline like little balloons.

In the Gimbals, Black-Bob thundered up to the heavy door of Greystone's study. He hurled it open and found Greystone hunched over some strange paraphernalia on a long table.

"What did I tell you? I knew it would come to this," Black-Bob ranted in such a loud furious voice it caught Greystone off guard. And he nearly dropped the glass vessel he was holding.

"That was close," Greystone said sternly. "Weeks of hard work almost wasted." He sighed and placed the beaker on the table.

"Now what's all this about?" he asked sharply.

Black-Bob drew himself up and reported what he had discovered.

"That young Mopley and Higley have somehow per-suaded my understudy Rebecca to break every cardinal rule in the Binders' Manual. I told you that boy of yours would be trouble. I'm not too bothered about the book not being returned to the Scriptorium, but I will not tolerate unauthorised entry to the Map Room. And now they have broken into the museum and taken some exhibits. I just hope those stolen travelators have self-activated their stealth devices."

Greystone wandered over to his desk and sat down wearily.

"Do we know where they are going?" he asked in a soft concerned voice. He knew this would not be some light-hearted prank.

"We don't," Black-Bob said. "The hydro-simulator was going through an upgrade. When pressure built up in one of the relay valves the Map Coordinator shut down, resulting in Cavalla suffering short-term memory loss."

Greystone rubbed his forehead and for a moment said nothing.

"What book did they take from the Scriptorium?" he asked.

Black-Bob referred to his notes: "The book they didn't return was The Thirteen Deadly Secrets by Jeremiah Foghorn."

Surprise crossed Greystone's face. He had all but forgotten that name.

He stopped to think, before ruminating: "As I recall, Foghorn was obsessed with finding Raven's Wood. I wonder if our three students have stumbled upon something in the book and are now trying to find Raven's Wood by themselves."

"We'd better find them before anyone gets hurt," Black-Bob said anxiously.

"The Imps will know where they are before we do," Greystone said, with a raised index finger. "Let's ask them first. Our students won't be able to get passed a gate keeper without the correct password so they can't leave our world. Chickens always come home to roost. Whether good or bad, they will learn."

Black-Bob was a little more doubtful and took the practical approach.

"In case they are gone there a while, we had better send their changlings to their homes."

It was agreed. Black-Bob hurried away and made arrangements.

The flying trio arrived high above Wanty-Tump. Simon gave the order to descend and the sheep below scattered.

"Not far now," he shouted as village houses came into view.

But Rebecca had other ideas and shouted, "I think we should get off these before we bring attention to ourselves."

Moments later, they spotted a good landing site and with a small little bump their Travelators were down. They folded them away like a city gent's umbrella. Tucking them under their arms, they set off across the fields.

The villagers of little Wanty-Tump looked on with curiosity at the youthful trio. The children passed two old ladies outside a neat row of cottages. One lady said to the other: "Either it is going to rain or that must be the latest fashion with kids these days!"

Outside the village store, Rebecca brought them to a stop. "You two wait here while I go buy some milk for the badger," she said, shoving her Travelator into Simon's hand.

But a few minutes later she came back with nothing.

"They've run out of milk and won't get another delivery until tomorrow," she said and despondently took back her Travelator.

"What can we do?" Ralph wondered but Rebecca was out of ideas.

"Don't worry me now. We'll have to sort it out later," she told him.

They quietly turned into Pennyquick Lane and hiked up a short, steep hill to three massive stones, the Shire Stones. The crooked stile Cavalla had mentioned was overgrown and unused. They climbed over and followed the twisted path down into a small valley with the Shillings Brook stream at the bottom. Tired, they all flopped down on an old tree trunk by the water's edge.

"What a brilliant stream," Ralph said, peering into its babbling waters. "It's so clear. I bet it has minnows and sticklebacks."

Ralph's enthusiasm rubbed off on Simon who wanted to look for newts and fresh water shrimps.

"I could do with a jam jar or an old tin," Ralph said to Rebecca but she was deep in thought.

"I'm not getting you one," she said, peeved. Ralph dived under some bushes, searching for a jar. She heard twigs break and a curious clink as Ralph reversed from the bush. He shouted for joy, for he had found a tin and lid.

The tin reminded Simon he had forgotten to feed Flame his dragon. He abandoned the fishing and over-turned large stones near the muddy bank. He told the others he was meant to have fed Flame two hours ago.

Under one stone he found a grub and a small black beetle under another.

"Hold these, Ralph, while I let Flame out," he asked pushing the wriggling insects towards Ralph.

"Synge likes flies better than beetles," Ralph remarked with a smirk. Simon replied, "Flame would starve here, if I had to catch flies".

Simon unscrewed his Binders Shield but Flame re-fused to come out. So he laid the shield on an old tree stump and gently coaxed him out. The tiny dragon rolled out looking rather crumpled but with the first breath grew to full size.

Flame was neither magnificent nor big. Actually, he was scraggy and tatty with a ragged ear. A wonky left eye gave the impression he looked the other way.

As Ralph passed Simon the beetle, he asked if he'd had seen Flame fly, as he'd never seen Synge fly.

"Not really flying," Simon replied. "He hops a bit, but I know they can fly when they want too."

While Simon held the beetle Flame sat up and begged like a dog. Rebecca was mortified that Simon made his dragon do such a thing.

"He just came with that trick," Simon said. "I didn't teach him."

Flame swallowed the beetle and jumped down to splash in the stream. It was then that Rebecca spotted his ear.

"Poor thing. It's as if somebody's chewed it," she said.

"It happened when he was very young. An older dragon savaged him and burnt his ear before the others could stop it," said Simon with compassion.

Ralph complained about Flame's splashing and said his chance of catching fish was ruined, but Simon and Rebecca didn't care.

Unhappy, Ralph wandered downstream a little. Simon and Rebecca followed after Flame was returned to his shield.

"Look, there's the bridge. So where's that badger?" Simon said.

The bridge was made of flat stone and looked hundreds of years old.

Rebecca knew the Ghost Door had to be found first.

"It's going to be impossible without Gonoculars," she said.

At the bridge Ralph felt tingles in his fingers and saw sparkles of tiny light dance on the leaves of bushes. These became long strands of light that streamed towards a big tree.

"I can see light swirling into the bottom of that tree over there," he told them excitedly.

"Light! What light?" Rebecca said. "Can you see anything, Simon?" she asked with doubt, but Simon didn't and nor was he going near any tree until he knew where that badger was.

"I can see it clearly," Ralph said to his doubters. "And there, in that trunk must be Iron Gate."

"How can you see that?" Rebecca asked.

"I just can," he replied.

It was then Rebecca realized there was a lot more to Ralph and remembered something obscure about Ghost Doors.

"I should have guessed," she said, "It's a rare type of Ghost Door called a tree gate. I didn't know we had them over here. They're mostly found in the massive trunks of redwood trees in America."

"Sometimes things don't look real," Ralph said and shrugged his shoulders. "It's like a heat haze. Then other times it starts with a tingle in my fingers, like this time."

Ralph stepped a little closer and Brockus the Bold appeared. The badger looked at him fierce and no one except Ralph saw the light as it turned into outlandish armour and covered the badger fully.

But they all saw the badger's snarl and a mouth full of sharp teeth that glistened.

"I'm not going near it! It looks too fierce for me and I don't want to get bitten," Simon said, edging away.

"He looks ready to bite," Ralph said concerned. "Perhaps we can lasso him?"

Rebecca rolled her eyes.

"This is not the Wild West," she told them. "We are going to do this properly and give him some milk!"

"But we don't have any," Ralph reminded her.

After a while, with no ideas from the boys, Rebecca announced her plan.

"We are going to get the milk from those cows in the next field," she said but the boys were shocked and together chorused: "No way!"

"Come on," she told them. "This is fun, I used to milk my uncle's goat on his farm."

"But cows are a lot bigger than goats," Simon said, not persuaded. "They can kill people. I read it in a newspaper!"

"Well, if you think this is too dangerous," she mocked, "we'd better all go home now and not bother with saving Evan."

"No! We'll do whatever it takes," Ralph declared, prompted into bravery. "I don't think cows can be worse than snargs." and he nudged Simon till he nodded in agreement.

As they stashed their Travelators under the fallen tree, Rebecca claimed Ralph's tin for her milk jug. They followed the path along to an old wooden gate where a lovely caramel-coloured cow leant over. Rebecca immediately greeted the cow in a calm voice.

"What a pretty Jersey cow you are," she said, petting its' head.

"Come and make friends with her," she ordered the boys. They approached cautiously and stroked the cow's nose. The beast licked each of their hands and Ralph chuckled.

"What a sharp tongue," Simon said as he snatched his hand back.

Rebecca climbed over the gate and Ralph started to follow.

"No, you two stop there. Go and pick lots of grass to keep her happy while I try to milk her." Rebecca said and pointed to the long, and lush grass. She waited, tin in hand, until the boys had collected a good grass pile and were feeding the cow over the gate.

Rebecca rubbed her hands together and warmed them as her uncle taught her. She moved to the left hand side of the cow and begun to milk with a teat in each hand.

"Is it working?" Simon asked as he peered down the side of the cow.

"Give us a chance," she said as the milk squirted and hit the side of the tin.

"Good girl," Rebecca said over and over. The boys kept handing grass to the happy cow until Rebecca announced they had enough milk.

As they returned to the stone bridge they caught sight of the aggressive Brockus staring out from a clump of brambles. Rebecca gave the tin lid to Ralph and poured in as much milk as she could.

Then she pointed and said, "Go the long way around. Get as close to Brockus as you can, then put the milk down."

Ralph gingerly walked in a wide arc towards the brambles. He was only a few feet away when the bush shook violently.

"Put the milk down there," Rebecca whispered to him urgently.

Ralph's hands shook as he put the lid carefully on the ground. Only a small drop of milk spilled on the long grass. But the ever-vigilant Brockus saw it and looked ready to charge. The badger's nose wrinkled in the air and it bolted out of the bracken towards Ralph. Terrified and horribly exposed Ralph looked for a safe place to hide.

sixteen: wychen rats

Ralph anxiously turned and saw his friends as they waved frantically for him to return. He felt the badger snuffle at his heels so he was forced to run.

Once he reached the safety of the bridge, he found the courage to look round. He discovered, with great relief, Brockus was simply after the milk. Fresh milk was a treat for Brockus and quickly he finished the lot. He sat looking less ferocious and licked his whiskers.

"What happens now?" asked Simon.

"We wait and see," Rebecca said patiently.

Brockus lifted his head, gave a humongous yawn and then dropped to the ground, fast asleep. Then before anyone moved, there was a fierce wind that pulled dust and debris towards the big tree.

"Look, the Ghost Door is opening," shouted Ralph. Then he remembered the Illuminatus riddle and how the door would not stay open.

"Quick," he yelled. "We have to go now."

They ran headlong towards the dust cloud and tree. But the Door was dark and ominous, not the enticing tunnel of light they had seen with other doors. Simon hung back but Rebecca seized his hand and pulled him through.

"We all go together," she yelled.

Then they were gone from Shillings Brook, sucked into blackness in a flash.

In the strange dusky red light, three bundles of ragged clothing stirred. The first rose and gave a long murmured groan.

"That was a bad landing, it nearly knocked all the stuffing out of me," Ralph winced as he tugged Rebecca's arm and helped her up.

"That was awful," Rebecca said in dismay. "I nearly tore my best jacket on that branch and now my hair is all in knots."

"I've twisted my ankle," Simon groaned as he tried to get up and flopped down again. Rebecca told him to wait, as he might feel better in a minute.

Ralph looked at where they had arrived. They were in a gloomy forest that looked as if it had been broken and battered by a terrible storm a long time ago. Fallen trees lay moss-covered, rotting and the ground was dank and swampy.

"I don't like this place. It all looks scary," Ralph said nervously.

Rebecca glanced up; patches of fog in long wispy layers drifted and swirled around the few trees that stood.

There was a green soggy weed that clung and dangled from everything. She reached up and pulled down a handful.

"You're right," she said and flicked the foul weed away, "this place stinks."

Simon looked around and felt it was time to move.

"I'm alright now," he said and hobbled in a circle. "Perhaps we should get going."

Ralph stood up and started to lead the way.

"Are we going the right way?" Rebecca asked nearly on Ralph's heels.

"I've no idea," Ralph said. Then he whispered, "Don't forget we need to look for a gold and blue tree. It's the only clue for old Foghorn we have." As Simon flagged behind he heard none of their conversation.

After a while the path opened into a small narrow clearing on firm ground. They were in the middle of an ancient ruin. On one side a low broken-down wall ringed the clearing. Behind the wall the ground dropped away and rose sharply to a small hill densely covered with trees. Everything was coated in thick moss and through those trees they saw a more intact ruin, bathed in an outlandish green and velvety light. Now opened to the elements, its roof had collapsed and wrecked timber beams hung down. Broken tiles littered the floor, and glass panes that had once graced the tall arched windows lay smashed on the ground.

The most extraordinary of all was the enormous broken spire, snapped at its base as if it were a tree trunk. The bottom of the spire rested on the end wall of the ruined building. While its twisted tip lay entangled in the remaining trees.

Rebecca wanted to explore.

"That place looks like it hasn't been disturbed for over a hundred years," she said. They were just about to scramble down the crumbling wall when Simon saw movement in the ruin.

"Wait! Something is in there and it's big," he warned her. Just then they saw the white body of an enormous animal move slowly though the hilltop ruin, a long tail dragging behind it. Rebecca and Simon knew immediately what creature it was.

"It's a Wychen rat," Simon whispered loudly. Suddenly, the partially broken wall gave way and he tumbled to the bottom. The others stood on firmer parts and watch helplessly as the clattering echoed over to the ruined building.

Broken timbers were thrust upwards as the heads of six huge rats popped up. Their noses sniffed to taste the air, as blood-red piercing eyes were seen against the white of their fur.

"Oh no! They are on a scavenging run," Rebecca whispered with horror. When Ralph asked what they meant, she answered replied: "It means they're adding us to their menu."

The rats had the human scent as more old timbers flew and quaked as a wall of white fur swept towards them.

"They're coming," Rebecca screamed to Simon. "Get up here now."

Simon saw the danger but in his desperate attempt to scramble up he slipped. His knee was sliced open on a jagged stone. Ralph leant down and grabbed Simon's hand. Somehow he managed to pull him to safety. But the rats spilled from the ruin, through the old doors and broken windows. Rat after rat hurtled towards them with nightmare speed.

The trio dashed across open ground in the mad hope of cover amongst the trees. From behind them came the terrible squeal of rats as they scaled the derelict wall. The children needed shelter. But before they reached the woods, the rats closed in.

Ralph seized a long and hefty lump of wood, although it felt inadequate. The rats swarmed, surrounding them. Ralph stood his ground. A hungry rat the size of a large dog bared its long sharp teeth and jumped for his throat. Ralph swung and knocked it firmly to the ground. A second rat leapt and he clubbed that one senseless too. Simon also had a weapon, a stout wooden stick that he waved while he yelled madly. Rebecca too had a weapon, although only a rock she held it high and yelled for all she was worth.

The rats went into a ravenous frenzy once they smelt the blood on Simon's trousers. Huge gobbets of saliva dripped from their mouths. The children looked at one another. It was hopeless. Tears filled their eyes, as it was a fight till the bitter end.

But then, miraculously, above squeals and war cries came a blood-curdling roar. Tree branches snapped and broke as an enormous brown bear crashed towards them. It struck left and then right, each crushing blow sending a rat to its death. The few rodents that survived fled for their lives.

The bear halted in front of the children, dead rats sprawled at its feet. The air filled with the acrid smell of dead rat and the musky smell of angry bear. The monstrous creature roared into the children's faces. Ralph dropped his club of wood, which was useless as a weapon against the might of a bear. The others followed suit and dropped their sticks and stones to the ground.

It was a strange bear, as Ralph could see. On its head it wore some kind of tin hat with a headlamp, the sort of helmet miners wore. Then it started to speak.

"Kids! What do kids want in this place?" the bear bellowed. In any other place except Wychen a talking bear seemed bizarre. Rebecca was the first to gather her wits.

"We are on a search for the legendary Jeremiah Foghorn," she said in her most plucky voice, but then her voice tailed off nervously. "Him, or a golden blue tree."

The bear licked rats' blood from its claws then stopped abruptly and growled at them.

"Look around. All this place offers is an early grave. Now go home before it's too late."

"We can't," Ralph said desperately. "Not without finding Mr Foghorn. Only he can help save my friend Evan from the snargs."

The distrustful bear cast its dark eyes over the children then grunted and swayed ominously. Ralph knew from his wildlife books that bears were notoriously temperamental. And many were solitary and had no wish for company. Sensing the children's uneasiness, the bear began to calm down.

"A Mr Foghorn, you say?" he mumbled with a deep, rasped voice. "Never heard of him." And with a monstrous sigh the huge bear grabbed the largest dead rat by the tail, threw it over a shoulder and sloped away.

"You'd better follow me," the bear said sternly.

The children hesitated.

"There is no time to waste. If you stay out here you'll be carrion, just like these rats. I have my dinner, as you can see, and besides I never eat children. At least not on a weekday," and the bear rumbled with a strange gruff belly laugh. The children glanced at one another to reassure themselves and without further words they followed, albeit reluctantly.

They soon reached a small clearing. There, beneath a sheer rock face, the children saw a most extraordinary tree. The trunk and branches were a splendid colour of deep dark blue and it had leaves that gleamed gold.

"That's our tree," Ralph whispered to Rebecca.

"We must be close to finding Jeremiah now," she quietly replied, excited.

The bear lumbered up to the magnificent tree and whispered something. The tree shook and then the ground shook too. Behind the tree there was a dull scraping and a mighty stone moved slowly from the rock face. A deep cave was revealed, lit dimly by a few old oil lamps. The bear carried the large rat into the cave and beckoned the children. They entered the cave with great uncertainty and hoped Jeremiah was close by.

The bear nonchalantly flicked on its helmet lamp and carried the rat over to a small dark alcove. There it hung the carcass high next to another dead creature. Over in another corner a foul smell and steam rose from a very large iron pot that rested on a hot griddle.

"I shall look forward to that rat in a week's time. Well cooked rat tastes better than hog roast," the bear said, grinning.

Revulsion crossed Simon and Ralph's face but not Rebecca's. She had eaten snared rabbit on her uncle's farm and understood the virtues of eating things you catch.

After Ralph gained enough confidence he looked around the cave for clues to Jeremiah. But he soon grew impatient with the bear.

"You must know this Mr Foghorn. So where is he?" Ralph asked as he peered into every corner.

"You children had best forget Foghorn," the bear said sourly. "He's long gone. Long gone and nobody cares."

Seeing the bear was reluctant to answer direct questions Rebecca tried another approach.

"I'm sorry. We were rude and didn't introduce ourselves. I don't even know your name." She paused but the bear's wasn't listening. "But we are desperate, you see. We must find Jeremiah because he knows how to find Raven's Wood and what a beggar gave to the Abbot of Dunton Abbey."

The bear glared into Rebecca's eyes.

"Well, now, little girl. And how have you heard of such things?"

"From his famous book," she answered.

"So, you're Binders," the bear snarled.

"Well, sort of," Ralph swelled with pride, and smiled politely. "We are serving our apprenticeship at the moment."

The bear turned up his lamp and looked at them better. He scowled at Ralph.

"Binders! Piffle. A load of nonsense, they think they can bind a person to a great cause. You dare have a mind of your own and that High Council of self-serving scoundrels will cast you out like a flea-ridden dog!"

Rebecca caught the bitterness in the bear's voice and wondered why. The bear fussed then fidgeted with pots and pans noisily, when a suddenly realization struck her.

"It's you," she said. "You're Jeremiah Foghorn!!"

This startled the boys who stared at the bear in a new light. The bear guffawed loudly at Rebecca's accusation. The children ignored his protests and disbelieved his denials. The bear grew frustrated with them and growled and swung his massive shaggy arms around dangerously. This scared the children, as the bear saw. The bear switched off the lamp and slowly lowered to the floor. The bear held its head between paws the size of shovels and complained.

"You're going to bring me trouble," he growled. "I don't want your trouble. Not any! I should have let the rats make meals of you. Now look where all this kindness has brought me."

Rebecca stepped closer and rested her hand sympathetically on the bear's hairy shoulder.

"You are Jeremiah, aren't you?" she said softly. "We understand how you feel. The thing is: we need the truth about Dunton Abbey. I swear we won't tell anyone, not a soul. We broke Binder rules to come here so your whereabouts will stay a secret."

The bear lifted its head out of its paws and looked at the children. The boys smiled with encouragement and nodded their heads but the bear continued and sat in glum silence. It was a while before the bear finally cleared his throat and spoke.

"I can see you are brave and determined. So I will come clean, I am Jeremiah Foghorn. The once Binder Extraordinaire, for all the good it did me. I discovered there were a few nasty Binders at the top of the guild and they just laughed at me. Well, now I don't want anyone round me and that's the truth. I don't want visitors!"

For the first time, the children could see beyond the bear's brutish exterior. They squatted beside Jeremiah and formed a small circle while Ralph recounted his story of the snargs and the fate of Evan. Jeremiah listened intently. When the tale was finished Jeremiah suddenly roared: "And you say the High Council did nothing to help?"

He stood and growled, then looked down at his massive paws and flexed his dreadful claws in and out.

"Some things never change. I must help you! I will reveal two of my great secrets. I wrote them all down in my book, or nearly all," he said, then paused.

"It was my belief that the clue to Raven's Wood was concealed on the bowl a beggar gave to Abbot Locke. Mark this carefully. It is possible this beggar was not who he appeared to be. Perhaps he was a sailor, or someone of importance. But do not forget its importance."

"Did you see this bowl?" Ralph asked.

The bear's eyes sparkled with excitement.

"No never! But I knew the Abbot had it hidden in his study. The bowl itself is not valuable. What is priceless is concealed in the abbey's tower."

At last Simon's shyness disappeared.

"Has some old pirate stashed his treasure in there? Is that what it will tell us?" It was a question of great concern to Simon. His big dream was to one day unearth pirate treasure.

Jeremiah gave Simon a withering look.

"Had you finished my book you would know the answer and not be asking nonsense. Now listen. This whole business goes right back to Judge Majestic and his snarg encounter. You do know the story?"

"I do," Ralph piped.

"Good," said Jeremiah and beckoned him closer.

"There is a strangeness in your eyes, young man," he whispered. "If I'm not mistaken you have the eyes of a twister!"

The bear tilted up the front of his tin hat and continued.

"Judge Majestic had a terrible dilemma after seizing the Shine. What was he to do with it? There were many who wanted to possess it. But it would not work in human hands except perhaps for a twister like you? My task was to solve these clues.

"The best clue was the story of the priest who gave the Judge sanctuary. Like any priest he was sworn to secrecy. But I soon discovered he wasn't a priest, he was a monk from a monastery where the Judge sought sanctuary. This led me to Dunton Abbey. There the records show the monks built Brimley Tower, though not without vital help. The tower has all the hallmarks of imp design. No monastery had a tower taller than this. Why it's been made so high I cannot guess. But it means something."

He paused before continuing. "That tower was built for one purpose and that was to hide the Shine. If it was fortified in some way you cannot tell from the outside. And no one dared look inside, not since the monks spread rumours that the tower was full of dead knights. Legend says this tower had an evil side and can kill people. Now why should it?

"Finding the bowl and Raven's Wood is itself not enough to get you into Ragna Doom, he warns. "You must also procure the key because without it you cannot unlock the Great Seal and that is your only doorway into Ragna Doom. I never finished my quest. Perhaps you will complete it for me." These last words the bear spoke only to Ralph.

The weight of this task pressed down on Ralph as he mulled over the story and the failure of Jeremiah, the great Binder Extraordinaire.

"What if I can't find this key or it's not in the tower?" Ralph asked, as he tried not to cast doubt on Jeremiah's story.

Jeremiah looked in dismay at Ralph.

"Do you not believe me? Jeremiah snarled. "It's there. I have told you the truth. Just look at me now. Who is ever going to let me, a great bear walk freely around a monastery?"

Rebecca saw Ralph had upset Jeremiah.

"Don't worry, Ralph," she said, "I know Jeremiah is right and that we must find it. But I also know it won't be easy, so let's rest and in the morning we can start." Her words calmed the bear.

In the morning Jeremiah opened the huge stone door and the children woke to bright sunlight. It was time to leave.

"We can't thank you enough for all you have done," Ralph said enthusiastically. Simon nodded effusively.

Jeremiah looked sorrowful as his visitors prepared to leave. Rebecca sensed his feelings, reached around and hugged his huge furry body.

"I won't forget you," she said as she clung to the lonely bear. He patted her back awkwardly with a huge paw, and was almost lost for words.

"You are the first people I have seen in over two hundred years. Nobody cares these days. But you are good children. You give me hope. You must go and bring those lost children home."

With a final wave to Jeremiah, the children returned to the Ghost Door.

seventeen: dunton abbey

When Mrs Ridley stepped from the drab taxi outside Dunton Abbey she was carrying a large sketchpad. She looked up daunted by the height of the tower and barely noticed the blue cloudless sky. The taxi-driver pushed up the peak of his grubby cap.

"That will be twenty quid, missus."

With a hard stare she pushed a £10 note towards him and snapped, "I'm not paying that!" The driver glanced at the note and across at the abbey's high gothic walls. He repeated, "It's twenty quid!"

Mrs Ridley looked over her long fingernails contemplating her next move. Momentarily she thought of paying him nothing, but she needed a ride home. Miserably, she relented.

Searching for the extra money she failed to notice the three Travelators and their occupants descend from the sky and land in a clump of trees only metres away.

She held the extra money close to the driver's face. "Return at seven," she commanded him. The man muttered what sounded like a prayer and pointed to a furry rabbit's foot that dangled from his rear view mirror.

"There's creeping death in them walls," he babbled, "and for my little baby's sake I won't come here after dark. I'll come at five o'clock or you'll need another taxi." The man wiped his forehead anxiously with a grey stained hanky and stared wildly at her.

"Beware the abbey curse," he said gruffly.

Mrs Ridley dismissed his ramblings as worthless. She leant forward, thrusting the final banknote coldly in his hand.

"Five o'clock. And if you're not here, I'll give you the creeping death!" she said menacingly.

Failing to hide his fear, he took the money and drove off in a cloud of dust.

From behind the trees, Ralph, Rebecca and Simon had finished furling their Travelators only to see that Mrs Ridley had beaten them to the abbey! Through its heavy open gates the atmosphere of the place felt sinister.

"That wicked old trout, I bet she's worked out the abbey's secret from our book," Ralph spat.

"She looks nasty," Simon said, his face drained of colour. "If she catches us we're mincemeat. Who'll save us then?" he whimpered.

"We'd better watch where she goes," Rebecca whispered.

Mrs Ridley entered the large open courtyard and waved at two hooded monks to attract their attention, but they took no notice and hurried away.

"Stupid monks," Mrs Ridley muttered to herself.

She stepped inside the main door and was startled by a dark figure in long flowing robe that appeared from nowhere.

"May I help you?" he asked. A large silver cross hung low around his neck.

"Oh, yes, I'd like to think so," she stammered. The monk was round, and his large eyes bulged. Mrs Ridley wanted to see the rest of his face but his cowl obscured it.

"I am Abbot Glutch," he said then adjusted his cowl but made no attempt to lower it.

"I'm Mrs Ridley," she replied "from Broomfield," she peered into the shadows of his cowl.

Never comfortable with strangers, Abbot Glutch looked at her warily.

"Are you of the faith?" he asked.

She nodded in affirmation, smiling to hide her lies. Mrs Ridley appeared a harmless old woman when suited and she fooled Glutch quickly.

She held up her drawing pad and asked if she could sketch his lovely chapel.

Glutch dropped his guard.

"By all means," he mumbled and clasped his silver cross, "but please don't sketch inside. The brothers need utter stillness for their prayers."

As he walked away slowly his right leg dragged and he shuffled on the stone floor.

Before the children could enter the abbey gates, Mrs Ridley returned to the courtyard forcing them to hide behind the high wall.

"That was close," Ralph whispered.

"Did she see us?" Simon asked. Ralph watched her and knew they weren't observed.

"What is she doing now?" Rebecca asked.

"She's looking at her drawing pad," Ralph replied, peering over the wall.

Mrs Ridley was poised in the middle of the courtyard her sketchpad raised in disguise. An older monk walked slowly towards her from the tower. With each step he muttered.

It sounded a bit like a chant – but it was, in fact, a warning.

"Beware the beasts," the monk wailed, "beware the beasts," then unnervingly he jangled his keys. "With these little soldiers I keep them out, but some always get in."

Startled by the monk's behaviour and alarmed by the mention of beasts she glanced round.

"What beasts?" she said but the old monk ignored her, and jingled his keys with another crazed look.

"Brother Jangles knows," he persisted. "I've seen 'um, the Corpse Scratchers lurking in that tower for lost souls. Takes 'em back to the old graveyard. They think I don't know? I know all about their forty-two dead. The brothers and the Abbot won't listen. So lady, keep out of that tower."

Behind the gates, the children could hear his loud rambling.

"I have only come to do some sketching," Mrs Ridley said, hoping to placate the mad old monk.

Then Brother Jangles suddenly stared at the gates blankly and without another word walked away abruptly.

"What a fruit cake," she muttered, smiling as it reminded her of Aunty May.

The thought of Aunty May, made her glance down at her shoes strangely, and she turned her ankles, checking to see if her soles were clean. They were spotless. No one could see her guilt. Mrs Ridley took comfort and pushed from her mind the burgeoning memory of Aunty May's death and how she really acquired Nettles End Cottage.

Unfortunately, she couldn't push the mention of Corpse Scratchers from her mind and an itchy rash broke out on the back of her hand. It was some time before the "curse of Aunty May", as she called it, passed.

And without any attention drawn to her, she withdrew and sat in a corner of the courtyard and quietly played the role of artist. Foghorn was right, she thought, the Shine must be concealed within the tower.

Eventually she crossed the uneven cobbles to a small chapel built directly on the tower's side. That seemed to be the only access. She found a narrow door and slipped inside unaware that the three children watched her.

"I think the old witch is going for the tower," Ralph told the others.

"Now's the time to search for that Abbot's bowl," Rebecca said eagerly.

"We need to talk to that funny monk," Simon remarked. "I bet he knows where this bowl is kept. He's the one with all the keys."

"That's a good idea!" Ralph said. "Come on, he went this way."

They dashed across the courtyard and hurried down a narrow alley until they were at the back of the Abbey's kitchen. Delicious cooking smells made their tummies rumble. Through a small doorway two monks stood preparing food on a long refectory table. The monk near the door turned and smiled blissfully at the three children. The children smiled back. They had found their funny old monk.

"Well bless my soul," Brother Jangles said to his fellow cook, "Look, Brother Sebastian, we have three little visitors."

"My goodness, Brother Jangles," Brother Sebastian smiled, "these poor things look as if they have come a long way."

Calmed by the children's presence Brother Jangles asked, "Would you like some like some freshly baked apple pie?"

Ralph and Rebecca looked at Brother Jangles anxiously and replied, "No thank you." However Simon licked his lips and said, "Yes please!"

Furious at Simon, Rebecca dug him in the ribs and whispered, "We don't have time for pie. We have to find the bowl!"

As Brother Sebastian went to the larder, Rebecca wasted no time and engaged Brother Jangles in conversation.

"You are all very kind," she told him. "But can I ask a favour?"

"I am one of heavens helper's," answered Brother Jangles as he held his big silver cross lightly. Rebecca felt encouraged.

Once the pie was on the table Brother Sebastian sliced Simon a piece. As Simon ate, the kind monk left for an overdue errand.

Rebecca continued chatting to Brother Jangles.

"We are doing a history project about pots and chalices of the Middle Ages and we heard a story about one of your abbots having an old bowl. We were wondering if such a bowl exists, could we possibly see it, please?"

She didn't like telling an untruth to such a devout old man but felt she had no choice. So to ward off any fibbing curses she kept her fingers crossed behind her back.

The old monk looked around carefully then made sure no one would hear.

"Brother Jangles has all the answers. Old bowls and new bowls, I know them all. Then evil things came crawling. I could hear scratching at the cupboards doors. I couldn't see them when they slither up and down the corridors. Looking for something? Maybe it is this bowl you've heard about, with all its pitch-black devilry."

Ralph didn't like the thought of things that crawled.

"Excuse me, Brother Jangles," he interrupted. "What do you think these crawling things are?"

The monk had the glazed stare of a visionary… or a lunatic.

"I know they are not Corpse Scratchers. I see those ugly bug-eyed scratchers all the time, looking for bones and souls to take away. But these stink like rotten eggs. One night they came gnawing at my door but I wasn't going let them in. I rattled my little soldiers and they scuttled away. But they will be back. Those who do the devil's work always will?"

Brother Jangles unclipped the bunch of keys from his sash and gripped them tightly. Indeed, the keys resembled little solders. As Rebecca and Ralph tried for a closer look, the monk waved the keys in front of their eyes hypnotically, briefly transfixing the pair. The old man made the keys dance and they turned from little disciplined solders into malicious little skeletons.

"Now you have seen them!" the monk laughed. "I don't show them to many people. The brothers think I am mad so they won't be seeing my soldiers."

A strange mist swirled around Brother Jangles during the brief moment the skeletons danced. Once the keys reverted to normal he slipped them back on his belt.

Ralph and Rebecca were all but dumbstruck.

"I saw them," Ralph said and shook his head. "Dancing. We can't be going crazy. These must be Skeleton Keys. Everyone has heard of them but we saw them work!!"

Rebecca never answered for she was glowering at Simon as he bushed down his pie crumbs.

"Have I missed something?" Simon asked.

"Nothing," Rebecca whispered blankly. She then turned to Brother Jangles with a probing question.

"So this bowl of yours," she said, "Do you know where it's kept?"

The startled monk smiled.

"For Abbot Glutch I keep it safe," he whispered then drew them closer. "It's a dark treasure so I lock it away from night thieves. The bowl is crafted from beggar's strife and filled with barrels of bad luck. I will show it to you but you must not touch it. It's not a child's toy."

The monk led the children out of the kitchen and into the inner rooms of the Abbey.

At the Abbot's study door Brother Jangles knocked twice. There was no answer so he peered in. Once inside he beckoned the children. They followed and he closed the door quietly.

Sunlight streamed into the large room through two tall and magnificent stained glass windows. Each was arched with the picture of a knight and a beautiful peacock. In the middle of the room stood a plain wooden desk and a robust wooden chair.

Brother Jangles dragged the chair back and took a single key from his belt. He crouched and laid the key delicately on the flagstone floor.

He smiled and stamped his foot violently close to the key.

The key leapt into life and danced a little jig. The trio watched in amazement, especially Simon. The key spun and turned first into the shape of a tin solder and then into a bony white skeleton.

The key danced faster and faster then melted into the floor. That strange mixture of stone and bone resembled a million-year-old fossil.

Below the flagstone was an eerie sound like the bubbling of mud.

Vine-like fingers sprouted around the edges of the flagstone and pulled it down a few inches. Within seconds the flagstone was gone and an inky black recess was revealed. The monk knelt then plunged his hand deep into the darkness and retrieved something equally dark.

The children gasped when they saw the bowl cupped in Brother Jangles' hands. He allowed the stained glass to bathe the bowl in magical light. Brother Jangle's laugh was almost infectious.

"Look at this bowl," he said with exuberance. "See how the sunlight fills it. I swear I can see all the stars of heaven in its darkness. The deeper you look the more you see."

The bowl was unnaturally black except on its inner rim. Ralph pointed to an inscription and each word he read aloud.

"Fill me like the sea
A Davy's Locker you will see."

"What do you think it means?" Simon asked the monk.

"It's just a sailor's curse," Brother Jangles said, after he carefully placed the bowl on the desk.

While the children puzzled over the inscription, Mrs Ridley had reached the small chapel. There she walked between the simple carved pews until she came to a large door behind a wooden lectern. The door opened with a creak onto a large spiral staircase of dull grey stone.

The tower. As she climbed the staircase her steps quickened when a sharp draught sent icy shivers down her spine. Although the steps were wide she felt hemmed in between the central pillar support and the outer circular wall.

At the top it was nothing like she imagined. There were no splendid views to please her. Stood on the last step she faced a huge triangular block, it was placed strangely like a stone shield. It was also wedge-shaped and wide like the steps. The shield jutted across to the central pillar and extended up into the roof. Ten feet above her head a short bell rope swayed from the strong breeze that howled through slats in the tower's pinnacle. Daylight cascaded through the slats, casting eerie shadows.

Mrs Ridley ignored the rope and concentrated on the triangular stone block. She ran her fingers over dark shapes in its middle. These were small skulls arranged in a rectangular grid. Forty-two, she counted. The grid was circled by several carved snake motifs that could be part of a puzzle. Below these she discovered an inscription. Perhaps this was her vital clue.

The inscription started with the symbol Alpha and ended with the symbol Omega. Silently she read it:

"Climb ever upwards towards Heaven. Perilous is the beast of the night; that retches in the four dark recesses of the World. Nine Knights of valour, each with a true heart, came into this Tower and laboured for fourteen days. Then twenty-four angels with heavenly wings wept in the darkness of night. For these knights endured thirty-three deadly wounds and suffered. By sunrise all was lost. These knights had fallen to the forty-two deaths. With a blackened heart the Reaper came, claiming a soul every hour until they all perished. Yet truly, only with each step will the truth be revealed."

She read the inscription over and over; convinced the Shine's hiding place would be revealed. She drummed her fingers thoughtfully and muttered: "Remarkable. Most remarkable."

As she looked upon those snake drawings a revelation struck her. These skulls and the grid reminded her of a simple but timeless board game she once played with her Aunt May.

"Snakes and ladders," she exclaimed and returned to the inscription to confirm her theory.

"In the text each number," she said to herself, "is a specific skull on the grid."

Convinced she was right she went to work with four, the first number in the text. She counted the skulls from the start position, Alpha in the bottom left hand corner. As she reached the fourth skull she noted it smiled, which was surely a little odd for a skull? But certain one was right, she pushed on the skull. The skull was forced into the wall where it left a square recess in the grid. Deep below the tower she heard large counter weights scrape the hard stone.

She moved on to the next number and the next until she reached forty-two, the last number in the text.

The tiny Omega symbol confirmed she was nearing the end of the sequence. At skull forty-two she sighed with anticipation. It was covered with gooey black mould. She pushed on the last skull with her eager bony finger. Her face contorted with disgust.

When all was finished there was a greater rumble below. She smiled and waited for the reward for all her hard work.

The stone steps slid away and stacked one upon the other, like a giant stone puzzle. Each stone step lined up with the triangular block until a vertical wall was made.

When she realised her terrible mistake, her smile died. She was trapped. Only one step was left, and that was the one she was standing on. Then beneath her feet there was inevitable grinding of stone on stone as the step moved. She stared at her shoes with terror as the step edged slowly into the sheer face of the wall.

She crept backwards impulsively toe to heel until there was nowhere else she could go.

The step locked into the tower wall. Mrs Ridley was pressed away into nothingness and plunged downwards. Her long screams filled the tower. Her last sight was of a long snake carved on the edges of the steps. Her scream ended with silence.

With her lifeless body laid on the ground there was the ominous rumble, as the steps unwound to their original positions. The ancient puzzle had guarded the tower's secret well.

It was Brother Sebastian's turn to sweep the tower steps. But he was late and felt guilty when he arrived. He found Mrs Ridley's body and he didn't react well. He was naturally superstitious and most of the monks played on this. Brother Jangles hadn't helped with his constant stories of a haunted tower. Ashen white he wailed as he ran back through the small chapel. Unfortunately, he ran straight into Mengius, who was an assistant to the Abbot but not a monk.

"What are you running from Sebastian? Your own shadow?" Mengius shouted.

Mengius was a powerful man with a head and neck like a bucket. Brother Sebastian stopped as Menguis's huge frame blocked his way.

"She's dead, Oh saints preserve us, she's dead," trembled the Brother. "She on the floor in the tower. It's Brother Jangle's curse!"

"Get the Abbot. I will go and look," Mengius grunted as he curled his top lip.

The monk dashed in a panic towards the Abbot's study. He arrived in extreme distress and banged very hard and loud on the sturdy door.

But it was Brother Jangles not the Abbot who opened it.

"The Abbot is not here," Brother Jangles snapped, awkwardly trying to close the door again. But Brother Sebastian was not leaving with his news.

"Quickly, fetch the Abbot. There's a dead woman in our tower. It's that curse of yours."

Brother Jangles remembered the sketchpad lady and clasped his silver cross then whispered some strange words.

Brother Sebastian was still in shock and burbled on.

"I left Mengius waiting at the tower for the Abbot."

In the room, hidden behind the door, the three children stood in a haze of shock. The horrible, vindictive Mrs Ridley was dead. Finally they were free of her, and their lives seemed much easier.

However, that relief was short lived. The tower now posed a great danger and suddenly this had become a serious game. As the monks hurried for the Abbot, the children knew the task ahead was going to be difficult. One mistake and anyone of them could be next!

eighteen: the tower

Alone in the study the children gazed at the dark antiquated bowl and could hardly believe their good fortune.

Ralph took the bowl from the table.

"This is so odd. It feels like ice. See what you think," he said and passed it to Rebecca.

"It's been hidden under this stone floor for ages, that's why it must be so cold," she said. "Look at this inscription, it must be a clue to our lost Ghost Door. But what does it mean?"

Minutes ticked by but no one could think of a solution. They knew another monk might come along at any moment. Ralph fretted and Rebecca looked at him crossly. If the Illuminatus was in his pocket he hadn't offered to use it.

"We need a solution. Use the Illuminatus, there's no time left," she snapped.

"No," Ralph snapped back.

Simon looked puzzled.

Ralph wanted its existence kept between just him and Rebecca. He tried to brush Simon's confusion aside. "I haven't a clue what she means," he said.

Frustrated, Rebecca decided to reveal all. "Ralph has a device that will help and he won't use it because it's a big secret."

Ralph was livid and flared up at Rebecca.

"You had no right to tell. What's the point of a secret if you keep doing this?"

Simon winced, hurt that he was excluded.

When the arguing stopped Ralph produced the Illuminatus. It was then activated straight from his pocket. Familiar buttons were pressed and bright words painted themselves on the wall.

'What is your question?'

Seeing the writing, Simon forgot about how he hurt he was as curiosity took over. He watched, transfixed.

Ralph cleared his throat.

"Illuminatus, please, can you tell me what this means? When you fill me like the sea, Davy's Locker you will see."

Light flickered deep in the machine. More writing appeared. Ralph read it aloud: *"When I'm full of the sea I'm sunk. You must look for a treasure that isn't junk."*

They were all baffled. Ralph was dejected.

"It's answered us with another riddle. And now we can't ask any more questions for twenty-four hours."

Rebecca tried to lighten the gloom.

"Does anyone have a plan B?"

Ralph gave no response and stuffed the device in his pocket. Then Simon had a simple idea.

"What if we take these words literally? Put seawater in the bowl? I wonder if that would satisfy the inscription."

"He's right! We might see some real treasure and not just this junky old bowl," Rebecca replied hopefully.

"Or just doubloons and pieces of eight," Simon said dreaming of pirates.

There was one major flaw, which Ralph pointed out.

"We are miles from the sea, in case you'd forgotten. So where's the seawater coming from?"

"I don't know," Rebecca said, dejected by Ralph's negativity. "It's Simon's idea. I'm only trying to give a few suggestions. As usual."

Then Simon came up with another good idea.

"If we don't have real sea water we can try to make some by adding salt to tap water."

They realized Simon might be on to something. "Come on," shouted Simon as they ran towards the kitchen with the bowl.

Not far away Brother Sebastian and Brother Jangles had tracked down the Abbot to tell him about Mrs Ridley's death but he didn't believe them.

"Brothers I reassure you, it is not possible. I helped the lady only a few minutes ago into a taxi. Look she even dropped her sketch as the taxi drove away."

The monks were stunned when the Abbot held up the drawing.

But Brother Sebastian knew of what he had seen and would not be convinced otherwise.

"No. I saw her on the ground. Dead. By all the saints, I'm telling the truth. Come and take a look."

Reluctantly, the Abbot and two worried monks rushed to the tower. There Brother Sebastian spoke before he even looked on the floor.

"There, I told you she's dead," he said triumphantly.

But the body was gone. Desperate to find the missing corpse, Brother Sebastian scrabbled around on the floor.

Mengius entered the tower and Brother Sebastian seized his arm

"You saw her. You must have," he shouted. But Mengius shook his head.

"Are you mad?" Mengius said and gave the Abbot a sly look. "There is no dead woman."

Brother Sebastian knew what he saw and was convinced of a conspiracy.

"You moved her body didn't you," he raged and pushing Mengius in the chest.

Mengius grunted and muttered a denial.

Brother Jangles then added confusion with his own brand of madness.

"It's the Corpse Scratchers. They want her flesh and bone."

The Abbot had heard enough. He waved his hand portentously and their talk stopped.

"I will hear no more of this woman. Are you trying to turn this monastery into a house for fools? May be its time to reopen the abbey's dungeons."

The two Brothers looked at one another. The dungeons were dark, dirty and deep underground. Their only food would be soiled worms and wriggly maggots.

Brother Sebastian was certain about what he had seen, but with the threat of dungeons that woman was best forgotten.

Sea salt was easy to find in the kitchen and Rebecca stirred a spoonful into a jug of water. Once the salt had dissolved the brine was poured into the bowl.

In the blink of an eye, the bowl changed from abyss black to blood-curdling red. The boys huddled round and watched as the saltwater swirled and the bowl changed again.

Around the bowl's edge tiny tentacles rose up like a sea anemone and projected a three-dimensional image of a lake. At first no one identified the lake until Rebecca saw a tower in the foreground. It was the abbey's tower.

"I wonder why we have never heard of this lake before?" Rebecca said.

Suddenly Simon felt an overpowering desire and poked his finger into the image.

Rebecca scowled and Ralph snapped.

"Mess it up, why don't you?" Ralph grumbled, his fears confirmed about Simon tagging along.

When Simon pulled out his finger, the image was stuck to it as if it were a luminous strand of glue.

"Wow," he said, as the strand of light snapped free and dropped into the lake, like a pebble that rippled the water.

After the image settled Ralph saw a tiny dark spot that shimmered right in the middle. Yet none of the others saw. Then, strangely, Ralph remembered a line from Sir John's book and muttered: "And a watery chasm was breached unto another world.' I think I've found the lost Ghost Door," he blurted. But then he looked disheartened. "The Ghost Door is in the middle of the lake, right at the bottom but it looks deep, deeper than I can go!"

Rebecca emptied the brine into the sink and watched as the image and tentacles dissolved. The bowl was left black and uninviting once again.

They were about to return the bowl to the study when voices were heard out in the corridor. One belonged to Brother Sebastian.

"Brother Jangles is right. Devils are coming and Mengius is one of them. That woman was dead and he dragged her body away. The Abbot hushed it up."

"But the Abbot is a good and holy man," they heard the other voice say.

"Not any more," condemned Brother Sebastian. "We are living under tyranny."

The voices faded, along with the monk's footfalls.

"So old Mrs Ridley really is dead," Ralph said, without remorse. "Good riddance, I say but it sounds like we need to steer clear of that Abbot."

After the bowl was returned to the study, they started to wonder, what next…

"That tower killed Mrs Ridley so we need to be extremely careful when we go in," Rebecca warned them.

"Go in?" Ralph said ominously. That comment surprised the other two. "Why risk our lives in that tower, if I can't swim down to that Ghost Door?"

As Ralph and Rebecca argued Simon drifted away and sat on the rim of the fountain. He twirled his fingers in the cool water and noticed a small metal ring that hung on the fountain's edge. It reminded him of an object he saw recently in one of the Binder Labs. Simon interrupted them.

"There is an Imp gadget that lets you breath under water," he said. "I saw one being tested in the Blue Lab."

"It's called a Nautilus Ring," he said, shaking the water from his hand. "I saw Black-Bob diving with one in a big floatation tank. It's really simple. Put it around your neck and press a green button. The ends of the ring snap together and a force field over your head keeps the water out."

"That sounds good," Ralph replied excitedly. "How long can you breath underwater?"

"Oh, ages!" Simon told them, "Black-Bob said it is a miniature aqualung."

"Can you get me one?" asked Ralph.

Simon wasn't happy and ummed and aahed.

"Getting one is not easy, not without the Binders knowing. Those tram drivers are very loyal and by now I bet we've been reported. The only way to sneak past the imps is to use an end of line tram with no stops. If I'm lucky no one will notice me. Otherwise it's a security lock down and I'll be caught."

"I know this is difficult," Rebecca pleaded, "but you're the best one to give it a try. Ralph and I will solve the tower. And if you're in and out quick," she said optimistically, "you could fetch Jeremiah's book from Mrs Ridley's house. The Sentinel will want it back."

"Right," Simon said unenthusiastically, "but what about getting in?"

"Oh the key!" Ralph said. "The next-door neighbour keeps an eye on things when she's away. So a spare key is stashed under a big flower pot."

Simon grabbed his Travelator.

Wishing their friend luck, Ralph and Rebecca watched him leave and then entered the chapel. Deserted they found the tower's door and opened it. Rebecca stared for bloodstains on the floor but there were none.

They climbed the tower, Ralph asked if she recognized a motif carved on some of the steps.

"Do you mean that squiggly thing?" she replied.

"Actually it's a knotted snake," Ralph answered, for he knew a little more. "The knotted snake is Judge Majestic's seal. It was on the Sir John's book. Perhaps it could be a clue?"

At the top of the tower they were confronted by the same stone block and inscription as Mrs Ridley and like her they counted the revolting grid of carved skulls.

"These must be the forty-two deaths." Ralph whispered. Rebecca hushed him and with burned concentration she read the inscription.

"I think I have it," Rebecca said. "This inscription is a mathematical puzzle. The numbers in the text, such as the 'nine Knights of valour' refer, I am sure, to a particular skull on the grid. They don't mean anything themselves but they do give us a combination. Each skull sits on a little square block. I bet if you push them they will move. This is basic imp technology. This grid is a medieval keypad and it may unlock a secret compartment." Rebecca's eyes blazed with excitement.

"So Mrs Ridley got it wrong. And now she's dead," Ralph said.

"I don't understand how she could get it wrong?" Rebecca said, confidently.

Ralph looked apprehensively at the skulls and their dark empty eye sockets. Suddenly, his fingers begun to tingle. It was a Twister warning.

"Something's wrong!" he cried. "You are wrong but I can't see how yet." Ralph muttered. He was certain they mustn't use these numbers.

But Rebecca hadn't heard. She was pre-occupied with the text and she ran the numbers through their sequence.

"Four, nine, fourteen, twenty-four, thirty-three and then finally forty-two," she whispered to herself. Then she pointed to a skull and said: "Now all I have to do is punch these numbers into the grid."

"No! Stop! We've missed something," Ralph yelled, snatching her hand from the grid.

"Don't do that!" Rebecca yelped. "You nearly gave me heart failure. We can't have missed anything. Go on, you show me then?"

"Most of the inscription is a fake," Ralph said, with his new brain wave. "It's a trap. All to mislead you except the last line, "Yet truly remember this, only with each step will the truth be revealed?" What it means by 'each step' is each step up the tower. Those knotted snakes are real clues to solving this puzzle."

"All right…" she mumbled, "so, if it's…." but her thoughts were slow like treacle and she knew it was inspiration beyond her powers of rational deduction.

"That's why the tower has been secure all these years. No one has ever cracked its meaning," Ralph said smugly.

Rebecca had to concede.

"You could be on to something. There could be a number sequence between the steps. If we can work that out maybe something will unlock."

"I'll count the steps between the snakes and you note the numbers," Ralph said, as he shrewdly took control.

At the bottom, Ralph started counting while Rebecca waited with pencil and paper at the top.

"Two steps up, we have a snake," Ralph shouted.

Rebecca wrote down the number two.

"Another three steps up and another snake."

Rebecca wrote three. Ralph climbed to the top and called out the intervals between the snakes while Rebecca wrote down the numbers five, seven and eleven.

"Let's put these into the grid and see if you're right," Rebecca said with a waspish grin.

She counted two from the alpha symbol and pushed the first skull home, this left a hollow square in the grid. Below them clattered the counter weights.

"It's working!" Ralph said, delighted.

As each number was pressed the movement of metal pulleys was heard. But after the last number and the fifth skull was pushed all was silent. They looked at one another perplexed. Rebecca checked each number to the grid.

"Perhaps Mrs Ridley broke it," Ralph said.

"Look at this grid," Rebecca told him, as she pushed back her hair. "I'm sure there is a number missing."

"But I used all the snakes," Ralph said, defensively.

"No, I don't think it's just about the snakes," Rebecca remarked as she held her scrap of paper. "It's in the numbers but I don't understand."

"If I count the steps and not the spaces in between," Ralph said, "we will have different numbers."

"Spaces in between," Rebecca mumbled, as Ralph sighed and scratched his head. Then Rebecca giggled loudly.

"What's so funny?" he snapped.

Rebecca composed herself.

"I've just found the answer," she said. "It's like walking down the road and not noticing lampposts because you see them everyday. These numbers are lampposts, except one is missing."

"What have lampposts to do with skulls? No you're talking in riddles." Ralph said irritated.

"Listen. Two, three, five, seven and eleven are all prime numbers, aren't they?" Rebecca said. "These are numbers divisible only by themselves and one. The prime number after eleven is thirteen, the great Wychen number. Any Binder will tell you that!"

She counted another thirteen and landed on skull number forty-one. Her fingers hovered over the skull as Ralph took a deep breath and whispered, "Do it!"

Rebecca pushed hard. The skull moved into the square recess and there was a loud sound as the top step moved. Afraid they would suffer the same fate as Mrs Ridley they clung to one another. But the staircase moved in a different way this time. The top step rotated anti-clockwise with the children balanced on top, stopping only after it came up against the other side of the wedge block.

Then the steps on the far side of the tower slid towards them until a new staircase was built and spiralled down in the opposite direction. The inside of the tower had changed.

"Let's see where this leads," suggested Ralph.

At the bottom they found an opening and another set of stairs that led underground. The new staircase blocked the doorway to the tower, so the only way out was down.

The stairs were gloomy and almost in darkness. Rebecca stumbled but Ralph steadied her. Above them the ancient mechanism of the tower was heard as the steps reset to their original position. They continued down for they couldn't go back.

The passage led into a large vaulted crypt lit by dozens of candles. It was a worrying sight. Something or someone had been there very recently.

Like a mole, Simon climbed the dark narrow stairs out of the Gimbals. He had his prize, the Nautilus Ring. On the last step he found a rusty old lever and pulled it hard. A door opened and he stepped into a tiny, dark room of brick and concrete.

He was in an old pill box built for soldiers during the Second World War and long abandoned. Three walls had gun slits, like letterboxes.

One slit gave a clear view of a river and another a view of the road into Broomfield. His last mission was to retrieve the book in Mrs Ridley's cottage. He took off his jumper and slipped it over the Nautilus Ring to keep it hidden. Once the coast was clear he was off.

Simon approached the deceptively quaint cottage with caution. It was empty so he crept up the garden path to the front door. There were flowerpots on either side. He found the latchkey under a pot and unlocked the door quickly, before creeping inside.

He entered an untidy sitting room where papers and books littered the floor. He knelt amongst the papers and searched for the book. Suddenly at the far end of the cottage there was a terrible crash like the back door had been ripped from its hinges. Something had knocked over the furniture. The pictures were down from the wall. In the passageway he heard an ominous crunch just like a heavy and clumsy creature had trod on broken glass.

There was no time to escape. He grabbed his jumper and Nautilus Ring and crawled behind Mrs Ridley's armchair. The door flew open and in burst a machine that resembled a huge insect. Terrified, he snatched a glimpse of the robot; it was the size of a washing machine. It moved on eight weird legs, like a mechanical spider. Simon shuddered. He hated spiders. The legs and body were black and leathery. As it moved a liquid whoosh was heard inside, like the dull continuous thump of a mechanical pump.

The insectoid had one large eye. It glowed and pulsated blood red in the middle of what was a small head attached to a large abdomen. Its brain worked with a loud rhythmic tick, tock, click. The motionless creature scanned the room with a brief swivel of its head. It was hunting, perhaps for Simon, or possibly something else?

The insectoid rummaged the books and papers with its two flexible arms. It scattered them violently but found nothing. It searched on top a sideboard. Again, nothing. It stopped and focused its terrible eye on the armchair where Simon was hidden.

It crossed the room like a rocket and Simon closed his eyes. Flinging the seat's cushion aside and seizing the very book Simon searched for, Simon was left trembling behind the chair. The monster's search disturbed a lot of dust. Some went up Simon's nose as he felt himself about to sneeze, no matter how hard he tried to stop.

"Aaah -choo!"

The machine knocked aside the armchair with a powerful arm and found him cowering. It seemed baffled. This was not what it came for. The machine clicked louder as it worked out its next move. Simon screamed and in defence the machine swiped at him wildly. Forced to duck, Simon made a dash for freedom. With the insectoid rushing after him. Each swipe of an arm was closer than the last. Simon weaved towards the front door. He had no book. But this was not the time to worry about that.

nineteen: the old crypt

Grey shadows shimmered high on the ceiling of the old crypt. Ralph and Rebecca each took a tall candle and explored the maze of rooms.

In some rooms rats and spiders were thriving on scary piles of bones that littered the floor. Ralph was curious to know what an old bone felt like, and picked one up.

In the candlelight Rebecca frowned with disapproval.

"You shouldn't touch those bones," she warned. "What if they're cursed?"

Ralph looked shocked and stared at the bone cautiously before replacing it gingerly.

"There are too many rooms to search," Rebecca said. "Do you know what this Shine is like?"

"It's like a twisted key. That's all I know," he replied.

"I hate saying this but we are going to die down here if we can't find a way out," Rebecca said ominously.

"Of course there's a way out," reassured Ralph. "After all someone lit those candles?"

"And if we're found they'll give us the guided tour they gave Mrs Ridley," Rebecca replied sharply.

"Let's hope these bones don't belong to people who couldn't get out," she said.

The stark reality hit Ralph.

They searched for hours without success. Then in some far off room they heard a terrifying noise like a dog's snarl. Rebecca panicked. She wanted to get out.

"That could be one of those Corpse Scratchers," Rebecca said with dread.

Ralph refused to listen and searched another room by himself.

"I think I've found something," he shouted.

Rebecca hurried and found the room filled with stone coffins. On each coffin lid was an ancient effigy. Enormous stone pillars supported the roof. Some pillars had animal sculptures that clung to their sides. These looked afraid and appeared to be escaping. Astonished she walked through the coffins to where Ralph stood smiling.

"How many coffins are here?" he asked excitedly.

"Forty two," she answered, catching his enthusiasm.

"Yes. But that's not all. The stone plaque on that wall has the names of all the knights who died in the tower. The ninth and last knight was Edmund Leversedge. I think that's the coffin we need to find," Ralph said.

Only a few of the effigies on the coffin lids were knights in armour so they checked those first.

"This is the one," he called confidently to Rebecca.

Sir Edmund's effigy was unlike the other eight. While the other knights had their hands clasped in prayer, Sir Edmund held a stone tablet in one hand and pointed to its inscription with the other.

Ralph bent and looked closer.

He pointed to the tablet. "I can read the first bit, it says, 'Here lies the noblest knight of all, Edmund Leversedge of Selwood' but I can't read the writing underneath. It must be another language."

Rebecca read the epitaph herself and smiled.

"It's Latin," she said, doubting Ralph had much idea of Latin or even English. "Latin sounds special. It's a pity my Latin isn't better. The trouble with a translation is these first two words can have two meanings, depending on grammar. Look, this gives a warning."

Ralph was impressed by Rebecca's talents and told her so.

"I've studied Latin for a couple of months. It helps on field trips. You see the early Wychen language and Latin have very similar linguistic roots."

"So what's the translation?" Ralph asked.

"It begins: 'Graviora manent' which is either 'Greater dangers await' or 'the worst is yet to come". And it ends: 'Ad lucem', which means 'towards the light'. So the warning is 'great danger awaits towards the light."

"What light? There's none down here?" Ralph said.

"I don't know," she said exasperated. "Everything's a riddle. It's making my head feel as if it will explode. I hate it down here. I told you earlier."

"You didn't," Ralph grumbled.

Losing his balance Ralph grabbed at the candle, which kept it upright. But he burnt a finger and squealed with pain. As the candle flickered he realised the inscription referred to the Shine itself.

"What if the inscription is not just a warning, but a voice command like Simon's trick with the Binders Badge?" he said excited.

Rebecca was speechless. Could he be right?

"Ok, I'll read it louder this time," she said.

"Graviora manent ad lucem," she boomed.

Suddenly there was a loud clunk from Edmund's coffin lid. Then a clockwork noise whirred as the effigies pointing arm moved upwards. It pointed to a roof pillar. As the children looked closer they saw a large statue. It was of a serpent hissing.

"Why do snakes always look so vicious?" Rebecca whispered.

"Those fangs would be full of poison if it were a real snake," Ralph said. He loathed snakes and that brought an intense interest.

Rebecca not only saw fangs but also its strange serpent tongue.

"This Shine. What does it look like?" she asked.

"I remember reading its shape was funny and all twisted."

"Twisted like that snake,s tongue?" Rebecca replied and pointed to the serpent's mouth.

"Do you think it's the Shine?" he whispered.

Rebecca held both candles while Ralph climbed the serpent's stone coils as nimble as the rungs on a ladder. He held one fang and reached for the serpent's tongue when Rebecca screamed. Instinctively, Ralph drew back.

"For goodness sake," he shouted as he clung hard, "I might have fallen."

"Your hand," Rebecca said. "The moment you touched that tongue it wasn't your hand anymore. I saw a monkey's paw!"

He looked at her incredulously.

"Does that look like a monkey's paw?" He said and waved his free hand.

"Not now," she replied. "But I swear it did."

Still grumpy, Ralph removed the serpent's tongue and jumped down.

The rusty red tongue was definitely funny, twisted and key-like. It had to be the Shine. He slipped it firmly into a pocket.

Then in a distant room they heard a great rumble.

"We'd better get out," Rebecca said and handed back his candle. The candles had burned steady in the air of the crypt but all of a sudden they were caught in a strong draught.

"Let's see if there's a way out," Rebecca said and pointed to her flame that flickered.

The chilled air led to a small room full of old cobwebs that fluttered in the breeze. In the far corner was a small newly-made hole and behind that a narrow tunnel.

"Look how this candle blows," Ralph said. "This must be a ventilation shaft and that could lead to the surface."

"Let's try it," Rebecca said, removing cobwebs from her hair.

Carefully they squeezed through the hole.

"We're going uphill?" said Ralph.

Their journey was slow and ended with a tight exit into an overgrown ditch.

Scrambling from the undergrowth they found themselves outside the monastery's high wall. Not far from the main gates they retrieved their hidden Travelators. Neither worked.

"What's the matter with them?" Ralph moaned.

"Look at this pop-up notice," Rebecca pointed, "it says the batteries need re-charging!"

Set in the handle was the warning: 'Low energy - rotor failure'.

"Great, Now it will take ages to find that lake," Ralph sighed.

Glumly, they folded away their redundant Travelators. Leaving the abbey despondent and behind, they stopped when they saw a man working in his garden.

"Do you know the way to the lake?" Rebecca asked. The man looked startled.

"To the lake you say," the man pondered the question. "That would be the Dead Pool. But nobody goes there, not after all those drownings!"

Ralph wanted to know more. After all, he was the one who would be taking the plunge.

"There's rumour of a creature lurking in its waters," the man said. "A huge monster. Some say its skin is shiny like a devil's mirror. They call it the Ice Phantom. When some lunatic family bought the lake it was closed. Their big house overlooks it. So they don't allow fishing and only fools swim there."

When Rebecca asked for directions the man chuckled.

"Follow this road to a humpback bridge then take the old footpath on your right. But you'd better hurry. It'll soon be the beast's feeding time!"

The man turned and with vigour continued to cut a hedge.

As the children walked down the road Ralph asked Rebecca if she believed his story.

"I hate to say it, but I think it's true," she answered.

Ralph dismissed it all as an old monk's story, but Rebecca disagreed.

"If a Ghost Door is at the bottom of the lake," she said with unease, "then who do you think is its gatekeeper?"

They made their way along the path next to the bridge. As they arrived at the Dead Pool Ralph looked fearful. The surrounding trees were bare and lifeless. Fluffy moss dangled like green garlands from smaller trees. In the water trees lay fallen with strange weed clung to their branches. Nearby was a small slanted signpost with faded words that read: 'PRIVATE. NO FISHING'.

On the other side of the lake Ralph saw a large house. Its three gothic turrets made it look like the setting for a horror story.

"Simon should be here soon. If he can't find us with his Travelator, there's something wrong with him. You could spot that lake from the air miles away," said Ralph. "And those stranger houses give me the creeps."

Rebecca peered into the lake and saw a rocky ledge. Where the ledge ended, dark water plunged into the unknown.

A sudden movement in the water startled her. It was a small shoal of fish. She felt anxious and stooped to stir the water with a hand.

Ralph also stooped and felt the water.

"It feels like the North Sea," he told her and shivered at the thought of the swim.

Overhead they heard a whirring and as Simon glided down between the trees. The Travelator landed heavily dumping Simon unceremoniously in the dirt. Simon climbed to his feet and furled his Travelator away.

Simon groaned, shook the soil from his coat and said, "I'm fine, thanks for asking!"

But Rebecca was concerned and asked about the flight.

"The flying was fine until I was over the lake and then it played up. There was a strange air current pulling me down. I really had to work to keep the thing in the air."

"Did you get a Nautilus Ring?" Ralph asked impatient.

"Of course. And I also got these," Simon replied and held out three little black rods with an outstretched hand. "These are new power packs for the Travelators so we don't have to walk home."

Rebecca was impressed but Ralph had other things on his mind.

"And Jeremiah's book?"

Simon's eyes were cast down as he relived his adventure.

"I went to the house but something came there just after. It searched the house and took the book."

"What sort of thing?" Rebecca asked, looking worried.

"Something really big and robotic," Simon said without it named. "It had eight legs. It was like being chased by a spider the size of a fridge. It tried to kill me. As I made a run for the front door I heard someone whistle. When I looked round it had gone. But so had the book."

Concerned less about the book Rebecca said, "My guess, whoever controlled that thing didn't want to be seen."

When Simon heard they had the Shine he wanted a look.

Ralph passed it over but soon became restless and wanted it back. Simon returned it reluctantly.

"I need to get going," Ralph said put it back in his pocket.

As Simon gave Ralph the Nautilus Ring his face was lit with its blue glow. Asked how it worked, Simon smiled. He had a passion for gadgets and loved the chance to share it.

"This is clever stuff. You see these metal fins on either side of the ring? They work like gills. Water goes in through these fins and air is extracted from the water. See these three holes?" he said, and pointed to the Ring's front. "Air is pumped through these into a force-field dome. You switch this on and the dome over your head keeps the water out."

Ralph listened then snapped the Ring around his neck. It was time. The water was even colder than he expected and he waded in trying not to shiver.

"I could be away for hours or days," he told them. "There's no point in staying here. Go back and tell them it was all my fault."

"I'll leave your Travelator by this tree stump. Take care and good luck, Ralph." Rebecca called out.

Ralph double-checked that the Shine was safe and pressed the green button. The force field activated. As the Ring hummed, he plunged into the deepest blackness of the lake. Bubbles swirled to the surface.

Rebecca and Simon drew closer to the water's edge. Concerned for their friend, they watched until the water was still and calm. Reluctantly, they picked up their Travelators and were airborne. They circled once, looking intently over the spot he was last seen. Finally, they peeled away and made for Broomfield. The flight back was quite. They wanted Ralph and it played on their mind.

Down and down Ralph sunk into a silent aquatic world. The intense cold sucked his breath away and the fear of drowning took him close to panic. But the Nautilus Ring detected changes as he breathed and fed him extra air to compensate.

The water at the bottom of the lake was strangely warm but there was another strangeness patches of algae glowed on the lakebed rocks. As Ralph drifted along the bottom, he saw immense rock formations. Some were like tall chimneystacks and others were deep wavy grooves that stretched beyond his sight.

He remembered from the bowl's image he had to swim towards its centre.

He swam for a long time before his fingers tingled and shook; a Ghost Door was close by. He was amazed when he rounded a tall rock and saw the light stream from his Ghost Door. But then he sensed danger. Away to his left, in a patch of dark water, something silver and shiny moved at speed. Beneath the rock chimneystacks a very large creature headed his way.

The creature twisted and turned, like a huge eel, at least eleven metres long. Ralph dropped and hid behind a rock. No story had prepared him for the Ice Phantom!

He hid for ages and when he thought it had gone he swam for the door. Suddenly something smooth and immense brushed against his right leg. He turned in terror and saw the creature's shiny body raised up and its huge head turned downward. It opened its massive jaws and looked ready to swallow him whole, Ralph froze. It was the Ice Phantom and it was defending the Door.

Ralph scrabbled clear and backed against a tall rock where he found he couldn't wriggle free. The Ice Phantom's eyes were grim and soulless. It was poised to strike a lethal blow. Ralph was terrified.

But then, above the Ice Phantom another creature cast a dark brown shadow in the water.

Ralph sensed powerful jaws and saw paws that had long razor-sharp claws.

The shadowy creature smashed into the Ice Phantom, knocking it away from its deadly strike. It bit deep into the serpent's neck with long raked cuts. Ralph was saved but by what? Was he in even greater danger?

All hope appeared lost until he recognized new beast was the bear. It was Jeremiah Foghorn. The huge bear forced the Ice Phantom away and smiled knowingly at Ralph.

Grateful, Ralph left Jeremiah locked in combat and headed for the unguarded Ghost Door. Opening the door, the water churned into a gigantic whirlpool. The vortex stretched down like a long dry funnel with an irresistible force dragging him. Ralph glimpsed Jeremiah for the last time and was whisked into a lost and fabled world.

In Greystone's study Simon and Rebecca prepared for their grilling. Greystone glared and slammed his paper-work down on the desk.

"I have never known such disobedient students," Greystone told them. "Every student is handpicked. They are the best and most promising."

At Greystone's side a stern Black-Bob nodded with agreement.

Greystone held up an envelope and ripped it to shreds.

"That," he said, "was my invitation to the convention of Masters and Grandmasters in London. I had to cancel because of the chaos you both caused."

"We're so sorry!" Rebecca said trembling with remorse. "We only borrowed things from the museum. We put back what we could. But we couldn't sit and do nothing for those missing children."

Black-Bob accepted none of it.

"How can you ignore everything I taught you!" he said and shook his head, "and choose such a reckless path?"

But Greystone's anger had diminished.

"No one ever said being a Binder is easy," Greystone told them. "Our rules protect the Guild. Without rules there would be no Binders and no Guild. The rules bind us to Wychen and broken rules can cause Dark Doors to form, wild doors with no gatekeepers."

"What Mr Greystone is saying," interrupted Black-Bob, "is you have interfered with a strict balance. It could be months or years before we see the extent of damage you have done."

The children kept their heads down.

"So where is Ralph?" Greystone demanded.

The children looked at one another but it was Simon who spoke first.

"We went to this lake and I suppose he's now in Raven's Wood."

Black-Bob raised his eyebrows surprised, but Greystone was worried.

"This is grave news," Greystone said. "We can't send Binders in after him if he went through without permission."

Silence followed then Black-Bob tapped Greystone on the arm.

"A solution," he said. "You must go to the imps immediately and ask for a *Passe Gratelle,* a plea for safe passage. We can only hope this request will find its way into Raven's Wood, but what's to be done with these two?"

Greystone rubbed his chin.

"They will be excluded from Binder studies and receive only ordinary lessons until they can show responsibility. But first, they must rest the night in the Lab dormitory," he replied.

In the morning, as the children left the Gimbals, they saw a small, shy imp who did the job of a porter. He rarely spoke. But as he escorted their changelings back to the Labs he gave them a small wave. As of then their lives in Broomfield would be tame.

The school bell rung and they left the library. Rebecca was concerned they would be late for lessons, but Simon was preoccupied and lost.

"I don't know whose class I'm in," Simon said blankly.

"You're with me in Mrs Deacon's class, until this grounding is over," Rebecca said as she dragged him by a coat sleeve.

In the classroom Mrs Deacon had finished the register, just as the two latecomers arrived. She directed the two children to a couple of empty desks at the back and in a stern tone told them it was a history lesson.

Mrs Deacon opened the large windows as sun streamed through and heated up the classroom.

The pupils heard an unusual scratching, then Archie Baldwin, a cheeky round-faced boy heard a scurrying noise by his feet. He saw nothing, but realised it was a chance to cause mayhem. As Mrs Deacon read aloud she heard nothing.

"Excuse me miss. I think we have mice in the room," Archie said for maximum disruption. Two girls jumped and screamed as things moved in their bags.

Mrs Deacon stopped and looked over the top of her glasses.

"OK children, stay calm," she said looking at Archie with a suspicious eye. "All look under your desks and chairs. Raise your hand if you spot a rodent. No shouting, please. We don't want to scare them."

Of course, no mice were found and normality returned. But to make sure Mrs Deacon brought Archie to the front and gave him a globe of the world. Then she told him to point to Egypt. But something spun the globe fast and Archie couldn't point at anything. Mrs Deacon told him to behave.

Protesting his innocence, he tried to stop the globe but the class was driven to laughter and near hysterics.

Sensing something wasn't right, Rebecca tapped her jacket lapel and signalled to Simon to be Binder vigilant.

Two rows in front sat a very studious boy. He was writing in a notebook when the pen in his hand flew across the room. He looked around but he saw no one who could have touched it. Rebecca leaned and whispered to Simon, "I need to put my gonoculars on!" Simon nodded and replied, "I'll shield you with my book." Moments later, Rebecca was wearing her special glasses.

Invisible to class six, snargs were causing trouble. One had created a distraction and spun the globe while the others searched the schoolbags.

"They're searching for the Shine," she whispered. "They are trying to find it by smell. Its smell is probably still on you." Above the commotion it was difficult to be heard.

"Smell or not," Simon said determined, "I'll go and fetch Mr Brack. He'll know what to do?"

Rebecca removed her gonoculars and hid them away. Unnoticed Simon slipped from the room.

One of the snargs grabbed Rebecca's bag and she seized the strap firmly in clear defiance. The snarg was shocked and called for snarg assistance. With extra help they dragged Rebecca to the floor. The invisible attack terrified the class. The normally calm Mrs Deacon sensed near mass hysteria and sent the class to wait outside in the corridor.

Pinned down by six snargs, Rebecca couldn't get up. When Mrs Deacon rushed to help she was knocked over.

Shocked Mrs Deacon staggered to her feet, just as Mr Brack entered the classroom. The pupils jostled for a better look, so Simon closed the door. Alarmed, Mr Brack asked Simon to help the traumatized teacher outside. Once the classroom was empty of Fribblers, Mr Brack donned his gonoculars. He saw the snargs holding Rebecca down and from his pocket he pulled something that looked like a pen.

"You filthy creatures had better leave now," he said to the snargs. "This is a Bison-twenty-twenty Mark II and it's loaded."

The snargs paused, then gave an evil cackle, thinking he was bluffing and it wasn't just an ordinary pen.

Mr Brack aimed and clicked the button on the pen's top. It made a crackling sound and split opened in his hand. He smiled, aiming the device at the snargs. One howled with terrible pain, as a pellet of piping hot goo hit, before smouldering and hurling itself through the open window. The others saw their fate and released Rebecca and scurrying after their friend.

Mr Brack faced Rebecca and said, "I assume this is the fruits of young Higley's work?"

Rebecca nodded and looked at the floor.

Mr Brack sent Simon and Rebecca to Mr Greystone to report the attack and announced to the class it was only a small field-mouse problem. As the chaos died away the pupils gradually returned to the classroom.

twenty: ragna doom

Ralph felt dizzy as he opened his eyes. Soaked, he lay in a pool of water the Nautilus Ring deactivated by his side.

A mysterious wood of tall pine trees stretched before him. He held the Ring and crawled to his feet. The birds chattered and squawked and announced the comings and goings of every beast in Wychen. But was it the legendary place of Raven's Wood?

He twisted the Ring and the two halves pivoted together. It was now easy to put in his pocket. Looking around he had no idea where he was, but he was drawn to the birdsong. The deeper into the wood he went, the higher went the pitch of birdsong. Then everything turned silent as he entered a small clearing. Through a broken skyline of trees he caught a glimpse an old castle.

Unaware that he was being watched Ralph started down towards a path. Perched in a tree, a very large raven observed his every movement. A small breeze whistled though the clearing and the tree branches swayed. It was then Ralph saw the bird. It swooped and landed near him. A split second later it changed its shape from a raven to a man in a long black cloak. The man's skin glistened like gold. His large eyes were night black. In his left hand he carried a strange sword, translucent like glass but stronger than steel.

"Well met, Ralph Higley," the strange man said. "The young man from beyond a desolate Door. Your unauthorized entrance is the talk of our wood."

"You know my name?" Ralph answered.

"The Higley name is well respected here and with word of a Twister our chatter turns to song."

A mysterious spark flashed in the dark of the man's eyes.

"One day perhaps," he said, "you will understand the impossible songs of Longwings, the great bird spirit."

The man's presence and glistening skin captivated Ralph.

"I am Rex Corven, the Raven King. This is my wood"

To have found the King of the Wood made Ralph exuberant.

"I'm looking for the Great Seal," he told the king and was about to ask more when the king reached into a tree and caught something with his right hand. He held it out towards Ralph.

"Here is a true way to your story," the king said. "There are many things in this wood. Some have slipped from who knows where?" Gently he opened a hand and in his palm sat a beautiful spider of sapphire blue.

"These are oracle spiders. Their webs reflect images of the past, the present and even the future. Watch. I shall ask it to build one," Rex said.

He marked a circle around it and the spider ran under and over Rex's hand several times. Carefully, he placed the spider on a bush. There in the foliage a spectacular dark purple web was created.

As the spider moved slowly away, a single glint of light trickled from Rex's left eye like a teardrop. He touched the droplet with his finger and transferred it to the web. The droplet was bright and moved across the web until every strand glowed.

"Come Ralph," Rex said, beckoning. "Look deep and you will see many things."

As he stared Ralph saw himself climb the serpent statue with Rebecca.

"So you have uncovered the Shine," Rex said with admiration. "Your ability will grow but the snargs will be mindful of this. They can sense when the Shine is near."

New images formed, but they were of a time when Ralph was younger.

Ralph stared again and saw two boys.

"That's Evan and me, when we were at the old quarry." Ralph said, shaken. It was a memory he didn't want to relive. He struggled with his emotions and looked away just in case a tear should fall.

Rex watched the boy and the images. These told an important story of how one boy had slipped near a huge drop and other had pulled him to safety.

"Your friend saved you from certain death." Rex said gently.

"Yes," Ralph answered with a heavy heart.

The images stopped and the web faded into darkness.

"There's more to come," Rex said. "There are other things I must show you."

Rex took another tear from his eye and the web glowed once more. This time the image was of a boy bent exhausted over a huge machine. Ralph's face contorted with recognition. The weak and frail boy was still recognisable. It was Evan.

"What have they done to him?" Ralph yelled. Distraught, he dropped to the floor and sobbed his heart out. There was a moment's silence as he pulled himself together. "I didn't mean to," he sniffed, wiping the tears away.

Moved by the boy's distress, Rex vowed to help.

"I understand your drive to save him, but he has become a Grimraith," he said, saddened. "A child slave of the snargs. Under the influence of the Snargs, grimraiths forget their home world. The vast machine you see is called the Blood Grinder. It can make war machines beyond imagination. The snargs are building something new, perhaps something diabolical? But the grinder is also the powerhouse for every other machine in Ragna Doom. Destroy the grinder and the snarg kingdom will fall."

"Smashing up their machine, is that a good idea. Won't it anger the snargs?" Ralph asked. "I want to save

Evan – and the children, but to destroy that machine I will need help. Maybe you could come with me?"

"I will take you to the Great Seal," Rex said, "but as much as I want to go, I cannot. It is forbidden for any Wychen creature to go there."

"Saving the children comes first," replied Ralph. "If I can do both, I will."

Rex waved as the web sparkled and it fell dark.

"Follow me," he said.

They walked a long way into the woods and descended a deep ravine. Hemmed in by walls of rock a set of old steps took them down to a large door. Ralph grew excited. Was this the Great Seal?

At the bottom Rex pulled away the green ivy that partially obscured the door.

"This is the Great Seal, and behind it is a dark realm," he said, pulling away handfuls of ivy.

The perfect circular door was made of dark black metal. And on its solid surface strange writing was embellished.

With no visible door-handle or keyhole Ralph asked, "How does it open?"

"Wychen doors can be difficult," said Rex, "especially this one because it was designed to stay shut. Most keys are made to fit a door. But this door was made to fit your key."

Ralph pulled his twisted prize from his pocket.

"But there is no keyhole," he said, confused.

"The Shine is special," Rex said. "And a very dangerous instrument. That is why it was hidden. Just because you can't see a keyhole doesn't mean it isn't there. Pass it over the stonework slowly and the keyhole will be revealed." He cleared away more ivy from the stonework.

Ralph passed the twisted object over the cleared area and heard a hum as it made the invisible visible. Suddenly a small keyhole appeared in the door.

He inserted the Shine and turned it but the door didn't budge.

"Turn it three times," Rex told him. "Three is the usual for snarg keys."

Ralph turned the key twice more and there was a clunk but it still wouldn't open. He pushed and then impatiently kicked the door hard.

He looked angrily at Rex, who was taken aback by Ralph's sudden temper.

Rex pointed down at the conduits on each side of the door.

"Look. The door is melting," he said as two streams of molten metal trickled away like quicksilver.

Ralph watched as the door seemed to melt away like ice-cubes in the hot sun. With the door gone they stared into the dark snarg world.

"How will I see down there?" Ralph muttered apprehensively.

Rex pointed to the Shine in the keyhole.

"It wasn't named the Shine for nothing. When you remove the Shine from its lock you will have a good light."

Ralph turned it three times in the other direction and freed it from the lock. Its tip blazed with light.

"Be careful how you handle it," Rex said. "Firstly, it will stay lit only while the Seal remains open. Secondly, after one hour the Seal door will begin reforming and in one Wychen day it will be closed. This reforming causes the Shine to grow dimmer by the hour until it is extinguished. You must return to this door before midday tomorrow or you will be locked in for ever. On that side there is no place to insert a key. And don't worry about snargs escaping. This Seal is like deadly poison to them."

"How do you know all this?" Ralph asked bewildered.

"It isn't difficult. It's written on the Seal!" Rex laughed raucously.

Ralph smiled and shone his light in Rex's eyes with cheek. But those were dark serious eyes and he waved Ralph to enter.

He bid Rex farewell but asked him to wait until he return with the lost children. Rex nodded and said he would remain until the Seal closed.

Ralph stepped with fear into the bleak darkness guided by the strange light.

The tunnel was large and sloped steeply down. He soon realised he was in a network of tunnels.

"Fed up with the tunnels," Ralph's anger and behaviour worsened. When he remembered he hadn't fed Synge his frustration increased further. He searched for small grubs and grumbled about his useless dragon not feeding himself.

After a while he caught a poor beetle and popped it into his matchbox. He released Synge from his shield.

Ralph opened the matchbox and grabbed the beetle before it ran away. Exasperated he cursed: "Come here, you ugly cockroachy thing." Synge looked at him perplexed as if he were a stranger. His nocturnal eyes reflected against the dark.

"What's that look for?" Ralph snarled. "I'm feeding you, aren't I?" He thrust the beetle at Synge. But the hungry dragon stepped back as if the food was tainted.

"I haven't time for your fussiness," Ralph snapped impatiently. His dragon then dashed away and left him with a beetle.

"After all my trouble!" Ralph grumbled, throwing the beetle down in temper.

Ralph hadn't realised it, but since the Shine was activated his temperament had changed. In his constant state of anger he hadn't grasped Synge was gone.

"Come back, Synge," yelled Ralph, suddenly remorseful as he struggled with his temper. But there was no sign of the dragon.

In the distance Ralph heard a faint voice and it sounded like a snarg. But it was from a little man that swept the tunnel. The man shouted incoherently as Ralph approached.

"Hello," Ralph said and hoped he was friendly. "I don't suppose you've seen a dragon?"

The man swept continually and babbled in a strange language.

"A dragon about this high," Ralph said with his hand held at waist height.

"Good gracious," the man paused on his broom. "However did a Door-hopper get here?"

"Well, it's a long story," Ralph said as he noticed the Shine dim. "So tell me so I can be on my way."

"A dragon? About this high?" the little man said as he held his hand an inch or two above his head.

Ralph felt he had achieved a good result.

The little man eyes shone in the dark just like his dragon's, and Ralph understood how he worked without a lamp. But the little man eyes were wonky. One was large and bulged while the other smaller one squinted.

"Then you are responsible for the dragon mess in my tunnel," the man griped.

"Mess?" Ralph said indignant. "My dragon's always tidy."

"That's what they all say," the man groaned. "No one cares. I've more tunnels than I can clean, just because some snarg bigwig wants to make a secret visit. I can't cope with dragon pooh dotted down my tunnels."

Any apology was abandoned with the nasty effects of the Shine.

"I don't care about your tunnels. I have important things on my mind. Not tunnels or pooh." Ralph snapped.

"For a boy in a strange land you have a high opinion of yourself," the man answered, his tongue as sharp as Ralph's. "If you don't change your attitude you won't get your dragon back, never mind anything else."

"I'm sorry, I don't know what's the matter. I've been feeling angry ever since I came down here." Ralph said mystified.

Leaning on his broom, the man looked at the young boy and then at what he carried. As he recognised its importance his large eye grew even larger.

"Surely it isn't possible! Can I take a look?" he said astonished.

"It's mine. You can't touch it," Ralph snapped protectively.

"I won't," the man said. "I just need to see if it's what I think it is."

Ralph held the Shine a little nearer.

"It's the Shine. I know it well from a carving in the snarg castle. So I know it's precious." And with courtesy he introduced himself as Gallybagger.

"Call me Ralph," Ralph replied with trust.

"The Shine is cursed. You shouldn't have brought it here," Gallybagger said. "It leeches the happiness of its bearer. That's why you're short tempered. Bringing it here is trouble. But I tell you what, just because it's you, I'll get rid of it," Gallybagger said and held out his hand.

But Ralph, not to be parted from his prize, stepped away.

"That place?" Ralph said. "I don't suppose was Croucher's castle by any chance?"

"Why yes," Gallybagger replied. "But you can't go there carrying that."

"I have to," Ralph said and explained about his friend and the missing children.

"Children in the castle," Gallybagger snorted. "Not likely. Not in his precious castle. That Croucher hates children like I sweeping these tunnels. He keeps them deeper along with his Blood Grinder. I can lead you there. You'll not get passed the gogaknights or the stealers?"

Casting aside his broom, he beckoned Ralph to follow.

Struggling to keep up Ralph quizzed the man about stealers.

"Stealers are black hairy things that come out of little cracks in the walls and snatch anything they can. The ones with whiskers smell bad. Once caught, they drag you to a secret lair to be eaten. No, we don't want stealers to catch us. If you hear a clicking in the walls it's them, talking to one another. But don't worry, old Gallybagger will see you safe."

As the little man rushed along the tunnels, Ralph was forced to keep up.

"Don't forget to look out for my dragon. I can't lose him. If I do...."

But Gallybagger interrupted him.

"Do you know how many dragons I find wandering lost?" Gallybagger laughed.

"No" Ralph answered.

"None," the man replied. "Because dragons don't ever get lost. They see in the dark even better than I do and they are the best navigators of any creatures born."

Ralph was never told that.

After they raced through the tunnels they emerged into a vast cavern. In front of them stood an enormous castle bathed in a mysterious green light. Its fortified turrets stretched to the top of the cavern's roof. Small windows broke up the heavy stonework. Most were in darkness but a few glowed eerily from candles that flickered.

As they drew closer to the castle huge stalagmites almost blocked their way. It was then Gallybagger revealed Croucher's Blood Grinder was directly below and that it was too dangerous to be reached through the castle.

"We must use the service tunnels," he said. "I know all the tunnel runs and ones the snargs never use."

Through a small crevice in the rock, Gallybagger disappeared. Ralph followed and squeezed behind into a very narrow tunnel. Its tightness was either a potholer's paradise or a chimney sweep's nightmare.

After a steep descent Ralph could see though a crack in the tunnel wall into yet another tunnel. He saw two snargs. Each held long sticks with bright oil lamps that swung on their ends.

One snarg was ugly and looked deformed. He grunted loud commands as a cart came through pushed by three small children. Ralph didn't understand the strange words but a guttural snarg voice made its meaning clear. The children moved the cart faster.

"Heave and push! Heave and push!" The children were wholly subservient and devoid of emotion. They heaved and pushed the cart until some of the curious metal ore it contained spilled out.

Ralph pitied the children, their faces covered in dirt with cuts and bruises. He felt helpless and struggled not to yell at the snargs. But Gallybagger slipped away into the dark and Ralph had to follow. They pushed through another narrow hole and arrived in a long circular conduit made of brick. Ralph brushed the dust and dirt from his clothes as Gallybagger waited for him. On both sides Ralph saw metal pipes.

"These pipes feed water to cool the hot core of the Blood Grinder," said Gallybagger as he rapped on a pipe. "We are not far now. You can hear it."

Ralph heard the deep low sounds of a huge machine that thumped out a rhythmic beat.

"Some say the Blood Grinder is Croucher's evil heart beating darkly," said Gallybagger. Ralph gave him a frightened look.

The ground soon quaked under the machine's power.

Finally, they reached the Blood Grinder. It was enormous, like an ocean-going ship, and filled the huge cavern.

Its massive frame and four tall storage tanks were illuminated with bright lights. There was one storage tank on each corner, linked by a web of metal gantries. Beneath the machine a mass of gears turned and flywheels spun, all were intricately joined together.

"It's a monster of a thing," Ralph said amazed. "How can we destroy it?"

As steam hissed from the pipes, Gallybagger groaned with the idea of such a mammoth task.

"With an army you couldn't destroy it," Gallybagger said. "You really have no idea. Some very nasty snargs are here just waiting for someone to meddle with it. They'll tear you to shreds. I took risks bringing you here and that's your lot. If I get caught, Croucher will have me fed to something horrible with lots of teeth. And believe me, there are lots of things down here with teeth."

Suddenly the Shine dimmed again.

"If I'm not out of Ragna Doom before this light goes out I'll be stuck here," Ralph said.

"How did you get here?" Gallybagger asked puzzled.

Ralph explained how the Great Seal was opened but for a short time only.

"Let's hope it doesn't bring bad luck," Gallybagger remarked, "It's not like opening the door of your old backyard!"

At the far end of the machine a small group of children shovelled dusty ore into a hopper. Ralph felt the machine's oppressive and gluttonous appetite.

Suddenly the Shine's caustic anger boiled up inside him and he lashed out at the ghastly machine with his foot. The vibration made a small flywheel splutter and a whistle blew loud with warning. Ralph jumped and Gallybagger scowled at him.

"Well done young man," the little man said with sarcasm. "That will bring those evil watch guards."

Ralph had no time to apologize. Two snargs headed their way and each sniffed the air with purpose.

"Snargs," Gallybagger said dismally. "I bet they smell the Shine. We need to hide. Quickly, I know a good place."

They slipped through a tiny door and disappeared from view. Ralph found himself in a warm dimly-lit room that housed four small ponds. Gallybagger beckoned him over.

"We are safe here," he said. "Only high ranking snargs enter this chamber. These warm water ponds are the nursery pools where the snargs nurture their young. Take a good look."

In the turbid pools of slimy water Ralph thought fish swam, except they were black and furry.

"What weird fish," he said. "I've never seen hairy fish before!"

"They're not fish," the little man laughed. "They're Smutts. Little baby snargs."

"They look cute and cuddly now but they turn into something as evil and ugly as a grown-up snarg."

Gallybagger raised his eyebrows and pointed to a smutt with its first tooth.

"Don't be fooled. Two weeks more they'll have a full set of teeth and hearty appetites. Put a finger in that pool and they'll have it off."

Ralph moved away and then his eyes lit up.

"I know," he said. "We can set the Blood Grinder on fire. Will that work?"

Gallybagger shook his head.

"It's made of hard snarg metal. There's nothing to burn."

Ralph was downhearted. Then the Shine's reflection in the water reminded him, his Illuminatus was still in his pocket.

"Can you solve riddles?" he asked Gallybagger.

"You mean like, 'riddles and fiddles are like pots and griddles'," the little man sang.

Ralph smiled and pulled the familiar gold object from his pocket.

"I have something that will tell how to wreck the Blood Grinder," he said and he activated the Illuminatus. Gallybagger looked intrigued.

"That's a fine old lamp," he said mesmerized by the burnished gold.

Already Ralph had prepared a question.

"Illuminatus, please, how can I destroy the Blood Grinder?" he asked.

A green light was projected and bright swirls of writing formed.

"One stone upon another;
one castle above the other.
Use your firebrand of brightness
and command the sky to fall
with the Devils Hunch and all.
Unlocking its power will topple the tower.
But use only words that won't make it sour."

Ralph was slow to understand the puzzle. But the meaning was simple once he grasped it.

"Can it be that easy?" he asked aloud. "Do we make the castle collapse on the machine and flatten it?"

Gallybagger was excited too.

"The firebrand of brightness is your Shine. There is enough rock above us to bury the Grinder for ever. There's just one snag, once set in motion, you don't want to be underneath at ka-boom time."

Ralph hadn't thought of that. He had thought only about how to bring the roof down.

"Well," Gallybagger said, "the words that won't make it sour must be snarg, so simply command it in snarg."

Ralph smiled.

"OK, but first let's get those children out."

First Gallybagger checked the snooping snargs were gone.

"The coast is clear," he said, "You know it's a mystery how those grubby little things can smell anything except themselves."

Ralph giggled nervously then they crept towards the machine where the ore was tipped. As they hid between the array of pipe work they saw a cart had toppled over. Its load was shed across the floor. Two snargs then forced a group of listless children to shovel the ore straight into the machine.

"The one holding the short whip is real nasty," Gallybagger whispered.

Ralph didn't respond. He was staring at something familiar. The recognition was gut wrenching and almost took his breath. In the weakest bunch of children, there was a child that looked like Evan. But the boy was so bedraggled he hoped it couldn't be.

Ralph knew at last he had found his friend. A wave of relief washed over him. But there was no time to dwell for another dirty face caught his attention. It was the little girl missing in the paper. Except if that was Alice Moore the sparkle in her eyes had gone. He struggled again to hold back the urge to yell and curse. A sad tear trickled down his cheek. He wiped it away clean and gritted his teeth. It was not a time for tears.

"How sickly they look," Gallybagger muttered. "They are grimraiths and they will stay grimraiths until we get them away."

Ralph was ready for action.

"I'll distract the snargs," he told Gallybagger, "and you lead the children away."

Gallybagger shook his head.

"No, they will catch you. I have a better way. I know how to throw my voice in a whisper and make the tunnels amplify it. Then it will bounce from another direction."

Ralph nodded.

Gallybagger screwed up his eyes and took a deep breath. He made the strangest sound. Sooner than he thought a voice echoed and boomed from a nearby tunnel. It sounded like the announcement over an old tannoy system: "All work masters report to South Control for free toad pies. Repeat all work masters to South Control. These juicy pies will soon be gone."

The vicious little snargs ceased their shouting and turned to each other with greedy eyes.

"I can't remember when I last had toad pies," said one snarg. "Beetle pies but not toad. I'll tell you what. You stay here and I will go fetch us some pies."

"No, it's alright," the equally cunning snarg said, "I don't mind going. I can carry more pies than you."

The first snarg realised his deception hadn't worked so he suggested they both go. The greedy pair soon abandoned the children and set off in a ravenous search.

Ralph rushed for the children and ignored Gallybagger's call to wait.

"Evan, it's me. Your friend Ralph," he yelled.

The scrawny dishevelled boy paused briefly to look in Ralph's direction then continued to shovel.

"What's the matter?" Ralph shouted, "I've come to get you out."

Gallybagger caught him up and with a hand on his shoulder pulled him back.

"They see you, but they don't understand you," he said gently. "You're not part of their world. They are living a snarg life controlled by snarg voices and snarg words."

Ralph appreciated their predicament, for he had struggled under the influence of the Shine.

Gallybagger searched his pockets and pulled out an old book. Quickly he flipped through its dirty and dog-eared pages.

"This book was once a bestseller," he mumbled to Ralph. "This is the deluxe edition of A thousand and one ways to upset Snargs'. It has an extensive compendium of snarg phrases in the back."

He turned the pages and read a couple of words from it.

"Bron Aganoff," he said in a low and gruff tone.

One by one the children turned and walked towards the little man. There were ten in all and slowly he led them away.

"You'll have time to bury this monstrous heap," Gallybagger shouted jubilantly. "I will wait for you at the Great Seal."

"How can I do it?" Ralph said and clasped the back of his neck in a fearful gesture. "I don't know any snarg words and commands for the Shine."

In a flash the little man tossed him his book.

"Look under 'ways to demolish'. You'll find the words, and good luck my brave little-fellow."

Gallybagger turned away and called to the children: "Follow me, bron aganoff ent grimraiths."

Within moments, Gallybagger and the children disappeared.

twenty one: deadly encounter

Franticly Ralph climbed the steps towards the machine's summit. They were ancient steps, worn thin by generations of snarg feet, and with his greater weight they twisted and bent.

The machine's thump, thump, pounded heavy on his chest. A final step and he reached a long platform on the machine's pinnacle. Two storeys above was the cavern's roof. Ralph had much to do.

He turned the pages of Gallybaggers' book until he found the right phrase. It simply read, 'to bring the roof down' with the snarg translation beneath.

"Aaaah," Ralph heard a guttural voice near by, "the snooping Higley boy. Human children never learn. You dare enter my kingdom!"

On skeletal legs, the hideous Lord Croucher scurried towards him. In an attempt to conceal the Shine Ralph dropped the book from his fingers.

The snarg saw the light in Ralph's hand and knew the object well. Without a pause, Croucher strode and held out his claw-like hand.

"The boy thinks he brings Croucher a sweet gift," Croucher bellowed. "The Shine is no gift here. It is always mine."

Croucher demanded its return and paced back and forth like a crow scrutinizing carrion.

But Ralph stood his ground. He no longer concealed the Shine and clenched a defiant fist.

"Never! You took my friend and all those innocent children. You're going to pay for the evil you've done," said Ralph angered.

Furious, Croucher swooped at Ralph determined to tear the lad to shreds as his shapeless black cloak fluttered about his grotesque body.

Ralph was desperate and he tried to fight. Slobber and slaver from the snarg's mouth splattered Ralph's clothes with a foul-smelling stench. It was a long frenzied attack. Claws slashed and penetrated Ralph's sleeve. The flesh of his arm was lacerated open.

As he retreated the Shine was knocked from his hand. His main weapon lost from his grasp as it slid along the platform. Croucher ceased his attack and scrambled after it.

But the Shine rolled and dropped from the platform. Croucher poised on the edge turned his hatred on Ralph again. His claws flexed as he muttered a vile curse. The words rolled in Ralph's head and brought another snarg phrase to mind. He recalled the words and shouted "Skug Rog", the last snarg phrase in Gallybagger's book.

"Bring the roof down." "Skug Rog" echoed round the cavern.

From below, a sound whirred and beyond Ralph's wildest dream he saw the Shine shoot upwards, like a miniature Travelator. When it reached the cavern's roof it glued itself to a vaulted keystone.

There the Shine turned the ancient stone into molten rock. Soon pyroclastic droplets like incendiary bombs fell on the Blood Grinder.

Croucher turned on Ralph with fury, blocking his only means of escape. He savoured his prisoner's predicament and stepped forward to finish the meddlesome child.

Ralph tried to ignore the pain in his torn arm as a dark shadow flitted overhead.

It was Synge! He was sweeping down to protect his master. Ralph called his dragon and it landed by his side. With wings outstretched, it breathed fire at the snarg. Croucher screamed murderously at Synge's intervention.

"You're no match for Synge," Ralph yelled.

"I will not surrender. I will break your dragon and drink his blood!" The snarg bellowed.

As fiery stone rained down there were terrible sounds of cracking rock. Croucher looked up and tons of debris crashed down. A near molten boulder pinned him by the leg. Frantically he struggled, screaming another snarg curse at Ralph.

"You cannot win. My master is more powerful than I. He is the Wolf Biter of legend, feared throughout Wychen. Destroying my Blood Grinder will bring his wrath. Run, little Binder run, and never let the sun set."

As Ralph looked at the trapped snarg, the Nautilus Ring bleeped in his pocket. But why had it woken? There was no time to dwell; the roof was about to fall at any moment. He had to escape.

The roof fell and Ralph froze with fear for he was beneath. Then a powerful force pulled him. It was Synge. Ralph felt the draught from a beat of wings and he was airborne. Out of harm's way he would never doubt his dragon's loyalty again. Then a huge rumble swamped the mad laughter of the snarg.

Synge rose and dodged the huge boulders that fell. Swiftly the dragon soared towards the dark hole that gaped above, while below, the machine vanished under a mountain of rubble.

Into Croucher's ruined castle they escaped and landed in the remains of a magnificent hall. Surrounded by crumbled walls Ralph dismounted and picked his way through the rubble. Because his wound still bled, he ripped his sleeve and bandaged it.

At a stone lectern in the shape of a snarg's claw he paused. He was astonished that a book had been left there. He told Synge to wait. The book lay open. He turned it over. There on the front-cover in gold bold letters was: 'The thirteen deadly secrets' by Jeremiah Foghorn.

It was the very book Mrs Ridley stole. He turned it back and by chance saw a reference to the Illuminatus. He read on:

I now come to the second and third secrets of my deadly thirteen.

Of Imps the most secretive group were Wychen's scientific explorers, so elite and secretive no one knew their name. Any records of their great achievements were few and far between. But I was lucky. I found one legend concerning an incredible device called the Illuminatus, or by some 'the illuminator of secrets'. Yet this device was not the whole thing. It was one part of a more complex device. Records of its history were lost during a war between the imps and snargs. Fearing the snargs might capture the machine they split the device into four components. As a further safeguard, they hid these in separate places in the world of men.

My third secret, uncovered during another long journey was by accident. I came upon a strange traveller with many tall tales to tell, of which I believed only one. He told me he once had a wondrous piece of this elite apparatus stolen. It was ordinary in appearance, like any short black metal bar easily held in the hand. But its extraordinary gift was to hide its user, or even a whole army. He couldn't recall its name, as it was foreign.

I knew at once it was a lost component of this secretive imp machine. I never learned anything more and it remained one of the most remarkable enigmas of Wychen.

"I knew there was more to Sir John's gift," he murmured. "Now I now know why he gave it to me!"

Synge swished his tail impatiently and tried to attract his attention. The Great Seal would soon close. Ralph slammed the book shut and pushed it under his arm.

"I know, Synge. Let's get out of here fast!"

Below them a sinister snarg sifted through the smoke-swirled rubble.

A blood-curdling war cry was heard as a snarg army gathered in the wasted corridors of the castle. Synge knew they would come and swept Ralph astride his back. Ralph clenched his book, but almost dropped it because of his injured arm. He grabbed the top of his dragon's wing and regained his balance. Synge was as quick as the fire he breathed and in no time they were out of the castle.

Behind them, hundreds upon hundreds of snargs swamped the broken corridors and tunnels like a massive black tidal wave. At the front rolled a hellish pack of gogaknights.

The mad gogaknights swished from side to side as their green rings pulsated. They screamed like banshees as their rings struck the walls. Sparks and slime flew.

Ralph gripped his dragon harder as Synge flew faster. In the bigger tunnels the dragon speed-glided. His fiery head tilted and he gained maximum speed. Ralph felt his dragon's unyielding power and knew that to survive they had to stay ahead.

The lead gogaknight saw the enemy flee and slammed his two green rings together. They merged and formed a single long board with a daggered point. The board sped on and changed from luminous green to a fiery red. As the other gogaknights copied, the pack gained like a flight of devil's arrows.

"Synge, they're catching us," Ralph yelled with terror. "If we can't make it to the Seal, we'll never survive!"

Synge swooped to the ground so fierce he almost unseated his rider. Ralph's eyes were wide with terror as the gogaknights bore down on them.

Like a glorious taut bow, Synge spread his wings. Then the dragon filled his lungs. Unflinching he waited his moment and with one huge breath, he blasted a massive fireball. In an instant the tunnel turned into an inferno and every airborne snarg dropped like a swatted fly. Like piles of burnt rags, they littered the floor. Ralph yelled in triumph.

twenty two: the dead pool

It was quiet in the Gimbals. Simon and Rebecca had just told Greystone about the snargs in their classroom but as they left his study Rebecca was filled with foreboding.

She grabbed Simon's arm.

"We have to get to the Dead Pool right now," she said. "I don't know why, but Ralph needs us."

"We are forbidden from doing anything," Simon said, unhinged by her temper and wishing for no more trouble. "We don't have transport, how would we get there?"

"I don't know," Rebecca answered. Her mind wandered as she watched a burly figure cross from one corridor to the other.

"I don't know," she muttered again, then in an instant she shouted: "Yes I do! Follow me."

Astonished, Simon followed loyally.

As they charged around the corner Rebecca rushed up to Black-Bob and told him it was urgent they go to the Dead Pool.

But Black-Bob was still unhappy with Rebecca. She had let him down and he saw no reason to help her. She was suspended from Binder activity. Nevertheless she had a very stubborn streak and wouldn't give up.

When she kept saying Ralph needed their help, Black-Bob looked at Simon quizzically. He felt more confident with this clever, obedient boy, after he realised Rebecca could be impetuous. Simon smiled meekly. Thinking that perhaps they had just cause to be determined, Black-Bob relented.

"Okay, I might enjoy sometime by a lake," Black-Bob told them. "You are both under my authority. Treat this as an excursion rather than an authorized field trip."

Black-Bob gave a knowing wink as the children followed mesmerised as his long flowing coat flapped.

Cocooned in darkness Ralph rode his dragon like a night demon. He saw nothing as the wind rushed by and masked the snarg screams. Synge banked to the left and Ralph saw a far point of light that gave him hope. As the light grew brighter, he knew the Great Seal was still open.

Synge scanned the area and landed safely. Ralph dismounted and patted his dragon on the neck. As he withdrew his hand away he found it wet from dragon sweat. His dragon had worked hard. The brief silence was broken by screams of snargs that poured from every corner. Each one carried a flaming torch.

Ralph ran towards the Seal and shouted for Synge to follow. The entrance was barely open and bit by bit it shut tighter.

That was a disaster for Synge as the hole had become too small. Ralph was not about to desert his loyal dragon. But he had to act quick. He dropped the book and fumbled for his Binders shield. He shrieked. "Synge, get back inside here now! They mustn't get us."

A second later the dragon's large frame vanished into the shield. He stuffed the shield into his pocket and snatched the book from the floor.

The snarg horde was just yards away and the fire from their torches shimmered in their evil sulphurous eyes.

Through the Door's narrow gap Ralph lobbed his precious book and then tried to wriggle from Ragna Doom to Wychen. But he was caught. Something held his foot.

The stench of sulphur was unbearable and the snarg shrieks stopped all his thoughts. He slipped backwards and screamed as he clung to the door. Then a powerful hand grasped his and dragged him through the shrinking gap. Safely on the ground Ralph looked up and saw the regal figure of Rex Corven. At first he saw neither Gallybagger nor the children but they were all there safe.

But the trouble wasn't over and there was no time to speak. Small snargs crawled through the Door's small opening. Rex took his fiery sword and struck these filthy fiends. He cut them all down. Not one was alive. He cut and slashed until the Seal closed for good.

Rex struck the hilt of his sword and its fire was extinguished.

"You said the Great Seal is like poison to them," Ralph said to Rex exhausted, "and they wouldn't come near it."

Rex looked down at the dead Snargs.

"Once you made them mad, death was the only thing to stop them!"

He nudged the snarg remains with a foot and made sure they were dead. Only then did he scabbard his sword.

Concerned, Gallybagger left the listless children and spoke to Ralph.

"Did it work?" he asked. "Is the Blood Grinder crushed?"

Ralph held his flesh wound.

"The Grinder was mangled when the roof came down," Ralph said. "And Croucher was squashed too. Synge came back and saved me."

The little man smiled.

"One minute dragons are soft as anything," Gallybagger said, "playing hide and seek with you. The next thing you know they are fire-breathing killing machines." But then he had a horrible thought. "Croucher might be gone but Snargs appear like mould on good bread."

Then Ralph remembered something embarrassing.

"I'm so sorry," he said, "but your book was buried under all that rubble. So I can't give it back."

Gallybagger looked across at the closed Seal.

"It doesn't look as if I shall be going back, so I won't need it. But I'm lucky, I have found another castle to clean."

And he glanced at Rex.

Rex had something serious on his mind and he spoke up.

"These children can't go through your Ghost Door because they didn't come that way. Once the Oaks have granted special passage I will return them. We need them home before the effects of the snargs have worn off or they will become halflings. A boy going home with donkey ears or a girl going home with a squirrel's nose will raise awkward questions in the human world!"

Concerned, Ralph looked at Evan and the little girl.

Rex continued: "If we get them home now, they will remember only seeing those little silver boxes."

"Then I mustn't delay you," Ralph said courteously.

"Take care young friend," Rex replied and patted him on the back. "And remember run with rabbits and you will learn to avoid the snares."

Ralph raised his good arm and saluted his friend, the King.

"Thanks for everything. Until we will meet again."

"Indeed we shall," the Raven King answered.

Gallybagger walked with Ralph to the Ghost Door and despite the pain in Ralph's arm they remained in high spirits.

As dark storm clouds gathered over the Dead Pool, a white car stopped at the bridge. Out stepped Black-Bob, followed by Rebecca and Simon. Frantic, Rebecca left the others and ran down the rough path.

At the water's edge Black-Bob sensed an eerie atmosphere. So he scanned the lake with his gonoculars and saw strange purple streaks in the water. He took them off for he had seen enough and he didn't like it.

Simon sat on an old log and watched for his friend. While Rebecca retrieved the Travelator left for Ralph and took it to Black-Bob.

"Where did this come from?" he asked with surprise. Then shook his head in disbelief when she told him it was for Ralph to get home.

Black-Bob sighed.

"I shall say this once," he said. "You can't leave equipment like a Travelator lying around. Fribblers might ask questions. They are a curious bunch. What if this fell into the hands of criminals? Always treat imp devices as secret treasure."

Rebecca wished there was a sign of Ralph to distract Black-Bob from his endless lectures.

Gallybagger and Ralph located the ghost door but before Ralph departed he had a question for the wise old man.

"Before Croucher was crushed he referred to the Wolf Biter," Ralph said. "Do you know who he is?"

Gallybagger looked full of dread. His mouth went dry with fear. He knew only too well.

"I won't speak that name and nor should you. Ask no more of this." Gallybagger said. "It is time to go, my friend"

As Ralph approached the threads, the dimensional flux thickened and twisted. The door opened. Air, dust, twigs and leaves were sucked into the churned vortex.

Ralph thanked Gallybagger for his help.

"If ever you come here again, look for the cleaner at the King's castle. You'll be welcome there!" Gallybagger said, with a raised hand.

Ralph slipped the Nautilus Ring around his neck and was gone from Raven's Wood, sucked into the vortex. He emerged roughly twisted deep in the darkness of the lake. The water greeted him like a rolling nightmare. Even before the water touched his face the Nautilus Ring activated, the vents opened and the tiny generator gave air. Frantically, he sucked the air until he breathed easy.

Suddenly, disaster struck. Small lights flickered on the Ring ominously and his airflow was shut off. Ralph usually banged things and made them work again but not that time. No amount of banging helped. With no air Ralph panicked and with the force field activated the Ring suffocated him. The safety lock prevented it from being ripped off. He was terrified. He couldn't breathe. He had to get to the surface but already he was losing consciousness. His thoughts grew cloudy and confused. As he struggled he tangled in weed and drifted slowly towards a comforting blanket of watery death.

At the lakeside Black-Bob had doubts. They sat for a long time and saw or heard nothing.

"Have you noticed there are no birds," frowned Black-Bob. "There is no goodness here!"

"I feel like we're being watched," Rebecca said.

Simon thought the place was haunted and dead people were watching them, but only he'd mentioned that to Rebecca. Suddenly she heard a knocking sound and jumped.

"What's the matter?" Simon asked nervously.

"Something is under this log," she said, pointing.

Black-Bob had heard enough about the supernatural. He pushed them aside and turned over the log. There a Binder's note glistened in a small hollow. It was addressed to him. He held the note in the palm of his hand and it opened. A flash of red told him it was urgent. He quickly read it before it turned to dust. Then he smiled with relief.

"I have good news!" he said. But he was interrupted when a huge swirl of water bubbled up in the middle of the lake. Moments later the disturbance was gone.

Black-Bob went to investigate with his gonoculars. "If this is caused by a vortex you should see the residual energy streamers," he said with vigilance.

He soon spied the light streamers and his mouth dropped. Below the surface was the outline of a motion-less body.

"That could be Ralph," Black-Bob said with great apprehension. "He's not moving."

He waded into the lake and swam into the deep water. The children stood by the lakeside and frantically waited as Black-Bob dived twice. Each time he surfaced he was empty-handed. The third dive he made deeper, his chest was tight with air as he forced against his buoyancy. Light from the streamers faded as he caught the glow of something within a hand's reach. His fingers closed on a jacket. He clutched something heavy.

Black-Bob struck for the surface. He had Ralph's lifeless body in tow. Rebecca and Simon helped him drag Ralph from the water. He lay on the hard ground, motionless.

"I must deactivate the Ring," Black-Bob said concerned. "But whatever caused it to malfunction?"

Ralph was pale and looked so ill, Rebecca was frightened he was dead. Black-Bob pulled the Ring away. He pressed two fingers on the young boy's neck and felt for a pulse. It was weak. Suddenly Ralph convulsed and took in a huge gasp of air before he breathed again.

Slowly Ralph saw three blurred figures over him. It took a few moments before he focused and recognised them.

"Hey," he croaked weakly. "I thought I was a goner."

Another minute and he would have been, thought Black-Bob, relieved.

"Evan and the children? Are they safe?" Ralph asked. Rebecca didn't know and looked at the others for an answer.

Dripping wet, Black-Bob smiled.

"Just before I pulled you out I received a Binder's note. It said, two hours ago a man calling himself Rex Corven brought some missing children to Broomfield's police station."

The news brought colour to Ralph's cheeks. As he shivered, he fumbled in his pocket and passed a book to Black-Bob. Black-Bob looked down and saw the words, 'The thirteen deadly secrets'.

"Nothing more to worry about, then," he said. "We'll get you back for a good meal and some well earned rest."

Rebecca and Simon were on their way to Ralph's. They met him outside Evan's house.

"I went to see Evan to make sure he was fine and that everything was normal," Ralph said. "With what happened it's strange seeing his parents act like they had been on a long vacation."

Simon smiled, "Greystone says thanks to you the Binders will look into the missing children cases, even in Wychen. There's to be a special bureau. And we aren't suspended any more. Isn't that great? It's Binder lessons as usual."

Relieved and happy, Ralph was glad at the news and proud he had a part in it.

"I know something no one else must know though," said Ralph.

"I've collected a drawer full of secrets with you," Rebecca said, "So one more won't make a difference."

Ralph told them how Jeremiah's book revealed the Illuminatus was one part of a mysterious machine. And it was broken up and kept hidden.

"I want to find the other parts and put it back together," he said.

"All three of us will find it," Rebecca replied, as if it were just homework. "We're a team now."

"We'll have adventures and maybe find pirate treasure," Simon said.

"I don't know about pirates!" Ralph laughed.

Above the children in a large tree a dark shape swayed in the breeze. Something was watching them, hidden by a tangle of branches. It moved closer and its blackness took shape. It was a magnificent raven. Its piercing eyes watched every movement and listened to every word.

Blissfully unaware, Ralph continued to chat. He told them how his cut arm had healed when he went through the Ghost Door.

"I'm as good as new," he said and wiggled his arm, "except I'm not sure I got off scot-free. Croucher said someone called the Wolf Biter would be coming for me."

Upon hearing the mention of the Wolf Biter, the Raven moved down a branch, getting closer to the children.

"Creatures just can't come through Ghost Doors," Rebecca said, as she displayed superior knowledge. "There are rules."

At that moment the raven flapped its wings. The noise startled the children and, unnerved, they looked up. Nothing was seen as the dense leaves hid the raven well.

"It's just the wind," said Rebecca with her gaze fixed on the tree. Relieved they continued alone the street.

"I don't think this Wolf Biter will care about rules." Ralph remarked as he resumed his previous conversation.

"That doesn't sound good," Simon replied.

"Perhaps Croucher was trying to frighten you," Rebecca said, without confidence. "I bet this Wolf Biter doesn't even know who you are."

"Gallybagger was scared to even to speak his name," Ralph said. "So he must be scary."

"More reason for us to stick together," Rebecca reassured.

"If we build that machine," Simon said with enthusiasm, "perhaps we can rid the Wolf thing with it?"

"Sounds like we have a plan," Ralph replied. "We can talk it over at my house."

"And I'll tell you what happened when snargs invaded the school," Rebecca said, "and the havoc they caused!"

As they walked through Ralph's garden they were still unaware that the magnificent raven listened and watched. Finally the three children disappeared into the house. And there in a tree, the raven glided from branch to branch. Majestically it stretched out its wings and took flight, and like a phantom it vanished into a misty sky.

Printed in Poland
by Amazon Fulfillment
Poland Sp. z o.o., Wrocław